THE HOUSE OF LONG SHADOWS

THE HOUSE OF LONG SHADOWS

Bruno Pirecki

Publisher's Note.
This is a work of fiction. Names, characters, places, and incidents either are the product of the author's imagination or are used fictitiously, and any resemblance to actual persons living or dead, business establishments, events, or locales is entirely coincidental.

Library of Congress Control Number: 2024920106

Published by Redfern Ink, Franklin, Tennessee

ISBN 978-0-9994690-5-7 (Paperback)
ISBN 978-0-9994690-6-4 (e-book)
ISBN 978-0-9994690-7-1 (Audiobook)

Cover design: Dan Harding of Blue Mile Design
Developmental editor: Scott Norton
Copyeditor: Carol Lynn Rivera
Interior layout: Andrea Reider
Editorial advisor: Ralph M. Rivera

1 3 5 7 9 10 8 6 4 2

First Edition

For Kim, Bobby, Tony, Tom, and Edward

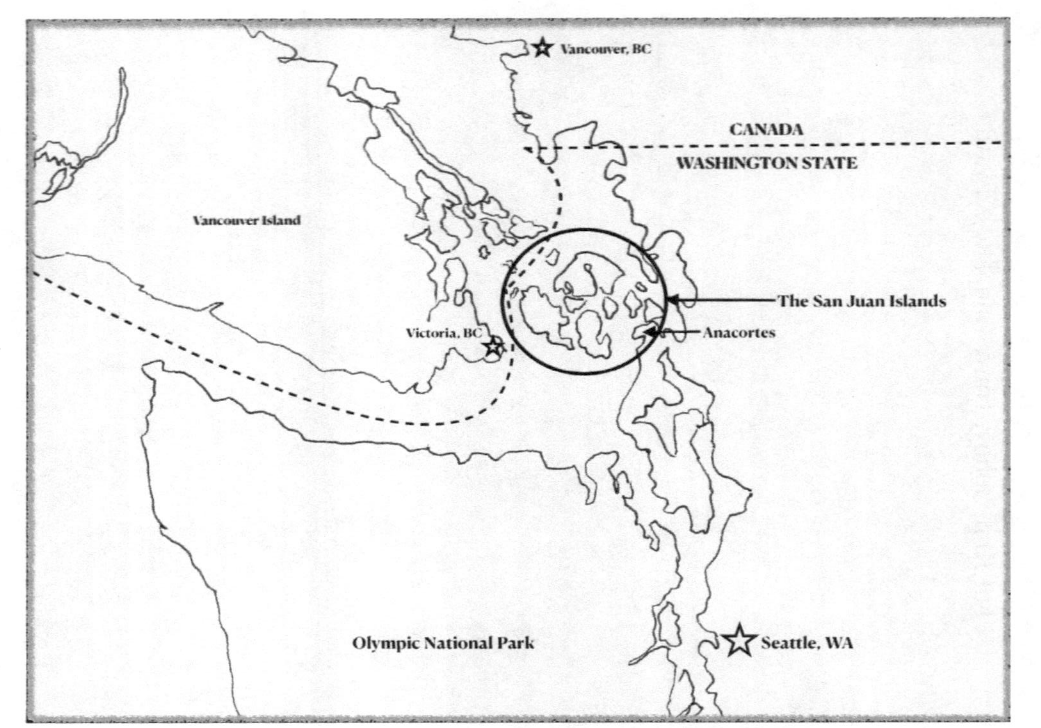

CANADA
WASHINGTON STATE
Vancouver, BC
Vancouver Island
The San Juan Islands
Anacortes
Victoria, BC
Olympic National Park
Seattle, WA

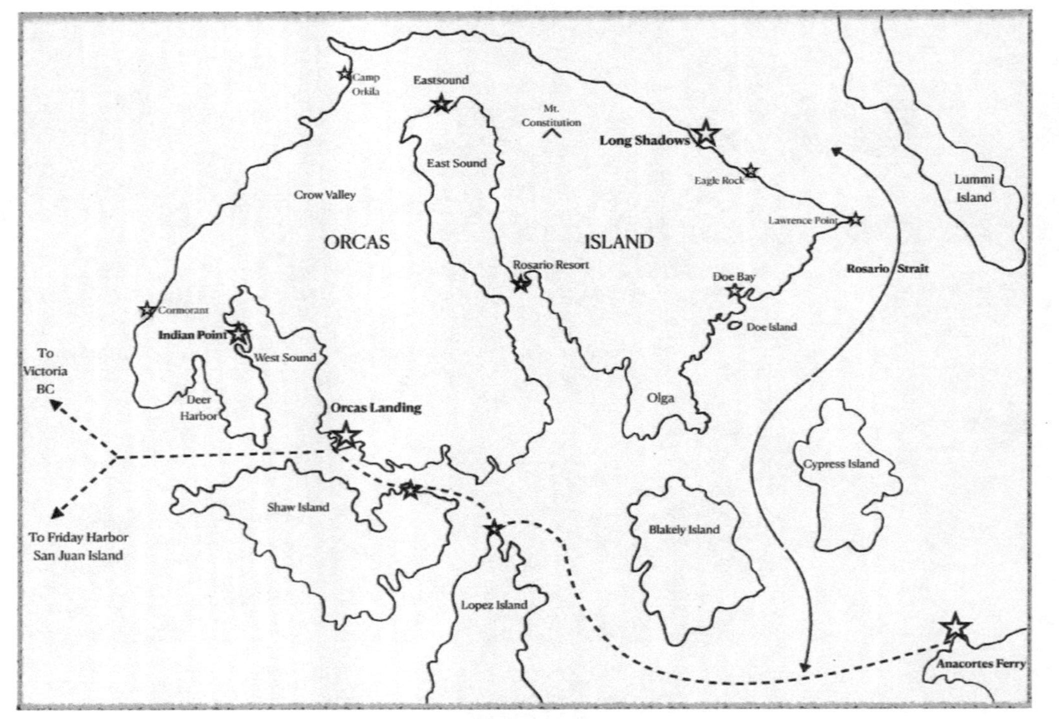
Camp Orkila
Eastsound
Mt. Constitution
Long Shadows
Eagle Rock
Lummi Island
East Sound
Lawrence Point
ORCAS
ISLAND
Crow Valley
Rosario Resort
Doe Bay
Rosario Strait
Cormorant
Doe Island
Indian Point
West Sound
Olga
To Victoria BC
Deer Harbor
Orcas Landing
Cypress Island
Shaw Island
Blakely Island
To Friday Harbor San Juan Island
Lopez Island
Anacortes Ferry

CONTENTS

JULY

THE MISSING

AUGUST

THE HOUSE OF LONG SHADOWS

JUNE

Haunted Houses

1

The Reprise

In many ways, an eternity has passed since I boarded that Washington State ferry at Orcas Landing. During my absence, I've created a life on my own terms, married a wonderful man, and gave birth to a son who is the apple of my eye. Welcome to the Charmed Life of M. G. Hawthorne, according to the recent exposé published in Sunset magazine. Yet beyond those glossy pages of finely edited words and perfect photographs, the painful imprint of my departure still lingers, as do the haunting memories that wake me in the middle of the night, even after all these years. I recall the promises to myself and those I left behind, promises that eventually evolved into obligations. Revisiting the list of those now realized, I confirm the one that remains unattended; today, this terrifies me, and not just for my sake.

~

"Follow him . . . and don't forget to put 'er in park and set yer emergency brake!"

"Aye-aye, skipper," Robert answers the ferryman, touching a finger to his forehead in a lazy salute as he drives us onto the San Juan Islands–bound vessel.

"How many times a day do you think he has to say that?" I ask, jarred from my contemplation.

"At least a few hundred if you consider the cargo capacity, give or take. Why are you shaking your head?"

"You engineers and your calculations," I laugh.

"You think we're bad? You're lucky I'm not an accountant!"

"Don't misunderstand. I still find your precise nature cute, but it's 1972—surely those kinds of announcements can be made with a recording like they do at Sea-Tac."

"Sounds like somebody's got a bee in her bonnet," Robert says with a smile.

I shrug lightly. He isn't wrong, but my emotions are too unsettled to be pinned down so neatly. "Sorry, I guess I'm a little on edge; please ignore me."

We come to a stop, and Robert shifts the station wagon into park, but it's the ratcheting sound of the emergency brake that confirms we are officially aboard.

"Hey, Mom, I'm finished!" pipes Edward from the back seat, followed by the triumphant thud of a large book.

"Was there ever a doubt?" I reply, turning to see his satisfied smile.

"Never! All sixty-two Sherlock Holmes stories, every single word!"

"I'm very proud of you. That took a lot of determination and patience, especially with the language differences since those tales were written."

"Thanks, Mom—reading *The Old Nurse's Story* last fall definitely helped with that."

"Congratulations," Robert chimes in, his proud grin as wide as mine. "I bet not many thirteen-year-olds, or adults for that matter, can say the same."

"That's exactly what Mrs. Barr said. I lucked out that she allowed me to pick something else when all the girls in the school book club voted for *Anne of Green Gables* and *Charlotte's Web*."

"Not surprising, honey—you've been one of her favorites since kindergarten."

"She knew I only had *The Five Orange Pips* left to read, and I promised her I'd be done before sundown, so today, in front of the whole club, she said it showed my ability to follow through on a highly formidable adult-level collection."

"That's a high compliment, Edward. I know you're going to miss her next year with the redistricting."

"I will, for sure." Edward's eyes scan the ferry, his insatiable curiosity gleaming with intensity. I can see him cataloging the details of our surroundings as he steps out of the car. "Are we going up on deck?"

"Absolutely, that's the best part of a ferry ride. Tell you what—meet Dad and me at the snack bar in ten minutes, and we'll grab a little something for the trip."

"Deal!"

"Now, you better scoot if you're going to see us get underway."

The ferry horn announces our departure as Edward slams the car door behind him and dashes up the cavernous stairwell to watch us pull away from the Anacortes terminal.

"Well, what about that?" Robert chuckles.

"His vocabulary is something else!"

"I mean, look who his mother is."

"Oh, stop—he's growing up so fast, Robert."

"He really is."

"I just pray it's not too fast . . ."

"As much as I wouldn't mind it, he can't stay our little boy forever," Robert says softly, his wistful tone matching my feelings exactly.

"I know, but I'd like to think we're giving him an extension is all; it's such a sweet time in life." The words sound like an attempt to convince myself as I speak them.

"Him?" Robert asks, resting his hand on mine.

"Touché. You've got me there." I meet his eyes with a half-smile.

Robert gestures toward the emerald waters of the Salish Sea. "How does it feel to be returning to Orcas Island for the first time since leaving?"

"I was fine until we boarded; now there's a bit of nerves, but I'm determined they won't spoil this experience."

"A little anxiety seems pretty natural. Don't be too hard on yourself—this is a big deal for you."

I smile at the man who has been the rock of my existence for fourteen years. "You've been so supportive through all this, especially with how I treated you and Edward while writing the last book."

"Water under the bridge, and for what it's worth, I've never questioned that this is the right thing to do. And I mean for all of us."

"I'm so thankful to hear you say that. I've been questioning myself quite a bit lately."

"You know this wouldn't have been possible without your success—"

"Our success, honey." I smile and peck his cheek.

"Regardless, it's hard for me to put into words, but being out on that property is something special, whatever the challenges of island life may be."

"I still remember that feeling . . . it's hard to believe we're actually doing this."

"Aside from everything else, it's an extraordinary opportunity for the price; you'd think the place was full of spooks or something."

"It's an old house, Robert; there are bound to be a few hanging around." I laugh. "But I thought you didn't believe in all that mumbo jumbo, as you so aptly put it."

"I don't know . . . the way the sellers jumped at our first offer kind of makes me want to reconsider my opinion."

"It just wasn't the right summerhouse for them, is all."

"Yeah, or the folks before them, apparently." He smiles, but there's something more behind his comment.

"I thought you loved the house."

"Oh, I do, spooks or not! I just hope they continue to mind their own affairs."

"All right, so what's the rub, then?"

"No rub, just thinking about the weekends I spent out there the past few months, is all." He pauses for a beat, then shakes it off. "Let's make our way upstairs and enjoy the rest of the boat ride."

"Robert—"

"It's nothing, really. Just stuff where your imagination can get away from you. Do you remember anything odd from when you were a kid?"

"Odd?"

"It's pretty remote. That side of the island is so isolated, and at night it's black as pitch when the moon isn't out."

"Which is part of the charm, right?"

"Indeed, I love the peace and quiet during the day—no complaints about that from me. Maybe it's just that I'm not used to that type of quiet at night, and my mind is trying to make up for it."

"That could be; we'll see if it's better tonight when we're all together. Guess we should get up top—Edward's probably already waiting for us at the snack bar. I think that kid's got a hollow leg."

Robert chuckles. "I shoveled away the food at his age, too. But I bet you he's still out on deck leaning over the rail and having a blast."

"You're probably right. Better grab his windbreaker and yours, too—it'll be chilly out there."

~

Edward isn't to be found at the snack bar, so we make our way through the main cabin until we spot him through a window at the forward rail. Robert and I laugh, and he joins him on deck, handing him his windbreaker while I find a booth inside the main cabin that allows me to observe my two boys doing what boys do best.

Witnessing their conversation and expressions from only a few yards away but separated by tons of steel and glass, I can only guess at their exchange.

The moment brings to mind a lecture I attended back at the University of Washington. The parapsychologist's theory suggested that spirits of the departed vibrate at such high frequencies that they're in another dimension and, as a rule, can only observe us. However, as all rules go, there are exceptions—something I can attest to from my own childhood experiences on the island.

Producing the small notebook and pen that once again serve as my constant companions, I recall that age when every new adventure is exciting and full of wonder.

The erosion of our youthful naiveté is a cursed path, but one we all must tread. Nonetheless, I still rue the memory of when Edward, then in the fourth grade, walked into the house so crestfallen after a neighborhood boy unmasked Santa Claus for him and his pals.

Now, as I sit here accompanied by the drone of ferry engines, my prayer is that this summer won't extinguish the last vestiges of his innocence, and yet, deep down, it seems inevitable.

Novels resemble life in that they're full of chapters, some to be reread, others to be rewritten, but all to be experienced. I learned this lesson early, as I was fortunate enough to have a good teacher. Without her, I'm not sure I would have had the resilience or fortitude to break away and craft stories of my own. This career in writing is something I've never regretted, but it's the casualties . . . there are always casualties, even when wielding Lytton's pen.

Survival demands that we learn to live with the consequences of our decisions, written or otherwise, and I'm only three ferry stops away from facing mine. Or so I think.

~

After a rough docking at Lopez Island, the boys join me inside the main cabin and apologize for their extended absence, explaining how they lost track of time looking for killer whales.

"Don't apologize; watching you two have a ball always does my heart good."

"Did you catch that dicey docking? Sometimes they come in a tad hot."

"Oh, we definitely felt it inside. Those poor folks over there almost had their sodas in their laps," I reply, gesturing across the cabin to an elderly couple playing cards.

"It's a good thing those pilings are designed to flex because we really whacked them that time."

"I thought it was cool!"

"That was evident from the grin on your face," Robert says, giving Edward an affirming nudge, then tipping his chin in my direction. "I've been wondering when that little notebook of yours would make an appearance."

"Just a few scratches is all," I smile.

"Edward, why don't you keep Mom company while I run to the snack bar for us, all right?"

"Sure. I'll have a Simba and some peanuts, please."

"You got it, champ. Coffee, honey?"

"Yes, please, unless they've started a wine service," I laugh.

"You know I'll join you if they have! Sit tight, and I'll be back in a jiffy."

As Robert heads off toward the snack bar, Edward slides into the bench seat opposite me, resting his elbows on the table and chin in his hands.

"Now that you're out of school for the summer, does anything stand out from this past year?" I ask him.

Edward reflects for a moment. "I guess one thing I noticed was how strange it is being one of the big kids."

"In what way?"

"Well, when I was in the lower grades, I thought they were so big and cool. Then, when I finally got here, I didn't feel that big and cool."

"That's a great life lesson and pretty common when we enter new environments, no matter what age we are. Think about all those younger kids who were looking up to you this year."

"That's kind of funny."

"Well, it's true—"

But before I can finish the thought, my throat goes dry, and my heartbeat accelerates as I lock eyes with the man making his way in our direction from the opposite end of the cabin.

I calmly stand up, and without raising my voice, I direct Edward to slide into my side of the booth. Sensing the urgency, he slips in behind me, and together we watch the man in his middle thirties with a cane and limping gait approach our table.

"You are Meredith Gaines, aren't you?"

"That was my name at one time," I answer, not tersely but definitely without further invitation.

"Oh, I see . . . yes, yes, of course," he replies with an odd look while taking stock of Edward over the top of his heavy black eyeglass frames. "Chase Stuart of the Shaw Island Stuarts—I'm sure you remember us."

"Indeed, I do. It's been many years."

"Things don't change much on Shaw, although Mother did die about four years ago in a house fire."

"I'm sorry for your loss," I reply, hoping this ends our visit.

"No loss, really—it's not a secret that she hated me. If I only had a dollar for every time I warned her about cooking in that nightgown . . . but she never listened. It was always Skip this and Skip that . . . Why couldn't you be smart like your brother Skip was? When any chump off the street knows that an open flame, hairspray, and a flannel nightgown are a bad combination.

"That evening, she was standing over the stove with her hair in rollers shellacked with half a can of Aqua Net and bent down to light a cigarette off the burner. When the flame got a whiff of that hairspray, up she goes like a god-damned dry Christmas tree, then ran through the house screaming and spreading fire everywhere. Next thing I know, the whole place is an inferno, and I have to fend for myself before the propane tanks explode! I mean, any sane person in that position would have done the same thing, right?"

"Undoubtedly." Now I'm so intrigued by his candor that I don't dare interrupt as he continues.

"You're a survivor like me, Meredith—I figured you'd see it my way, unlike some of the riffraff also-rans loafing on these islands. That same lot would have been roasted like pigs on a spit!" Stuart chuckles as he whips the cane hard against the side of his leg, producing a loud, unnatural crack.

The startled expression on Edward's face registers with Stuart as he ends the diatribe, and following another awkward laugh, he hikes his pant leg using the crook of the cane to reveal a medieval contraption fashioned of metal, canvas, and leather straps, cradling a grotesquely disfigured leg.

"I consider myself damned lucky to have gotten out of that house with some singed hair and this gimped leg after the tanks blew." He states before releasing his trousers to once again cover the repulsive sight.

"The entire ordeal sounds horrible; I'm sorry," I say.

"No pity, please. I'm the first to admit that the checks I received from the insurance company helped out, if you catch my drift." He winks.

Once again, I hope this concludes our conversation; he continues, however, carrying Edward deeper into uncharted territory with his dredging of the past.

"I recall reading in The Seattle Times that your father and that gold-digging trollop of his died in a car wreck on the floating bridge; that must be fifteen or sixteen years ago now."

"Yes, I'm afraid so," I reply, smirking at his description of Samantha.

"Considering the circumstances, I'm surprised he didn't blow his brains out or jump off Deception Pass bridge. I know plenty who would have preferred that to the humiliation of financial ruin and life among the rabble."

I nod without reply. Then he meets my eyes with a quick, cold stare that I haven't seen for almost two decades, and his carefully chosen words bring a shiver to my spine.

"Dreadful business, but alas, the worms have to eat too—don't you agree, Meredith?"

Everything about Chase Stuart makes my skin crawl, but I don't flinch from his flattened delivery or break from those empty eyes with my response. "According to the paper, they were cremated in the wreckage, so I guess the worms missed a meal."

"How delightfully morbid!" Stuart lets out an exaggerated laugh, narrowing his gaze as he searches my eyes for weakness. I refuse to show him one.

The chill in the conversation is palpable, and before he can comment further, Edward, who has been a quiet observer, stands up and shouts across the cabin, "Dad, we're over here!" waving his hand in the air as if his father doesn't know our location.

Robert sets the tray on the table and introduces himself while extending his hand in greeting.

"The name's Chase Stuart—a pleasure to meet you, Robert. Meredith and I have quite the family history together," he says coolly as the docking announcement for Shaw Island crackles over the speaker with their handshake.

"Ah, my stop approaches. I'd better not dally and get back to the car—these ferrymen tend to frown on tardiness, and it doesn't matter to them in the least if you're a goddamned cripple, either. Well, it's been nice to see you again, Meredith, and to meet you, Robert, and your son, I presume?"

"Yes, this is Edward," Robert answers.

"A nice strong name! Off to Meredith's old stomping grounds, are we?"

"I'm sorry, Mr. Stuart, it's a surprise for Edward," I intervene before Robert can answer.

"In that case, enjoy your surprise, Edward! It's supposed to be beautiful up here the next week or so—might even see a whale pod or two if you're lucky. I've sighted several over in Sullivan's Cove on Shaw!" he yells just before vanishing into the stairwell.

"Hmmm, that was interesting," Robert says with a lift of his eyebrows and a questioning smile.

"Astonishing is more like it," I answer, trying to conceal my trembling as the adrenaline from our exchange dissipates.

"You all right?"

"I'm fine. A bit of cat and mouse."

"I think it's safe to say the cat's out of the bag now."

"We both knew it was bound to happen at some point. I'm actually relieved that it's over."

"But do you think he—"

"Oh, he's a reader all right—a return one at that," I say with a nervous laugh and a thousand-mile stare, which Robert immediately recognizes.

"What's rattling around in that pretty little head of yours?"

"Sullivan's Cove—there isn't one on Shaw or any of the San Juan Islands."

"So it's something from your last book that only a local might catch."

"Yep, thinly veiled, along with—"

"Who is that guy?" Edward interjects. "He gives me the creeps."

"Excuse me? What have I told you about interrupting people?"

"Sorry, Mom . . . *it's inexcusably rude and a vulgar habit.*"

"Exactly."

"Aside from the interruption, I'm with you—that guy's a weirdo," Robert says, rolling his eyes and making Edward laugh.

"Dad, you should've seen his mutilated leg—it was super-gross, plus he was talking about worms eating dead bodies!"

"All right, now."

"But Mom, his skin . . ."

"But Meredith, that skin on his throat—I'm going to wash my hands in case he's got scabies!" Robert parrots as he laughs.

"You two are incorrigible! Now, gather up your stuff because we need to get back to the car in a couple of minutes."

The encounter with Chase Stuart at the outset of this trip was unsettling, to be sure. He's three years my senior and was about twenty when I left Orcas; today he's just a limping older version. The same height as Robert at six feet, but of a slighter build and wearing what's left of his orange hair in a comb-over so sparse, I think, why bother? Dressed in corduroy trousers and a waxed canvas jacket, the generous helping of Brut aftershave appeared to irritate his skin. It was outlasted only by the tension that hung in the air after his departure.

Although I wasn't around him much during my years on the island, there were the occasional soirees of affluent families who entertained at one another's estates. His awkwardness was abundantly clear from the start, as he lacked even the most rudimentary of social graces. Initially, this elicited compassion from people, believing that he might be a tad slow, but this opinion changed after just one conversation when it became apparent that there was an absence of right or wrong behind that unsettlingly vacant stare of his.

It's no secret or slight to locals to point out that the veins of Islanders run rich with gossip, and the more prominent the family, the more rancorous and salacious the whisperings. The Stuarts were never far from the top of that list, and after his teenage stint in a mainland reformatory for setting fire to the dock in Deer Harbor, Chase unseated his philandering father for top billing in marina gossip throughout the San Juans. As the younger and least preferred of two brothers, he survived the rest of his family and became sole heir to their once-sizable fortune, apparently boasting about acquiring his money the old-fashioned way—inheriting it.

Chase Stuart is the sleeping dog that I hadn't let lie in my latest work, and though he was cleared by the local authorities of the day, his proximity to several deaths, including that of a local girl who was pregnant, left many unanswered questions. His parting comment assured me that our next encounter would prove even more interesting.

Entertaining that suspicion as Edward and I make our way toward the stairs, I discreetly ask Robert to go to the bow of the boat to see what Stuart might be driving, as there won't be many disembarking at Shaw Island, even on a Friday afternoon.

The stop is brief, and Robert returns to the car as the docking horn sounds for Orcas, just minutes across the channel.

"Orcas! That's where we're going," shouts Edward, stating the obvious.

"The game's afoot, Watson!" Robert replies in the accent of a Londoner.

"I'm Holmes, Dad. You're Watson!"

"Tally ho then, Holmes!"

"Get those hands washed?" I ask Robert.

"Yes indeed, no scabies here," he answers the question I'm really asking.

Following the small line of traffic along a two-lane road, we reach the island's main village of Eastsound and pull into the parking lot of Templin's grocery store.

"Wow! It's nice to see the old place hasn't changed much," I say.

"According to the banner inside, they're celebrating seventy-five years this summer. I figure we'll grab some steaks for dinner and a couple of things for breakfast. You ready, or do you want to stay in the car?"

"Are you kidding me? I can't wait!"

The familiar smell of Templin's takes me back to the days when my tutor Edna brought me shopping with her. Somewhat indescribable, it's reminiscent of the cardboard boxes that apples are packed in, much like our Capitol Hill market on 15th Avenue during fall, minus the waft of caramel and cinnamon brooms from the neighboring bins. I return a welcoming smile from the clerk ringing out another customer, and the three of us set off through the narrow aisles with our shopping cart.

"Well, hello there, Robert," says the slim, attractive, doe-eyed brunette about my age, whom I barely avoid a collision with at the intersection of canned goods and condiments.

"Hi Danelle! We just got in on the five o'clock," Robert responds, as my raised eyebrow relaxes with the mention of her name.

"I figured. Welcome to Orcas, Meredith and Edward! I'm Danelle Sinclair—my husband, Kent, and I have the farm just down the road from you."

"Danelle, it's so nice to finally put a face to the name. I can't thank you and Kent enough for everything you've done."

"Aww, you're welcome. We're just glad to help out and thrilled that you're finally here. Edward, we have a fourteen-year-old daughter named Vivian, and she's very excited to meet you."

"Yes, ma'am," Edward replies, not quite knowing what to make of the situation.

"Would y'all come for dinner on Sunday? Maybe three-thirty or four—that way we can show you around the farm, too."

"That sounds wonderful, Danelle," I smile. "We'll be looking forward to the visit. What can we bring?"

"Yourselves, and please call us if you need anything in the meantime. Oh, and don't stock up on eggs or fruit—we'll be sure to send you home with plenty!"

~

Robert squeezes the groceries into the overstuffed station wagon, and minutes later, we find ourselves on a forested, twisting two-lane highway heading toward the eastern end of the island. A long stretch of trees that creep close to the road produces an overhang so dense that it practically extinguishes the daylight.

After a few are-we-there-yets from Edward, we turn onto an unmarked, unpaved road leading to a dead end. I feel the flutter of butterflies for the first time as Robert drives through the arched iron gate and we start down the cedar-lined lane. Rounding the final curve, we enter a large, open range, cordoned on three sides by a forest that closes its doors behind us, and a second later, my heart jumps at the sight of her.

The house is regally perched among the rock and cedars, her weathered shingles reflecting fawn and silver in the fading daylight, the exception being those yet to endure the prolonged exposure to salt air and unrelenting island sun. The white trim outlining the house is fresh and bright, giving added distinction to the windows, roofline, and several large pillars supporting the formidable front porch. She's breathtaking to behold.

"Oh, Robert, thank you! How on earth did you manage all of this?" I ask, kissing his cheek.

"Not a big deal, really," he answers nonchalantly, struggling to contain his smile.

And that's the moment when Edward puts the pieces together.

"Wait a minute—this is the project Dad's been working on, not something at Boeing?" His tone reveals the shock of his misperception and excitement for what lies ahead.

"Another case solved, Mr. Holmes!" Robert affirms.

In the preceding months, Edward had deduced that his father's weekend absences were due to an important deadline he was under at Boeing, and neither of us corrected him. First, his deduction was plausible. Every Seattleite knew that the aircraft giant had undergone severe austerity measures the past year and a half, with over fifty thousand losing their jobs in the downsizing. We were extremely fortunate, as Robert's knack for logistics was deemed essential, and our family survived the bloodlettings. So rather than correcting Edward, we reasoned that it would be a good lesson for him to learn about jumping to conclusions, and it just so happened to fit in with his current muse, the great detective Sherlock Holmes. But deep down, I felt it was more about preserving his innocence for one last semester of school in our Capitol Hill enclave, as everything was set to change.

The car stops a few feet from the house, and Edward naturally goes for the door handle.

"You stay put!"

"Better do as she says," Robert advises with a slight turn of his head as I step out of the car.

I stare up at her just long enough to draw in a deep breath and exhale a quick prayer before opening Edward's door with all the flourish of an Italian courtier.

"Edward, welcome to the House of Long Shadows."

2

Reacquainted

Seventeen years have evaporated since my promise to return, and as I stand before her today at age thirty-four, I feel a twinge of sadness that another full lifetime has been lived from the moment I uttered those words with such conviction.

I've often chided myself for looking back when Edna drove us off the property that morning, as the image I've carried is so tightly stitched to my soul that there are times it almost suffocates me. Though I was exiled, a part of me remained behind, marooned beneath the waves of passing years . . . waiting, watching, hoping, as countless ships navigated the dark green waters of Rosario Strait. At least that's how I imagine it's been for her.

Today, thanks to a loving husband who's remained remarkably steady through the rough patches of my writing quirks and dreams, this moment marks a huge milestone toward my reunification.

"Let's go, boys!" I say, pushing on toward the house.

My excitement is contagious, and Edward outpaces Robert and me, doubling the porch steps, then reaching for the ornately patterned bronze doorknob.

"Hold your horses, pal, you'll need the key."

He doesn't, and the mechanism lets out a substantial clunk as the large mahogany door pivots open with a welcoming gesture.

Robert shoots me a quizzical look. "That's strange—I know I locked up last Sunday. Kent must have come back to work on something or other."

A hint of linseed oil greets us as he turns on the lights, flooding the foyer with a warm incandescent glow.

"W-h-o-a . . ." is Edward's pithy take on the scene as his eyes wander around the large formal entry.

I had thought that my response in this moment would be more composed, if not somewhat dignified, but that notion turns out to be pure nonsense. Instead, the impact is so powerful that I let out a sob and smother an ugly cry, burying my face deep into Robert's flannel shirt.

"You OK?" Edward asks, touching my arm.

"Just grateful," I barely manage to reply through the emotions. "Really, really, grateful."

Long Shadows is not an average summerhouse. Woodwork with detail so finely crafted that one knows these artisans were dedicated to their skill. It was built in 1912 by many of the same craftsmen and shipwrights who constructed the Rosario mansion for famed Seattle shipbuilding magnate Robert Moran, and they utilized its overages of brass, mahogany, and teakwood throughout the interior.

"Kent brought the wood back to life. Lots of elbow grease, linseed, and beeswax," Robert says, his kind eyes finding mine.

"It shows! I can't wait to thank him in person."

"They're such great neighbors, Meredith; Kent encouraged me, and Danelle kept me well-fed over the last five months, that's for sure!"

The house is easily three times the size of our Capitol Hill home on 16th Avenue East. The downstairs has a sizable open foyer flanked by a living room on the right and a study on the left. A wide central hallway leads past the grand staircase with a large alcove underneath containing the telephone desk that I remember well as a child. Robert stops to run his hand over the intricately fashioned mahogany panels lining the space.

"They sure don't do work like this anymore," he points out, admiring the finer details.

"No, they don't," I smile and slip past him deeper into the alcove.

Before he can say another word I grasp the base of an old brass sconce with both hands and give a firm twist to the left and back to the right.

"You gotta be kidding me!" Robert exclaims as the cleverly concealed mechanism pops and releases its pins.

"Great Scott! This is like something out of 'The Musgrave Ritual'!"

"If you say so, Edward! But I'm thinking more like the Addams Family," Robert replies, as the panel now spins freely on a heavy brass rod, revealing the hidden room.

"This was originally built for the owners to secure their valuables. It also came in handy for stashing away liquor brought in from Canada during Prohibition," I tell them, thrilled by their surprised faces.

"It's the coolest thing ever!"

I can already see the engineer's gears spinning in Robert's head. "I can't wait to see how this mechanism works—it seems pretty sophisticated."

"Well, you two can explore that to your heart's content, but after the rest of the tour, please."

I quickly restore the panel to its concealed status, and we continue down the hallway to the main-floor powder room, followed by the butler's pantry, and pause briefly before entering the huge kitchen. It's one of three rooms that I insisted be completely redone, and when Robert flips the light switch, I'm stunned by how beautiful it turned out. While the trend is to do something in harvest gold and avocado green, I chose Thermador's lifetime stainless steel for everything—from the double wall oven, gas cooktop, and refrigerator to the dishwasher and trash compactor. No dark cabinets, either! Instead, they're cream, and the counters are topped with American walnut butcher block, creating a welcome contrast.

"Oh my . . ."

"It turned out great, didn't it? Take a look at the view."

At a rare loss for words, I walk across the room toward a wall of windows and through the French doors onto the rear porch. Some things haven't changed, and the view over the sloping landscape to the sea in the distance is one of them. I'm so entranced by it all that I don't notice Robert and Edward stepping outside to join me.

"The guys shored up the joists, replaced some decking, and widened the stairs going down."

"It's just hard to take it all in," I reply while trying to hold off the years of memories that are coming back.

"Well, come on, there's more to see!" Robert grins, corralling me with his arm as he leads us back inside.

To the right is the laundry, adjoining a utility and mudroom with its own door to the outside. The dining room is on the left and connects us to the living room, then into the foyer.

After scaling the wide staircase, we visit the rear two bedrooms—identical masters with full baths and individual covered porches providing the same magnificent east-facing views as the porch below, only from a higher perspective.

"Edward, this is your bedroom; it was mine at your age."

"Really?" he shouts, bounding across the room and diving onto the king-sized bed.

"The way the morning sunlight pours in here is something very special to wake up to. Leave the windows open at night for the cool breeze, and you'll sleep like a baby."

"Can I go out on the porch and check out the view?"

"By all means, it's your room—just stay on this side of the railing!"

As Edward hurries onto his porch, Robert and I continue the tour arm in arm, where he proudly points to each detail, conveying the amount of work it took to restore the house to its present state. "Kent did a great job working with Ralph, the contractor. It helped that his wife, Carol, is co-chair of the largest book club on the islands. She'll need an invite when we get everything situated the way you want."

"Absolutely! I've been excited to try out a dinner-gathering idea that's been percolating for a while now."

"It'll be nice to get acquainted with more folks out here. I'm sure there's already plenty of curiosity about your return."

"Oh, whatever—I'm just a simple girl who spent her childhood summers here is all."

"Yeah! M. G. Hawthorne, best-selling novelist and simple girl . . . that's you, all right!" Robert grins and shakes his head.

"Am I really that bad?"

"Not as Meredith, but that M. G. Hawthorne—she takes her writing pretty seriously."

"She has to—it's her name on the cover." There's insecurity in my wavering reply.

"I understand, it's your job. I'm just giving you the business is all. Fair warning, I haven't done much in the cellar or the attic yet."

"Ah yes, the cellar—I remember that massive boiler. Does it still shake the house when it fires up?"

"Oh, that monster's still down there, but thankfully in their brief stay, the last owners updated the heating system. Today it's just a backup if needed."

"That was smart. What about the attic?"

"Empty. I walked it checking for signs of leaks, rot, and creepy crawly things. It's in great shape like the rest of the structure, and plenty of room for storage."

"Don't worry, I'm not wondering if there's a place for my desk; how's the cabin?"

"Honey, I'm not all that worried about you having a temporary writing spot in the attic. As for the cabin, there are only so many hours in a weekend."

"I apologize. It's obvious how hard you've been working; I still can't believe my eyes."

"No need. I know you've been anticipating this for so long. But you should be down at the cabin when Edward and I clear it out just in case you recognize something. Looks like the last owners may have used it for a catchall, and they weren't too concerned about it when they left."

"Take your time, I've plenty of other things to do over the next few weeks," I say. "By the way, the house and furnishings are superb! I couldn't be happier."

"You picked everything out; I just made sure most of them got here in time."

"Once again, your logistical skills are impeccable, my dear. I was most concerned about the paint, but everything is perfect!"

"I agree. The neutrals are nice and don't distract from the beauty of the house itself," he smiles as his eyes scan the room. "We'll have to clear out the cabin sooner than later because the construction crew will be here in a week and a half, and Ralph says his guys don't lollygag; they really get after it."

"Whatever you need, and whenever you need it, I'm all yours."

"I'll hold you to that," he says, whispering in my ear while patting my bottom. My response is a cat-like smile and purr.

After a few hurried footsteps from above, Edward flies down the stairs, rejoining us in the foyer with a big grin. "This place is totally outrageous!"

"How's the view from your porch?"

"It's great—I can see everything! It looks like there are big cliffs down by the water."

"Yes, there are, and you need to be very careful around them. I mean it."

"Yeah, Edward, no goofing around! We'll check them out tomorrow morning when we have more light."

"Cool, Dad. Hey, is anyone else starving?"

"I'm famished."

"Well, that makes three of us," Robert concurs. "I'll fire up the hibachi so we can celebrate our first night with a steak dinner."

"Now that sounds divine. If you two unload and get the grill going, I'll do the organizing while the sweet potatoes are in the oven and throw a salad together for us."

~

It's already dusk as I step outside to the sizzle of Robert placing the steaks on the hot grill and Edward with his neck craned skyward.

"Wow! Check it out!"

"We don't see this back on the hill, do we?" Robert replies while pointing out Venus and Mars.

"No way!"

"Without the light pollution of the city, you'll see plenty of shooting stars out here and even a satellite orbiting the Earth if you can sit still long enough."

"Maybe we can get a telescope?"

"Vivian has one; you'll have to ask if you can look through hers first. I just toss a blanket on the grass and lie down with a pair of binoculars. It's amazing what you can see with them; they're in our bedroom if you want to try it for yourself."

"I wonder if Vivian's seen any UFOs with her telescope!"

"Go ahead and ask her. I mean, who knows, you might even catch a glimpse of the starship Enterprise!"

"Or a Klingon Bird of Prey!"

"Or a Romulan Warbird!"

"Don't laugh, Dad—wouldn't that be so far out?"

"Yeah, that'd be far out, all right!"

Edward turns to me after their banter. "Mom, you lived here and in Seattle?"

"Yes, I did. I spent every summer right here from the time I was six years old until I turned seventeen."

"That's cool! So, is this place ours?"

"Ours is a big four-letter word, honey. However, in the spirit of your question, yes, ours is now the responsibility of stewarding this place."

"The guys back home will flip out when they hear about this. How much land are we on?"

"I believe this parcel is a little more than a hundred acres—so, all the way to the sea and then well beyond the trees surrounding us," I say, making a 360-degree turn with my hands outstretched.

"Man! That's like the size of a whole neighborhood on Capitol Hill!"

"It is, or you can think of it as about the same size as two Volunteer Parks."

"Hey, it looks like these steaks are about ready to come off. Are we eating inside or out?" Robert asks.

"For our first night, I vote that we break in the kitchen table and give the house some well-deserved family time."

Over dinner, Edward peppers me with questions about my life on Orcas while Robert grins from the other side of the table, taking in all of his excitement. I find it comforting to know that at least a portion of his smile is rooted in the deep satisfaction of restoring this magnificent house to its current state, the other being how much he loves his family.

"Anyone up for taking a walk down to the barn to help digest that fabulous dinner?" Robert suggests.

"There's a barn too?" Edward whips his head around.

"There'd better be—it was here a week ago!"

"Yeah, I'll go with you, Dad!"

"You two go ahead—I'll finish cleaning up around here, but take a flashlight with you."

"Got one right here," Robert says, emerging from the utility room while staring into the dim yellow beam. "Nuts, I knew I forgot something at Templin's. This should get us there and back tonight, but next trip into Eastsound we need a lantern battery."

"Be careful and stay away from the cliffs until daylight," I say, tying on an apron.

"Yes, dear, we're not going all the way down there, just straight to the barn and back. You sure you don't want to come along?"

"Positive. I'll go see it tomorrow—you two enjoy yourselves!"

"All right, we won't be too long."

"Take as long as you want—we're on island time now," I say with a laugh.

The boys bid me farewell and set off on the three-hundred-or-so-yard jaunt to the barn. I suspect that Robert wants to show Edward the hayloft swing as well as that old workhorse Massey-Ferguson tractor I drove as a child.

After quickly finishing the dishes, I shed my apron and lay out Edward's nightclothes before embarking on my own excursion through the house, beginning with the attic.

Surprised to find the door wide open, I chalk it up to Edward's earlier explorations and flip the light switch to examine the same stairwell I summoned from memory for use in my last book. The cringe-worthy squeak of that first tread as my foot finds its center was something to avoid as a child, but tonight I find it charmingly nostalgic. At the top, I'm greeted by the familiar sharp fragrance of cedar lath that brings me back to the days when I played up here among the boxes of treasured memories, none of which were mine.

As an only child who was, for all intents and purposes, abandoned by my father and his new wife, Samantha, I had to create my own entertainment. There were no playmates out here, nothing but land, sky, and sea. At least my father and Samantha were selfish enough to recognize that unless there was someone else to pester with my everyday little girl things, I would forever be a nuisance to them. They argued back and forth over hiring a governess for me, but the last straw was when I kept talking about the girl I met out on the property.

She was about my age and, like me, very shy. Our first encounter was when I was singing songs and reading stories to my dolls outside of the cabin by the cliffs, something I had done without fail for about a week. She stood partially hidden by the low branch of a cedar tree at the edge of the woods and didn't speak; she just watched me. This continued for several days and I recall feeling sad for her, perhaps because of my own sadness, thinking she might be alone like I was. So, the following morning I carried along my favorite doll. She was an Indian girl wearing a beaded buckskin dress and moccasins that my mother brought home for me after a trip, and as much as I cherished her, I knew deep inside that the girl in the woods needed her more than I did.

The girl remained in the shadow of the cedar as I gently placed the doll on a large rock and said that she was now hers and would keep her company if I wasn't around.

When I returned the next day, she stepped out of the woods cradling the doll and presented me with a glass float, one of those spheres that break away from Japanese fishing nets and somehow find their way across the ocean unscathed. Her eyes were the same shade of palest green, but invitingly warm, and when I thanked her for the gift, she just smiled and bashfully pointed to the book I carried.

We sat among the rocks on a patch of grass close to the cliffs, and I began reading aloud like I always did, while displaying each picture to our audience of dolls. A giggle was the first sound she made; it was sweet, innocent, full of delight and wonder as she stared at the brightly colored illustrations splashed across the pages. When we parted ways that afternoon, she smiled and with her palm to her chest spoke one word:

"Lhaq'temish."

3

A Mother's Gift

"We're back!" Robert's faint voice from below returns me to the present like a hypnotist snapping his fingers.

"Be there in a minute!" I shout, dawdling down the stairs, concerned that I may lose the detail of that memory with each step.

When I reach the bottom, Edward is glowing with excitement. "Did you really drive that tractor?" he asks, half-skeptical, half-admiring.

"I sure did, and I was about your age, too."

"I wanna drive that thing!" he exclaims, taking an apple from the bowl on the counter.

"I'm sure your father would love to teach you; wash that first," I admonish.

"Sorry, but I've never even sat on a tractor before. I'm liable to run it through the back of the barn."

"Mom, you'll teach us both, right?"

"I guess I'll have to." I smile and wink at Robert. "How's the barn look?"

"It's in good shape, like everything else around here. Kent thinks we should update a few things if we plan to store hay in there, and it'd be a good time to beef up the workbench and service panel while we're at it."

"That all sounds great—whatever we need is fine with me."

"And that reminds me, do we want to donate this year's hay to Olga Livestock? I think they come to get it in August."

"Those are the folks who had a fire last year, right?"

"Yep, and according to Kent, they're gathering donations of straw and hay from around the islands to get their new barn and stables filled; I guess the Farmer's Almanac is calling for a harsher winter this year."

"Let's give it to them then; it sounds like they'll need it more than we will."

"Great, I'll call them Monday and deliver the good news."

"It feels nice to end our first day with a good deed." I smile.

"I don't know about you two, but I'm bushed, and a hot shower will feel really good about now," Robert says.

"Me too, I'll be up in a bit, I've still got a few things to set up for the morning. What about you, Edward?"

"I have a Thor comic to read, and he's about to team up with the Silver Surfer and fight Durok the Demolisher!"

"That sounds thrilling! Take your shower first, though—towels and washcloths are in the bathroom closet, and your new bathrobe is on the hook behind the door. I also laid out some very special pajamas; you'll have to roll up the bottoms a turn or two, and there's a nice pair of house shoes to keep those tootsies warm."

"Thanks, Mom, but Dad always uses up the hot water."

"Not here! There's two brand new water heaters in the basement and they're one-hundred gallons each —that's almost triple what we have in Seattle." Robert's voice trails off as he makes his way down the hallway to the stairs.

"I'll take mine after you're finished, Edward, so get going."

~

After his shower, Edward finds me stretched out on the living room sectional with the lights off, staring into an unlit fireplace.

"Who were you talking to?"

"Just myself. Hey, don't you look smart in your robe and pajamas." I smile, taking the sleeve of his cashmere robe between my fingers.

"They're the best! Thanks for not getting me the cowboy and Indian ones again."

"I brought these back from London—the man at the shop told me they're exactly what Sherlock Holmes would wear, same with the robe and house shoes. I know they're a little large now, but you'll grow into them. How was that shower?"

"Plenty of hot water, and lots of pressure too. The water feels weird, though, kind of slippery, like I still had soap on me."

"It's the well. Well water isn't treated with all the chemicals they use in Seattle."

"That's right, Dad did say something about a well on our way to the barn. Hey, can I ask you a question?"

"Of course you can, but in the interest of precision, that's now two questions."

Edward barks out a laugh, part amusement, part sarcasm. "In the shower, I wondered if you named your book after this house."

"That's a great question, and the answer is sort of."

"I deduced that it was. Why?"

"That's a story for another time." I smile and release his sleeve.

"OK, it just came to mind is all . . . goodnight, Mom."

"Goodnight, honey. Sweet dreams, and give Thor my regards."

"I will. Oh, I almost forgot, Dad wants you to hurry up."

I try to hide my smirk as I push off the couch. "Let's walk up together, then. Do you need any lights on?"

"No thanks, Mom, I'm at least a year past all of that now."

"I guess you are." My reply fades with the reality of his answer.

Suddenly the tears begin to come, but I hold them back and kiss Edward's forehead goodnight at the top of the stairs. I make it past Robert reading in bed and into the shower before the levee breaks, and when it does, my tears seem to fall at the same rate as the cascade of warm water around me.

Now here with my own family . . . the place I longed for during the school years, my summer respite from the constant clatter of other spoiled rich kids back in Seattle's wealthiest circles, all desperately caught in the snare of our parents' delusions of grandeur.

Though eventually banished by my father entirely, I knew from the moment I left that today would arrive. This place was never his sanctuary, and certainly not Samantha's. If anything, the house is a lone thread back to my mother, who insisted he purchase it. Tragically, she passed away shortly thereafter without a single summer here. Regardless, I always believed this was her final gift to me, and now, with my once-little boy teetering on young adulthood, I'm praying that this is right for him and Robert and that they aren't just passengers on some ill-fated voyage of my own invention.

The saint of a man I married is fast asleep when I crawl into bed and discover the note on my pillow. "My dearest Meredith, welcome home. With all my love, Robert."

4

A Lesson in Herstory

My eyes open to the faint bugle of a rooster and the predawn glow that testifies to an imminent Orcas sunrise. Catching a whiff of coffee, I roll over, surprised to find Robert still dead to the world, and quietly slip out of bed, donning my robe before heading downstairs to the kitchen for a cup.

"Why, good morning . . . it's only five o'clock—what are you doing awake and dressed already?" I inquire with a yawn, rubbing my eyes.

"Morning, Mom! Been up for an hour. I can't wait to go out and explore this hundred acres!"

"I'm glad you're so excited about it. How'd you sleep?"

"Like a rock. I was lying there just about to start reading Thor, and when I blinked my eyes, it was morning! Is your coffee good?"

"It's the best cup of coffee I've had all day!" I smile through the bite of Edward's attempt and move to the refrigerator for some cream.

"Where's Dad?"

"He's still asleep, surprisingly."

"He must have been zonked too. Do you think you can teach us how to drive the tractor today?"

"We have plenty of time for the tractor. How about you and I take a walk before breakfast—that way, I can point out some of my favorite spots."

"Sure! But do we have to wait for Dad?"

"Only if he gets up before I get dressed." I take another sip out of habit and immediately regret it.

"Good, because I'm ready to move out!"

When I return to the bedroom, Robert stirs and rolls over with a yawn. "What time is it?"

"It's a quarter past five," I answer. "Why don't you stay in bed? Edward and I are going for a walk."

"He's already up?"

"Up and dressed. He even made the coffee." I beam. "By the way, thank you for the beautiful note."

"You're welcome. I'm so comfortable, I think I'll snooze till you get back."

"Good, and if you're still there when we return, I'll make a fresh pot of coffee and serve you breakfast in bed."

"Like the full breakfast?"

"Robert Hawthorne! Really! Stay put and you'll find out." I wink and close the door behind me, returning downstairs.

The plan is to make a loop of the open range beginning at the southern tree line and then head east toward the water. After that, we'll walk north along the cliffs with the sunrise until we arrive at the cabin. Then we can poke around inside and return up the northern tree line past the house, ending our walk at the water tower.

"It's so quiet," Edward says, at a volume suitable for the city.

"That's one of the best things about being here. Now try using your inside voice outside, honey."

"I guess that was kind of loud. Back when you lived here, were you bored without a lot of other kids around?"

"I was a young girl when we first arrived, so I guess a little overwhelmed, but in all those years I don't recall boredom being an issue."

"I can see how reading is like its own adventure every day."

"Indeed, and when you discover some favorite places to read, it makes it all the better. I had a few hideouts here and there where I might disappear and read the entire day away."

"What if it rained?"

"It doesn't rain a lot up here in the summer, but when it did, I'd either go down to the cabin or stay in the house. At the house, I'd sneak up to the attic or to the secret room downstairs, where I wouldn't be distracted."

"You mean by your parents?"

"Well, mostly Samantha."

"You never talk about them . . ."

"I guess I've been so grateful that you've grown up around the Mels and with Carver and Calvin that I didn't feel the need to."

"But who were they? What were they like? That weirdo guy on the ferry wasn't very nice about them, that's for sure."

I pause for a breath and shake my head with a rueful grin as I recall our exchange with Chase Stuart. "You're right—his delivery definitely lacked decorum."

"Were they bad people?"

"Edward, something you're going to learn for yourself as you get out in the world is that people are complicated. There's good and bad in just about everyone, and sometimes that good is buried under scars from their own past. It took me years to see it, and I think that was the case with my father."

"I'm pretty sure his name was Marvin because when I was staying with the Mels last weekend, Aunt Melanie was talking about the time you moved in with them—it was right after you left the huge house where Uncle Carver worked—but then Aunt Melinda gave her the big eyes, and she changed the subject."

"You don't miss a trick, do you?" I reply, concealing my wince at the name never mentioned in our house.

"Elementary! It's all the Sherlock Holmes I've read."

"Apparently so. All right, let's see: his name was Marvin Gaines; he founded Cascade Timber and Truss, a very large lumber company, and made a lot of money providing lumber to the government and other suppliers throughout the Pacific Northwest."

"Wow! That's that huge place next to the Fremont bridge! He must have been rich!"

"Yes, that was one of four yards that he had around the state. Beyond the money, he was extremely rich. He had a wife who loved him and a daughter who thought he hung the moon in the night sky just for her. But he became impoverished by his money and the power he wielded with it."

"Wait, how can having loads of money make you poor?"

Edward's wheels are turning and a flippant answer won't suffice, so I scan the landscape and find a place for us to pause while I offer an explanation worthy of his inquisitiveness.

"Let's have a seat on those rocks by the barn because it's important for you to understand this part of the story." Once seated, I brace myself and begin.

"Money and influence can be wonderful tools to build things, just like a hammer and nails. However, it's the love of money and the unquenchable thirst for power that becomes a Faustian bargain."

"OK, only I don't know what that last part means."

"The term comes from an old German legend and play, where Faust, a brilliant man in his own right, sacrificed all he had, including his immortal soul, for more knowledge. In essence, my father sacrificed his love of family for money and power. It was a soul trap—he lost it all, and as you heard yesterday, he died, leaving only a legacy of ruin behind."

"That doesn't sound very good." Edward's contemplative look tells me he's thinking it through.

"It's awful, but as I said, people are complicated, and we all make mistakes. With some distance from it now, I see that my father was victimized by his own wounds, and that played a part in his tragic fate."

"What about your real mom?"

I take a breath with his question. If I'm going to lose it, it will be here.

"Her name was Lila—that's where I get my middle name from—and she was an absolute wonder of a mother."

"She already sounds like you!"

"There's my sweet little man, still inside that growing body of yours."

"What was she like?" When he turns his gray eyes to meet mine, I see the sincerity.

I smile and quickly glance towards the water reminding myself to keep it together for Edward's sake.

"She was stunning and vibrant, full of life. I can still see her jet-black hair and bright green eyes. They twinkled when she smiled, even when the cancer came for her. She died when I was five. I think that was what finally turned my father's heart into stone because he was never the same afterward, even toward me. Then he married Samantha."

"I—I'm sorry. I just realized that your mom died when you were way younger than me."

"Honey, these bodies all die someday; it's part of life . . . what matters most is how we live while we're in them. Don't look so worried—I don't plan on going anywhere anytime soon."

"Promise?"

"You know what I say about promises, but I'll do my best to stick around for as long as you need me—how's that?" I reply with a nudge, attempting to restore some levity to our conversation after clearing my own emotional hurdle.

"I guess it'll have to do. So, was Samantha like the wicked stepmother in 'Cinderella'?"

"That, and the evil queen from 'Snow White' all rolled into one! But in fairness, as with my father, she had her own demons tormenting her, most of which lived in the bottles she'd uncork every night. I kept my distance from her, especially when she was in that state, which was most of the time."

"Oh, she was a drunkard!"

"That's a much coarser characterization than I would use, but unfortunately accurate," I say with a chuckle and shake of my head.

"And they died in a car wreck?"

"Yes, driving across Lake Washington on the floating bridge, right where the bulge is. That happened just a year or so after I moved in with the Mels." My gaze wanders to the southern tree line and back as I recall reading about the accident in the newspaper.

"I never knew."

"I'm glad you asked, and as tough as it is for me to admit, you're old enough now to understand these more difficult themes of life."

"Thanks, Mom."

"Now, what do you say we keep moving and go have a look at that tractor?"

"Really?"

"Don't get too excited—it'll be a miracle if it runs. Probably hasn't been started since who knows when. Lend me a hand to open these barn doors so we don't kill ourselves with the fumes if we do get this beast going."

I climb up on the old tractor and take a couple of minutes to reacquaint myself with the controls. "All right, let's see . . . key's already in the ignition, choke pulled, out of gear, and here we go."

Click-click-click-click-click.

"Darn, dead battery."

"Let's jump it with the car—there's cables in the station wagon," Edward suggests.

"This is about half the voltage of a car battery, and we'd fry the electrical system. We'll have to get a new battery in Olga or Eastsound."

"How do you know all this stuff?"

"Edna—she's the one who taught me how to drive it."

"She was your tutor, right?"

"Yes, she was, and I learned a lot of things from her besides schoolwork. Let's close up the barn and walk along the cliffs to catch the sunrise."

The slight westward breeze at our backs ushers us down toward land's end as the orange rays begin to rise out of the sea and cut through the haze of marine layer lingering above the horizon.

"I think this is where I saw some deer this morning from my porch."

"I'm not surprised. They love this tall grass to bed down in. Look over there—see how it's lying?"

"Yeah, it's in a bunch of swirls—that's cool."

"I used to watch them play out here from that porch as well. I'm happy they're still around for you to enjoy."

When we arrive at the cliffs, the incoming tide washing over the rugged coastline presents us with magnificent easterly views, and we pause until the sun skips off the water like a mirror, making it impossible to see beyond the glare. As we continue in the direction of the northern tree line, Edward moves closer to the edge for a better look at the gulls and seabirds soaring in and out of view as they search the water and rocks below for breakfast.

"This is what Dad and I were talking about last night at dinner. I want you to promise me that you'll always stay back from these cliffs; it's a long, unforgiving fall. I'm tempted to put a railing out here, but that'd be a shame, so let's just be smart about it, OK?"

"I will, I promise. But how do we get down to the water from way up here?"

"The closest way down is from over at Kent and Danelle's farm."

"Where's that?"

"You see the cabin up ahead sticking out of the woods? There's a trail next to the cliff, and if you walk in that direction, you'll eventually pop out onto their property. There were some switchback stairs not too far from the tree line."

"Will they mind if I check it out?"

"I don't think so, but you need to ask them about it when we're over there for dinner tomorrow."

A few steps further, we find ourselves next to a cleft in a large rock that instantly broadens my smile, and I have to touch it out of sentiment.

"Here's one of those reading hideaways we were talking about; the wind can't get to you and the view is heavenly. I used to drag in a chair, so I had something to sit on."

"It reminds me of a goose pen in a tree trunk."

"I guess it does!" I laugh and bristle the top of his crew cut.

"What's in that cabin up ahead?"

"Besides a bunch of memories, I'm not sure."

"Huh?"

"That's where Edna lived. After you and Dad clear it out, we're going to renovate it into my writing retreat—no more attic."

"Oh, that's what he was talking about. It's cool the way it sits back in the woods a little; we can barely see the house from down here because of the hill and those huge boulders."

"It's perfectly tucked away, isn't it? That makes it nice and private for me to work from." The excitement in my voice is evident as I reflect on the blueprints.

"I like the moss on the roof and the tree branches scraping against the sides—reminds me of the witch's cottage in the forest from 'Hansel and Gretel.' Does it have a big oven?"

"I swear, Edward, sometimes you're worse than I am with that kind of stuff! You know it would have to be made out of gingerbread and gumdrops, right?" I laugh while pushing him toward the steps.

"Yeah, but wouldn't it be cool if it were haunted?"

"Maybe it is!" I say, tickling the back of his neck with a ghostly moan that makes him hop up the stairs.

We duck under the large cedar boughs that drape the roof and walk around the porch as we peer through the dusty windows that wrap the cabin's east side with a sea view through the cliff-hanging madrona. Rather than fight our way around the haphazardly stacked furniture, we forgo the inside and continue on up the northern tree line past the house and arrive at the water tower.

"Oooh, let's climb up there!" Edward points skyward.

"Not today! The ladder and walkway around the tank need a lot of work before anyone does that."

"Have you ever been up there?"

"Yes, I have, but it was in much better shape in those days, and it still took a lot of nerve to make it all the way up and around the tank."

"So that's where our water comes from?"

"Yes and no. The water comes from the aquifer deep underground. That's accessed by the well and then pumped up to the tower. Think of the tower like a giant storage tank, and in case there is a power outage or a pump failure, which is bound to happen every now and then out here, the water stored in the tank flows to the house by gravity."

"That's why they're always up so high."

"Very good! And in the best case, like we have here, they're positioned uphill from the house. Your father's already spoken with the steel workers to come out and assess what it needs in the next few weeks; it's too rickety and dangerous at the moment."

"But we can go up when it's fixed, right?"

"Sure. There's a terrific view if you have the courage to make the climb."

"What if I only went up a little way today, like twenty feet?"

"Edward."

"OK, I promise, I'll stay off of it until you say it's safe."

"Good. Now let's get back to the house, and I'll make us some banana-covered French toast with bacon and eggs!"

"Hash browns, too?"

"Of course."

"You know that's my favorite!"

"You know what else?"

"What, Mom?"

"You're my favorite!"

5

The Farmer's Daughter

Sunday afternoon arrives and Dad leads the way to the Sinclairs' farm while Mom and I lag behind his brisk pace. It's a twisting fifteen-minute hike through the heavy woods that separate our properties, and when we catch up to him at the tree line he points out the two-story farmhouse set nicely into the landscape.

From where we stand, the house is partially shielded by a group of large cedar and pine trees that add privacy from the rows of crops and open space on the western side of the farm. Continuing toward the house, we pass two barns, both easily twice the size of ours, and a large pond next to their water tower.

"Hey Dad, is that Mr. Kent up on the porch?"

"Good eyes! That's him all right; looks like he's relaxing with a book."

He soon catches sight of us and waves before setting off in our direction.

When he arrives, he slaps my dad on the shoulder, then Dad makes a quick introduction and Mr. Kent welcomes us to Madrona Cliff Farms with a booming voice and big smile. At about six-foot-four, with a face tanned from working outside and big hands that feel rough as sandpaper when we shake, it's simple to deduce that he's no stranger to hard work.

"Kent, I have a little extra thank-you for all of your beautiful work next door—she looks magnificent!" Mom says before handing him the tote bag she's been carrying.

"It was my pleasure, Meredith; all I did was give her the TLC the old girl deserves, but thank you just the same for this nice bottle of whiskey! We'll have to have a celebratory shot."

"I can go for that!" Dad says, laughing.

"How was the walk over, Meredith?"

"It's quite a trek, isn't it?" Mom smiles.

"I bet it's a half-mile door to door that way, with all the weaving through the rock and woods," Kent replies. "I'll drive y'all back tonight because we're sending you home with some farm goodies."

"Thank you, that's very kind."

"Think nothing of it; it's just a welcoming basket. Let's head around back—Danelle and Vivian should be about finished setting the outside table. With such a beautiful afternoon, we thought we'd eat on the rear porch overlooking the apple orchard and the water."

Vivian is placing a large vase of flowers in the center of the dining table as we round the corner, giving it a last touch to ensure that they're perfect. The blonde soon-to-be ninth grader with a shag haircut is about my height at five-four and approaches us confidently, wearing a bright smile and blue overalls with a faded pink T-shirt underneath.

"Hello, Mrs. Hawthorne, I'm Vivian. It's a pleasure to meet you."

"Why hello, Vivian, it's my pleasure to meet you as well. Now that we've met, why don't you just call me Ms. Meredith," Mom replies. "And this is Edward," she says, turning toward me with a smile.

Vivian's grin widens as her hazel eyes meet mine.

"Hi Edward, it's nice to meet you."

"Hello Vivian, it's nice to meet you too. And now that we've met, you can just call me Mr. Edward."

I try to keep a straight face, but when Mom bumps me, I can't help but burst out laughing, as does everyone else.

"All right, kids, we have about an hour or so before dinner. Vivie, why don't you give Edward a tour around the farm, show him where the name comes from."

"Sure thing, Mom. You ready, Edward?"

"Yep, anytime you are."

Our first stop is the greenhouse, where Vivian explains how they grow vegetables in the winter and nurse the starts before transplanting them into the outdoor garden beds.

Chatting casually, we cut across the apple orchard, making our way down the slope to the cliffs and the madronas dotting them. Their smooth trunks under the curling paper-like pink-orange bark make them one of my favorite trees, and it's cool to see them overlooking Rosario Strait. We squeeze around an outcrop of rock and brush to reach the large gray stone slab beneath the partially exposed roots of a beautiful madrona arching over the water.

"The farm gets its name from these trees, and this is one of my favorite places in the whole world," Vivian declares.

"I can see why—it's like we're in an eagle's nest here!"

"Sometimes I come here to read or just daydream."

"I would, too. What do you daydream about?"

"Just things like what it'd be like living in the city—you know, that kind of stuff. What about you?"

"I guess mine are more like how cool it would be to have a car."

"I think a lot of guys think about that. Hey, have you had a smoke yet?" Vivian asks, brandishing an unfiltered cigarette from the chest pocket of her overalls.

"I tried a pipe this winter, but it wasn't for me—it smells way better than it is. You go ahead, though, I'm not a narc."

"I can tell you aren't. This comes from Canada; my dad keeps a pack of them in the greenhouse bench, lasts him about a year. I've always wanted to try one."

Vivian scratches a stick match across the ledge, touching the flame to the tip as she puffs.

"Not to be a wise guy, but I think with cigarettes you're supposed to breathe the smoke in, not just hold it in your mouth and then blow it out."

She gives me a questioning look, then takes another puff and inhales about halfway before erupting into a coughing fit and dropping the cigarette onto the rock between us. I'm not sure if it's chivalry or what, but as she gasps for air, I pick up the butt and take a puff myself, with the same terrible results.

Soon our choking turns to laughter, and Vivian grabs the cigarette from me and throws it over the cliff. "That was a really bad idea," she rasps, wiping the tears from her eyes, still struggling to catch her breath.

"At least now we know!"

"They sure make it look cool on TV."

"I know, they always make everything look way better on TV than it is in real life. My mom says it's all marketing, and that's also why they call TV shows 'programming.'"

"I think she's onto something. You're a good sport, Edward. Here, have a Jolly Rancher—I hope you like sour apple."

"I already like it way better than that burnt tobacco," I manage from my stinging throat.

"So how come you tried it after seeing me about choke to death?"

"I read somewhere that misery loves company, and you sure seemed miserable."

"Yeah, I won't be doing that again anytime soon, I can tell you that!"

"Me neither!"

"Let me ask you something, Edward, but it may sound weird."

"Sure, ask me anything you want," I say, my interest piqued.

"Now that you've spent a few nights at Long Shadows, have you noticed anything strange about it?"

"Like what?"

"I don't know . . . like anything out of the ordinary?"

"Well, it's kind of all out of the ordinary. I mean, it's way different than our Seattle house, if that's what you're asking."

"Not quite. I guess what I'm getting at is folks here on the islands say it's haunted."

"C'mon! If you're trying to scare me, it won't work."

"No, I'm telling you the truth—that's why nobody has been able to live there, like since your mom did ages ago, anyway."

"You swear it?"

"Yes, I swear it! The last owners didn't make it through July, and that was four summers ago. The folks before them, less than two weeks. I was just a little kid back then, but I remember the night that lady showed up at our house white as a sheet—poor thing was shaking so badly, she could hardly hold the shot of booze that Mom poured her. The way folks talk around here, my guess is that they're betting on how long y'all will last."

"Have you ever seen a ghost for yourself, like with your own two eyes?"

"It's not a ghost; it's a witch! And no, I haven't seen her."

"If you haven't seen her, how do you know there's a witch, then?"

"Because last November, some vandals from Orcas High School tried to break into the house. My dad thought they were going to burn it down because he found gas cans on the front porch steps. Something scared them off before they could finish the job."

"Maybe they thought someone was coming and chickened out. I've been chased out of abandoned houses with my friends before."

"But those jerks left their car behind, still running! At least that's how my dad found it the next morning."

"That does sound pretty weird, but it doesn't prove anything."

"Proof? I'll give you proof. I overheard some parents talking this April at the Spring Farmer's Market saying that the witch chased those guys through the woods for miles, and a couple had to see the psychiatrist in Bellingham because they started peeing the bed!"

"That's not really proof; it just sounds like one of those bullshit stories adults spread around to keep other kids from doing that sort of thing. We have a couple of haunted houses back on Capitol Hill, so I believe they're real, but my mom grew up here—I think she would tell me if it were haunted, especially if there's a witch, for crying out loud!"

Her account suddenly brings to mind an incident that took place in our attic a couple of years earlier, but I don't let on.

"Your mom seems like a nice lady, plus she's famous," Vivian concedes. "All I know is something scared those dumbheads so badly that they won't even talk about what they saw over there. Oh, and last week when school let out, three of those four families left Orcas for good and moved to the mainland."

"Really?"

"I'm not kidding—someone said they're locked away at the insane asylum in Sedro-Woolley, but that's probably BS."

"For sure. So far, I love it there—you should come over and see for yourself."

"Whatever you do, please don't tell your folks that I told you about that because if it gets back to my parents, they'll put me on restriction for the summer."

"I won't, I promise, and I never break a promise. Plus, wouldn't it be kind of cool to live in a haunted house, anyway? Oh, and Vivian, my mom isn't famous."

"I don't know . . . she's pretty famous around here."

"That sounds so weird to me—she's just my mom."

"I get it. Hey, do you like to fish?"

"I like to eat fish . . . but I've only fished in freshwater."

"That's good because we're having some tonight, but I'll teach you how to fish in saltwater if you want—it's a lot of fun."

"Sure, I'll give it a try."

"There's a great spot right below us, and my dad made it safer to climb up and down, but you still have to be careful on the stairs, especially with a stringer full of fish or a bushel of crab."

"When my mom and I were walking along the cliffs yesterday morning, she made me promise that I'd always stay back and never try to climb down."

"It's way too risky over there," Vivian agrees. "If you fell, it's like a fifty-foot drop straight down into the water, and that's when the tide's up. If it's out, that's probably sixty, and nothing but a rock shelf and boulders below."

"I saw that. You're dead meat for sure if you go off and hit those!"

"You can always climb down to the water from our property when the tide's out; then you can pick your way back along the rocks to your property, but they're slick with kelp and barnacles, so you still have to watch out. There's even a cave over there, but you can only see that a couple of times a year when the tide is super-low, and you have to know where to look. Just don't get caught down there when it comes back in because you'll get cut off, and there's no way to climb up, so that'll be the end of you."

"Don't worry about me, Vivian, I'm a really good swimmer. I swim in Lake Washington all the time—if I got stuck, I'd just float along the rocks until I found a way up."

"Sorry, but this is way colder than some city lake, and there's a strong current that'll haul your ass out into the middle of the strait. If that doesn't do it, the killer whales or a sea serpent will finish you in one chomp!"

"A sea serpent!" I laugh. "I was born at night, but not last night!"

"No joke! Back in the early 1900s, one was spotted off North Beach at Parker's Reef! Just ask around. Every islander knows about it—they even named it Elsie!"

"Yeesh."

"Look, if you remember one thing out here, remember this: Four minutes in the water and you go hypothermic, then you sink like a rock. It happens every couple of years; if you live here long enough, you'll know someone who has."

"Thanks for the warning—I'll try not to let that happen."

"Good, because I'm starting to like having you around," she says with a smile.

"Hey, what's in that cave?"

"I didn't go very far inside because the water was up to my shins, and my ankles and feet were aching so bad from the cold, plus I was worried the tide would come in and drown me."

"You're lucky you got out in one piece—that sea serpent might've been in there!" I laugh.

"Don't think I didn't consider it! I know for a fact there's plenty of starfish lining the walls; they were orange and purple."

"That sounds really cool—can we go check it out?"

"Sure, I'd like to go back with someone, but I'd wear my insulated rubber boots this time. Dad's too big to get in there; he really bawled me out last time and made me promise not to ever try that alone again. Most of the time you can't get to it anyway, even when the tide's out."

"Hold on a sec, I don't understand. You said—"

"OK, so some tides are higher, some tides are lower; the full moon makes them more extreme, something about how gravity causes the earth to bulge. I have a book that explains all that stuff—it's kind of fascinating."

"You're pretty smart."

"Thanks. Even though you've only been here a couple of days, you probably noticed that there aren't any kids around, and with no brothers or sisters, I spend my free time reading and exploring."

"I can totally relate to the no-brothers-and-sisters thing, but back in Seattle, there are a lot of kids in our neighborhood, so there's always something to do. I like to read too—just finished all sixty-two cases of Sherlock Holmes."

"Wow, I'm impressed—that's like college-level reading. Sherlock Holmes . . . is that why you tried a pipe?"

"Brilliant deduction!" I laugh with admiration. "It's kind of funny to think about doing that now."

"We watch those old black-and-white movies whenever they come on television—they're cool."

"That's Basil Rathbone and Nigel Bruce—those two are the best."

"Any of the guys I know who read something besides comic books read on the level of the Hardy Boys. You'll have to meet my friend Mary Ellen—she lives on the next property north and loves Victorian-era literature. She gives me reading assignments all the time; I just finished *Anne of Green Gables*, and before that, *Oliver Twist* from Dickens."

"That's cool. The girls in my school book club read Anne with an 'E' this last semester."

"Have you read your mom's books?"

"Not yet. The last time I asked her about it, she said I should wait until I finished Sherlock. Now that I'm done, maybe that'll be next. Have you?"

"When I found out y'all were moving here, I started the last one, but my mom saw me with it and said I might have nightmares, so I chickened out after the first murder."

"You're fourteen—it can't be all that bad."

"That's easy for you to say. My chores start at four-thirty in the morning, and it's spooky enough in the dark out here if you let your imagination run wild—and trust me, I have an imagination!"

"That sounds completely reasonable if there's a witch prowling around—I mean just yesterday I told my mom that the cabin reminded me of the one from 'Hansel and Gretel,'" I nudge her.

"Hush! I'm not joking!"

"Sorry, I'll keep an eye out and tell you if I see anything weird, I promise. Hey, you said you like to explore—it looks like there's a lot to explore around here."

"There is! This whole area was full of Indians at one time, so every now and then I'll find something neat like an arrowhead—I have five of them so far—and a tomahawk head; that's what I think it is, anyway. Dad says it's a cutting tool like a knife for skinning animals or scaling fish; there's even bloodstains on it!"

"Wow! Will you show it to me?"

"Sure, remind me when we're back at the house. That's Lummi Island over there on the other side of the strait;

it was named after one of the tribes." Vivian points to a shoreline that I guess is three or four miles away.

"Are there any around here?"

"Probably, but Hattie Gil is the only Lummi I know on Orcas; she owns the Crow Valley Co-op and Dairy, and makes the best ice cream you'll ever have. I also went to school with a Samish girl named Caledonia, until she moved to Whidbey a couple of years ago. I visited her once."

"My aunt and uncle live on Whidbey, just outside of Oak Harbor."

"That's where Caledonia lives! We went roller skating in a big red barn when I was there—have you done that?"

"Yeah, that's called the Roller Barn; my cousins taught me how to skate there. It's pretty cool."

"I thought it was neat, too, but we don't have anything like that on Orcas. What do you think about driving over the Deception Pass Bridge?"

"It makes my stomach feel funny every time, and have you seen those whirlpools in the water below?"

"Yeah! People have drowned out there—they get sucked to the bottom!"

"My uncle Maurice told me that some workers fell off when it was being built, way back. You know, if you keep going inland, you hit the Swinomish Reservation. I was there last year with my folks for a salmon festival where Mom was invited to be a speaker. Dad snuck home some bottle rockets and Black Cat firecrackers for us to blow off; she wasn't happy about it."

"Every Independence Day some kid will go to the Lummi reservation and bring them back to Orcas, and unless there's been some rain, you can bet they'll start a fire with them."

"I heard about a fire last year and something about a barn burning down. I guess we're giving them hay to make sure they have enough in case the winter gets bad."

"That fire was down in Olga, at Olga Livestock. But it wasn't in the summer; it happened just before Thanksgiving, not long after we heard your folks were interested in the house. Some fool started it, probably with a leftover sparkler or bottle rocket. That's exactly why my folks never allow any fireworks on the farm. Instead, we go to the show over in Eastsound where they shoot them over the water. It's kind of fun to watch, probably boring compared to what you're used to in Seattle."

"Seattle's pretty cool for that stuff. There's a big show at Green Lake and another downtown over Elliot Bay—we've been to both."

"I've only been to Seattle twice—it's big."

"I know my way around pretty well, but our neighborhood on Capitol Hill is great—there's always something to do."

"I'd like to hear about that sometime."

"If you come down for a visit, I'll show you around!"

"Cool. Hey, my mom will be ringing the dinner bell soon, so we should probably start walking back to the house, plus I want to show you something else."

"All right, lead the way."

We march toward the farmhouse, traversing one of the garden spots that border the chicken coop, and then enter a large enclosure where the chickens roam and scratch the dirt looking for food.

"Have you ever held a chicken, Edward?"

"If fried chicken doesn't count, then no, I haven't."

"Shhhh, not in front of them!" Vivian says, putting her finger to her lips. "These are laying hens; they're a heritage breed. That means they haven't been messed with by some mad scientist in a lab. Mom is sending y'all home with four dozen of their eggs. I know, because I collected each one of them for you this morning."

"Sorry, that was a bad joke, and thanks for the eggs."

"You're forgiven. Here, you wanna hold Henrietta? She's a Rhode Island Red and my favorite; I raised her from a chick."

"Sure!" I try to sound a little more enthusiastic than I feel at the prospect.

"You have to hold her soft—don't squeeze her too tight. You know . . . it's like when you're slow dancing with a girl."

"Well, I—I—I . . ."

"Oh, come here, and I'll teach you."

Vivian sets Henrietta down and moves closer until we stand face-to-face.

"First of all, you're way too tense for Henrietta; you need to relax. Now put your arms like this . . ." Vivian embraces me and puts her ear against my collarbone. "See, just hold me . . . gently but firm—you'll get it." As I do, she begins slowly stepping side to side.

"Now imagine that song 'The First Time Ever I Saw Your Face' is playing—you know the one, it's all over the radio." When Vivian quietly hums the familiar melody, I feel the nervousness drain from my arms, soon losing track of everything but the sway and soothing tone of the song through my chest.

"You've got it! I think you're ready for Henrietta. Remember, just like with me," she says as she softly hums the song again.

My movement is smooth and deliberate as I gently pick up Henrietta with little protest and bring her close to my chest. She immediately settles as I cradle her and begin stepping side to side, just like Vivian taught me.

"Well done, Edward! You're a fabulous study," she whispers, quietly clasping her hands with excitement.

"Uh, Vivian, I think she just pooped on me."

"I probably should have warned you that she might; it just means she likes you. Don't worry about it—I have a shirt back at the house you can wear."

The dinner bell rings as we cut through the apple orchard, making our way back to the farmhouse. Just before we're within view of the parents, Vivian stops beneath the branches of a large tree in the center of the orchard.

"I think you're brave, Edward—thanks for being my friend," she says and kisses me on the cheek. Then, just as quickly, she runs off through the apple trees giggling, with me giving chase.

When we bound up the stairs, our parents are sitting around the table talking, and turn their heads in our direction.

"Wash up, you two, the food's on the table in five minutes!"

"Yes, Mom, but I need to get Edward a shirt first—Henrietta pooped on his!"

"She likes you, Edward!" Ms. Danelle laughs as Vivian and I continue on inside.

The smell of scented candle wax sets the stage for what the flip of the light switch reveals when we enter Vivian's bedroom, which takes up much of the top floor. Star maps, navigational charts of the San Juan Islands, and, after a short hum and clink, some fluorescent posters of fantastic realms ignited under the glow of a black light. Three large, neatly packed bookcases serve as her personal library, with an overstuffed chair and ottoman in a dormer facing the water.

"Whoa . . . great room, Vivian."

"Thanks. I wanted a waterbed and was even going to pay for it myself, but Dad said no way, they're too heavy."

"My dad said the same thing when my folks were talking about one, plus they can leak. I hear you have a telescope—can we look through it some night?"

"Sure, but I'll warn you, it's disappointing, not at all like those pictures you see in advertisements or on the box. I'd rather use binoculars any day."

"That's what my dad does."

"Who do you think told him to try that? Here, this'll fit you," she says, tossing me a sweatshirt that matches the paint on her walls and holds her soft, powdery scent.

"Lavender?"

"You're brave, remember? Go ahead and change in the bathroom," she laughs, pointing to another door. "Just toss yours in the hamper and I'll wash it for you."

"Can I see those arrowheads and that bloody tomahawk?" I shout through the door as I pull the sweatshirt over my head.

"Yeah, but hurry up."

When I exit the bathroom, Vivian opens a desk drawer and pulls out a cigar box containing five arrowheads and a palm-sized kidney bean–shaped piece of the same type of rock. The dark rust-colored staining along the edge definitely suggests a bloody history.

"Whoa, this is really cool! Hey, is that an Archie comic in your drawer?"

"Yeah, I know, it's corny."

"No, I have a Thor at home—I think comics are way underrated."

"Hurry up, you two, dinner's on the table!" Ms. Danelle calls from the bottom of the stairs.

"Coming, Mom!"

6

Table Talk

While Edward and Vivian are getting acquainted touring the property, we adults enjoy a glass of wine and some casual conversation about raising crops and *onlys* on Orcas.

"*Onlys* are a different breed of child altogether," Kent says; he had practically raised his younger siblings.

"I agree with you 100 percent," replies Robert, who comes from a family with a younger brother and sister.

"Since Meredith and I are *onlys*, I'm sure that's the highest of compliments from you two," Danelle says.

"Oh, definitely! I think they're the perfect balance of innocence and independence," Robert confirms.

"Cheers to the *onlys*, and those who raise them!" I lift my glass.

~

When our two *onlys* return to the porch after Edward's shirt change, Danelle taps her wineglass and makes the official dinner announcement and toast.

"Smoked cod with rock crab salad and rhubarb pie, all from within three hundred yards of this table! The wine, well, that's up from California. Here's to our neighbors, for whom we wish many wonderful moments and memories made."

Following brief applause, she adds that Vivian and Kent are responsible for the cod and crab, while the pie is an old family recipe that goes back to her great-grandmother in Wenatchee.

"Robert tells me that you and Kent grew up in Wenatchee, so what brought you two west of the Cascades?" I ask Danelle.

"We did. Right after graduating WSU, Kent accepted a job in Anacortes working for the state in hydro-engineering and water management. We'd spent all of our lives on the dry side of the mountains, and we had always dreamed about living by the sea. The job came with the San Juans as part of the territory, so it was a perfect fit."

"So no family connection to Sinclair Island?"

"Hardly! Just a fun coincidence. We bought a small house in Anacortes, and I went to work for the state's accounting office conducting forensic audits on contractors doing work for the state. I was there for a year and absolutely hated it."

"She was miserable," Kent confirms with a nod.

"Since we were both raised on farms and with Kent able to commute to the islands using the ferry system, we started looking for something manageable out here."

"I was over on San Juan in early 1957 doing an evaluation when I got wind of this property. A developer purchased the land the year prior just after it had been subdivided by your father. It was raw—none of the hydro or power had been engineered, that was all on the Long Shadows piece of property, and those were going to be challenging and costly projects to complete." he says, pausing to skillfully swat a yellow jacket off the porch before it lands on the pie.

"That's outta here!" shouts Vivian with a smile, and Kent gives her a wink, then continues.

"The owner wanted to focus on a much more lucrative option that came along in Roche Harbor, and he needed to free up some resources to do that. I made him a deal to engineer his Roche project on the side, in exchange for a sizable down payment on this land, and we bought it."

"I remember looking at Kent like he had two heads when he came home that night: 'Don't worry, Danelle, I know I can run the hydro, and Dave owes me for the well design I did for his place on Lopez; he'll run the power.' And as always, Kent got it done. By the time Vivian came along, we had all the water and power we needed."

"Vivian's grown up right alongside the crops," Kent adds, smiling at her as she blushes.

"Forgive me if I'm prying, Meredith, but how's it feel to be back here after so many years?"

"You're not prying, Danelle. I guess it feels like a homecoming. This morning when I was out for a walk, I thought about my first trip down the driveway with my parents when I was five years old. It was as if I could hear my father's gruff voice declaring: 'Our summers will be spent here,' —he was always one for making declarations," I reply, after doing my best to mimic him.

"You were only five when you started coming here?"

"No, that was right after they purchased the property, and my mother was still alive. We didn't begin summering here until the following year. By then, Mother had passed away, and within six months of her death, Father married Samantha."

"I'm sorry, I didn't know you lost your mother so young."

"It's just part of my story."

"Did the name Long Shadows come about because of your father?"

"Yes, and no . . . although the book might lead one to that conclusion. The naming happened when I was nine. One afternoon, my father was sitting on the rear porch looking down toward the water and overheard me say, 'long shadow,' as I came out of the woods next to the house. He stood up and confirmed what I had said, then immediately made the designation. He always believed it to be the perfect allegory of life and death after watching the summer shadows cast by the chimneys growing longer with each hour."

"He sounds like he had a real flair with words, too."

"He was an abstract thinker, that's for sure. I recall him saying that he found the chimneys reminiscent of fingers straining toward the sea but cruelly withdrawn by the setting sun, never able to satisfy their quest. Tragically, his interpretation turned out to be more of a self-portrait, or self-fulfilling prophecy, depending on your view."

"Like they say, truth is stranger than fiction," Danelle smiles.

"It sure can be. I remember within days of the book landing on store shelves feeling some hesitation about the title, like maybe it was a little too personal, but by then the book had taken on a life of its own."

"I'll say! The New York Times Best Sellers list that first week . . . and our little book club along with every other in the area was reading it. That must have been a very exciting time for you."

"It was, and still is!" I laugh. "I don't know any writer who isn't grateful when their work finds an audience, but I also realize that locals were a little put off because I didn't make a book tour stop in the San Juans. Or perhaps they thought I took liberties that some believed weren't mine to take."

"You know us island folks, Meredith, always needing something to gossip about, especially in the off-season, when we can't complain about tourists clogging the roads and leaving their trash all over the place." Danelle pauses for a sip of wine. "Folks who get their noses out of joint over a book, well . . . they have deeper problems."

"I agree," seconds Kent. "There's more busybodies here than anywhere I've ever been. That book is quite the tale, though. Interesting characters and fun to read about something set here in the area—so what if the content is shocking for some?"

"Thanks, Kent; as trite as it may sound, I'm just thankful to be back here with a chance to become part of the community."

"You're among friends," Kent assures me with his warm smile.

"And we're thrilled to have y'all as neighbors. It's as if that beautiful old house has rebuffed the other suitors, patiently awaiting your return."

"That's quite a lyrical interpretation. Have you tried your hand at poetry, Danelle?"

"Heavens no, I leave that to Vivian," she says with an affectionate gaze. "You'll have to meet Mary Ellen next door—she's the literary one in these parts and quite a kick, too!"

"Mary Ellen Carter?"

"One and the same—I see you remember her."

"Yes, but I only met her once. Didn't she live on the other side of the island?"

"She did, over in Deer Harbor, back in the woods just opposite of Indian Point Road. She had her cottage moved all the way over here. I think she still owns that property, too."

"Mary Ellen was a close friend of Edna's, my 'summer governess,' as Father and Samantha distastefully referred to her."

"Oh! The Edna you always mention in your acknowledgments; I guess she was a big influence on your becoming an author."

"Immense. Edna tutored me from the time I was six, taught me all the wonders of Dickens, Twain, and Wilde. My thirteenth birthday presents were rare first editions of Brontë's *Jane Eyre* and Austen's *Pride and Prejudice*. They're still among my most precious possessions."

"I just finished *Oliver Twist*!" Vivian blurts out, followed by an immediate apology for interrupting.

"Magnificent, Vivian! You feel free to interrupt me with classical literature anytime." I smile across the table, catching a glimmer of myself at fourteen.

"Yes, ma'am, Ms. Meredith."

"I'm afraid Edna would have found my latest effort slightly unrefined in comparison with the first two," I laugh. "She was a bit of a formalist when it came to her literary pursuits."

"Well, I found it riveting!" Danelle says, holding her wine glass aloft. "Especially—"

"Don't wreck it for me! I've got two chapters left." Kent jumps in, waving his hands.

"You better hang on, Kent. You're in for a ride." I shake my head and smile. "When did Mary Ellen move to this side of the island?"

"She bought the eighty acres the year Vivian was born. Kent helped her with the power and water, and she took to Vivian like moss to a rock. I understand that her acreage was also part of the original property."

"That's correct. When I lived here, the parcel was over three hundred acres, but because of the remoteness it may as well have been a thousand."

"Thankfully it still feels like it. She likes to keep to herself, a bit of a curmudgeon and pretty self-sufficient. I don't go over there very often, maybe once or twice in the winter to bring her a pot of chicken soup or check in on her if she's been sick. She has a nice little garden plot, some chickens, and even a cat or three keeping her company.

Every now and again she'll join us at the Farmer's Market to sell something she's grown."

"I think she grows her own herbal remedies over there, too," snarks Kent with a chuckle.

"Kent's just jealous because her tomatoes outsell his when she shows up at the market. Vivian gets along with her famously—right, Vivie?"

"She's really smart. Her house is full of books, and she knows something about pretty much everything!"

"Mary Ellen sounds like a very good mentor, Vivian. You stick with her, and I bet you'll get into any college you want, and probably with a scholarship."

"I like the sound of that!" Kent laughs, as he stretches across the table to refill our wine glasses.

"I know she's read all of your books, Ms. Meredith. I've seen them on her bookshelves, and she's read everything that's on those shelves."

"Then, I look forward to paying her a visit. It'll be nice to speak with a friend of Edna's and reminisce."

"I bet Mary Ellen would enjoy that when she gets back from the mainland; she and her cat are vacationing there the next two weeks," Danelle replies. "Until then, Vivian and I are keeping her garden watered and chickens fed."

~

When Kent drops us off at the house, I bring home much more than the bag of vegetables, flats of fresh cherries, strawberries, and eggs. I carry a relaxed trust, something difficult for me to imagine coming back to Orcas, and the fact that they're just next door makes it all the sweeter.

"What do you think of the farm, Edward?"

"It's really great, Mom; plus, Vivian said I could cut through their property anytime, and I told her she could do the same here."

"It sounds like you two made fast friends."

"I like her . . . she's different from girls back on the hill."

"She's a farm girl," Robert explains, "And farm girls understand that nothing gets done if you sit around and talk about it. They usually have a lot of chores to do and know that the sooner they start, the sooner they finish."

"She told me that during the summer her chores start at four-thirty every morning, rain or shine."

"Maybe you should offer her a hand and see what real farm life's about."

"I might give it a try. Who knows, it could be fun."

"She's a real cutie, isn't she?" I ask, trying to goad Edward.

"C'mon, Mom, she's a girl!"

"At least you noticed! Maybe your voice isn't the only thing that's changing!"

7

Whispers

om is right. I did notice Vivian, and more than any girl I've ever met. She's easy to talk to, and we like a lot of the same things, but there's something else that I can't quite figure out. I lie in bed, considering this before shifting my attention to the adult conversation around the dinner table. Until we arrived on the island, I had no idea that *The House of Long Shadows* was based on a real place, much less that Mom grew up in a rich family and spent her summers here.

When writing that book, she locked herself away in the attic from the time I left for school in the morning until I got home in the afternoon. A few nights a week I'd wake up to the squeak of floorboards above me and the muffled sound of her voice, as if carrying on a conversation or reading both parts of the dialogue she had just written. Sometimes when she sent me off to school with my lunch box and a kiss, I knew she hadn't been to bed. This went on from third through fifth grades; then one day she was finished and things went back to normal like she had just returned from a book tour.

She wrote her first two books downstairs in the study, and according to Dad, those didn't consume her. *The House of Long Shadows* had taken possession of her, he blurted out one night in frustration about her continued absence, setting off the only real argument I ever witnessed between them.

There was an afternoon a week or so before the manuscript was done when she ran out to the grocery store to buy a bottle of wine for dinner. My curiosity pulled me away from the math homework I struggled with and up into the attic, a destination that was off-limits to anyone else during the entire time she was working on the book.

I recall the eerie feeling of being watched as I walked across the attic toward her writing table and the window with its view overlooking the canopy of chestnut trees lining 16th.

The typewriter sat centered on her table; to the left was a tray containing a bottle of Liquid Paper, an eraser, and a few perfectly sharpened pencils resting atop a notepad, and on the right lay a glass ball in a shallow wooden bowl cushioned by a nest of old sea-rope. A pair of candelabras with half-burned tapers flanked the area, and a box of candlesticks on the floor, also containing stubs, told me that she sometimes wrote by candlelight.

A few sketches were pinned to the surrounding rafters, their edges rolled by the passing seasons, but my eyes were drawn to the three nearest the table. These were watercolors, tacked to the cedar lath at their four corners, which prevented them from curling like the others. The first featured two young girls from behind, one taller than her companion, standing arm in arm in a field of wavy dry grass and rock. They wore simple, tan-colored dresses that blended into the surroundings, with their long black hair blowing downwind in the breeze. The next picture was weird. It was a mishmash of black, gray, and white splattered with red, yellow, and orange that took up the entire paper, and it reminded me of a really bad elementary school finger painting. The third was a frightening portrait depicting a girl, her face partially covered by thick olive ribbons falling randomly about her pale skin, littered with green blotches.

Almost half the face was bone—her only eye was the shape and color of a mussel shell, with a look of sadness that struck me like an arrow to the heart. Unable to look away, I stayed there mesmerized until the slam of a car door broke the spell and sent me hauling ass back down to my room before Mom caught me.

But that image was burned into the back of my eyelids, and I slept in my parents' room for a few nights, conveniently blaming Hitchcock and *Psycho*, rather than confess to my trespassing. I hadn't thought much about it until Vivian's witch story brought it up. Now I'm intrigued that this house is somehow connected to that painting and to my mom's book—a bonafide mystery that I have the whole summer to solve.

~

Just as Mom predicted, I slept like a baby the first two nights, and by the third, I'm growing accustomed to the sounds of Long Shadows at rest. The creak and thump of wood contracting as she cools, an occasional groan from the pipes, and the odd tap from who knows where all have become part of my bedtime ritual as I drift off.

But it's the ebb and flow of the wind through the trees, the fresh island air, and the distant lap of water against a rocky coastline that lull me into the deepest, most restful sleep I've ever experienced; and despite Vivian's haunting story, tonight is no different, as far as my nodding off goes.

"E-d-w-a-r-d," an alluring whisper summons me from the galactic realm where I'm battling alongside Thor and the Silver Surfer.

"Wha-a-what?" I prop myself up on my elbows as the white form moves toward me and then retreats just as I'm about to scream bloody murder. I rub my eyes to be sure, relieved that my visitor is only the window scrim aglow in the moonlight, moving to and fro with the breeze. I lie there for a moment staring at the ceiling, trusting that my heartbeat will soon return to normal in the cool sea air; then, just as I'm drifting off again, the soft creak of a door tightens my chest and jolts my eyes back open.

If there's one thing I don't want to do, it's get out of bed, but after convincing myself that the great Sherlock Holmes would never pull the covers up over his head like a coward, even at thirteen, I rise to the challenge.

Quietly cracking the door an inch, I find the large hallway empty, and seeing my parents' bedroom door closed isn't at all comforting. Stepping out in my robe and house shoes, I creep along the wall of the corridor to the main staircase, pausing briefly to peek over the banister into the dark void. There's a splash of moonlight reaching up the stairs toward the first landing, accompanied by the rhythmic ticking of the grandfather clock in the foyer below; again, nothing out of the ordinary. Continuing down the hall past the two front bedrooms, I find both doors shut and ease around the corner before stopping cold when confronted by the open attic door.

My fear and dry mouth are instantly consumed by curiosity as I gulp hard and slip through the doorway in silence. One careful step at a time, I scale the stairway, mindful to keep each footfall on the outside edge of the treads to avoid any squeaks—a technique I picked up in one of my detective stories. About three-quarters of the way up, my eyes clear the top step, and my heart lurches as my knees turn to Jell-O and my feet to cinder blocks.

At the far end of the attic, silhouetted by the moonlight, stands a cloaked figure staring out the row of windows toward the sea. I watch the motionless specter for what seems like minutes but in reality is probably only a few seconds.

"M-m-m-mom?" I whisper with hope, doubt, and confusion all warring for space in my racing mind.

"Edward! For the love of Pete! Don't sneak up on me!"

"I'm sorry, but what are you doing up here? You about scared me to death!"

"I'd say we're even, then. I couldn't sleep . . . why are you out of bed?"

"I thought I heard something and figured I'd better check it out."

"Thank you for being brave enough to investigate—now back to bed with you." She shoos me off but I'm too curious to instantly obey.

"Are you thinking about writing another book?"

"I'm always thinking about writing another book—afraid that's part of the curse."

"Curse! Like a witch's curse?"

"Oh, for heaven's sake, figuratively, not literally! Writers have to write; it's what we do."

"But you won't disappear like last time, right?"

"Oh honey, no . . . I promise, not like last time," she says, rubbing my back gently. "All right, that's enough talk—let's get back to bed."

I agree, relieved, but I notice her parting glance out the windows before we make our way to the stairs.

"Do you think I could read *The House of Long Shadows* now that I'm done with all the Sherlock Holmes?"

"You're absolutely capable. Let me talk about that with your father first."

"All right. Before you went up to the attic, did you come into my room? I thought I heard my name."

"It was probably just your guardian angel watching over you," she replies with a smile, then kisses my forehead before walking across the hall and quietly returning to her room.

I close my door and hurry onto the porch to see if I might catch sight of whatever she was looking at, but all I see is a small herd of deer making their way toward the southern tree line. After standing in the dark for another minute, I give up and go back to bed, wondering if I'll hear that voice again.

8

She

She did the same thing to me in that bedroom. Mostly because she was lonely and wanted to talk, but the last time, she woke me with a dire warning. When I left, it was with her blessing, and I know that half the tears I've cried since are hers. She was alone in the world just as I was, and yet somehow in the economy of this vast universe we were knitted together, she and I.

My world shattered the day we were torn from the fabric of our embrace, only to be alone again. Edna told me that it was for the best, that I had to get out from under the weight of iniquity that would ultimately collapse my father's house, or it would destroy me as well. Of course, she was right, but that wouldn't mitigate the pain. No, my pain was the key, my rite of passage through a darkened corridor leading to the understanding that this level of anguish only testifies to love.

Edna always knew what to say to get me over the hump of stubbornness I'd inherited from my father, and thankfully that seemed to be the only trait of his that I carried.

The rest came from the mother I revered but lost far too young. So, when Edna said goodbye to me at the Orcas ferry dock that morning, her final words were:

'Be brave, be of good cheer, and above all else, be that woman I know you are meant to be. I love you as my daughter and always will.'

I didn't look back as I walked onto the Anacortes-bound vessel as if I were headed to the gallows. I couldn't, because I knew I would crumble, and then what? No, once aboard, I straightened myself, fixed my gaze on the rising sun, and took those crucial first steps into another life.

~

Sleep eludes me as I lie in bed sifting through the memories of that girl lost somewhere inside of me—the tales she told, the life she lived, intertwined and inseparable, still not knowing how our story will resolve.

When Robert awakes at sunrise, I'm exhausted but relieved to have someone besides myself to talk with.

"Morning—I noticed you were up last night. Everything ok?"

"Good morning, sleep well?" is my vain attempt to skip the conversation ahead.

"I slept great, always do out here. How long have you been up?"

"Not long; I'm just trying to clear myself of the muddle and get this new book straight."

"Meredith, I'll do anything to help, but please . . . I can't lose you again for two years. Neither can Edward."

"Robert, I promise I won't put us through that again. Wherever these stories come from, they'll have to find another set of fingers if that's the price."

"I'm sorry to bring it up."

"No, you've every right to, but Long Shadows is an entirely different matter; that's been an obligation hanging over me since the day I left here."

"I know, we've been over this ad nauseam. I just couldn't fathom the cost is all."

"Me neither, but I had to trust the process and hope that it would turn out OK in the end."

"Please don't take this the wrong way—I'm genuinely curious about your opinion. Has it turned out OK? I mean, beyond the money and all."

"The money was never part of the equation, and to answer your question, it's a process. Please don't ask me to explain it further; I'm not sure I can. What I will tell you is that I pray daily to Jesus for guidance—he's my Cudgel through the dark woods of the soul."

"That sounds pretty dire." Robert smiles, knowing my propensity for the dramatic. "Anything to do with Chase Stuart and that 'Sullivan's Cove' remark?"

"He's just an annoyance by comparison."

"But if you're right about him . . ."

"If nothing—I am right. By the way, what was he driving off the ferry?"

"Blue Ford Galaxie 500 two-door."

"Like the Morrisons'?"

"Same. Definitely a 1967 too—you can tell because that's the year they moved the turn sig—"

"Too much detail."

"You asked! Anyway, I watched him hobble over to it myself—that's quite the limp he has."

"He's an abomination. And for the record, I do appreciate that precision of yours... most of the time," I tease. Robert returns my grin and I'm relieved by the brief moment of levity.

"I've noticed him several times on that Friday ferry since I began working on the house."

"He must have business in Anacortes—as I recall, the Stuarts had quite a few properties on the mainland."

"What I'm concerned about is that nobody likes looking over their shoulder for very long."

"*Shadows* has been out for more than a year now; he's had time to settle down. The dumbest thing he could do is start trouble—it would only draw attention to him, and for no good reason. He's free and clear of those murders."

"I understand that, but just like in your book, a murderer can always be tried. For safety's sake, I think we should have a gun out here."

"Why? You're here to protect us. Besides, you just said it: he's badly crippled and drags that dead leg of his around like Boris Karloff did in *The Mummy*."

"I'm serious, Meredith. I have a lot of overnights in Seattle this summer, and I'd feel much better if we had at least one in the house and one down at your cabin."

"So, it's two guns now! I don't know how I feel about that, Robert."

"Correct me if I'm wrong, but I recall you once saying that you were a pretty good shot as a kid."

"While standing up I could shoot the heart out of an ace at twenty-five yards with my .22 Hornet, but that was a long time ago, when we had to keep the rat population in check. Frankly, I'm a little nervous about having an armory around here with Edward."

"Three or four guns hardly make an armory—"

"What? Three or four now?"

"I'm just kidding—relax. I understand your hesitation, but he's a good kid, Meredith, he makes good decisions, and I think he's ready to learn how to handle a firearm safely. Kent takes Vivian varmint shooting at the dump all the time; it's an important skill for anyone to have who lives in an isolated area like this."

"Let me think about it before you go pulling the trigger," I say with a sly smile.

"At least you haven't lost your sense of humor. What if I take him shooting the next time Kent and Vivian go? You can come too if you want."

"Sure, I might go along to supervise, maybe give you boys some pointers. Oh, and by the way, Edward asked me again about reading *Long Shadows*."

"What'd you tell him?"

"I said he's capable but that I'd run it by you first."

"That's completely your department, but I think he'll be fine with it."

"It's dark. Lord knows how many letters I've received; seems like there's a few complaints in every batch from Random House."

"You had a few of those for the first two books as well. For what it's worth, I found *Haunted Houses* and *The Missing* creepier, but *Shadows* is definitely an adult read. Still, it's not any worse than him watching *Psycho*."

"You seem to have forgotten that he slept with us for a week!" I laugh.

"OK, so not the best example, but that was two years ago."

"Yes, well—"

A knock and the bedroom door opening interrupts my retort, as Edward peeks his head around the door at us.

"Good morning, Edward, come on in," Robert says.

"Morning!" he replies and jumps between us on the bed.

"Able to get back to sleep?"

"Yep, no problem, but I have a question."

"Fire at will."

"Do you think this house is haunted?"

"Great question," Robert chuckles and looks over at me before punting. "What do you think, honey?"

"I think we're all haunted houses; it's just that some of us are more haunted than others—I wrote a book about that."

He contemplates my answer for a good thirty seconds. "So, it's all in someone's head?"

"Possibly, and it might be that it's in someone's heart, too."

"Ooooh, *The Case of the Haunted Heart*! That sounds like a great Sherlock Holmes case!"

"Better write that title down, Meredith, it's a good one!"

"I agree! Well done, Edward!"

"Thanks, Mom. So if a haunting is inside someone, there's nothing to be afraid of then, is there?"

"Now that's an excellent deduction, young Sherlock!" I say, pulling him close and kissing the top of his head. "By the way, Dad and I think you're ready for your next reading assignment, but it's a challenging one."

"Is it . . ."

"All three, in order, beginning with *Haunted Houses*, then *The Missing*, and finally, *The House of Long Shadows*. I will expect a book report for each one. Is it a deal?"

"And how!"

"That should keep you occupied through the summer. They're a bit scary in parts, so if any of them get too much, there's no shame in putting it down for a while, all right?"

Edward pounces on me with a kiss. "You're the best parents ever!" He exclaims, before announcing that he's off to explore and map the vast wilderness, then vanishes as quickly as he appeared, leaving Robert and me staring at each other.

"Meredith, I'm so proud of you!"

"See, I really am trying to let him go."

"I know how hard this is for you, but you're doing great."

~

There's little doubt in my mind that Edward can handle the suspense and the frightful nature of my books, even with the gruesome details of ripper-style murders that take place in a couple of them. My hesitation lies predominantly with *The House of Long Shadows* and Edward's penchant for sleuthing. After living on the island for a couple of months, he'll detect the similarities. But besides those revelations, it's his inevitable confrontation with the book's final chapter that I'm most concerned about for him.

9

The Cabin

Our first seven days have gone by in a flash, and between stocking the house and making several introductions around the island, there's been little time to dig in and corral the wisps of the new book stirring inside me. After promising Robert that this project would not reflect the obsessive nature of penning *The House of Long Shadows*, I intentionally include him and Edward in the wider net of my process, hoping to rebuild any trust that was strained by the former experience.

From an author's perspective, it would be unreasonable for anyone else to understand the isolation needed to accomplish that particular book; and as with a prolonged natural labor, I was just as exhausted from the journey as they were by witnessing it. Though Robert is a beautifully kind and caring man, the fear of his thinking I was completely off my rocker and having a nervous breakdown kept me from sharing any subtext of the story beyond the obvious parallels that he already knows about my upbringing, let alone what or who might come along with its publication.

After our conversation about my recent nocturnal visit to the attic, there's no way I'm going to mention waking up the following night outside in my nightgown halfway down the slope. I just knew it couldn't happen again.

The next morning, I established a writing routine that has me rising with the rooster, bundling up, and walking down to the cleft in the rock by the cliffs, carrying a thermos of coffee and a notebook. Once there, I tuck myself into an old teak deck chair and jot my notes while listening for the sound of her voice in the wind and the changing tide, something that's been elusive thus far. Still, I know she's here; I feel her, especially close to the sea. But there's another presence as well, one who softly whispers our names in the dark, the same figure I saw from the attic window standing by the cliffs; maybe it's Edna, maybe not . . . either way, she belongs here like I do, perhaps even more.

The day finally arrives to clear the cabin, and the boys are incredibly patient as I inspect everything they haul out, hoping to find at least one or two treasures marking my former life here. But that isn't to be. My father was a man true to his angry words and successfully purged every trace of my and Edna's footprints from the property.

"I'll clean up while you and Edward make the dump runs."

"Watch out for mice—I'm sure there're a few scurrying around," Robert jokes.

"Those cute little field mice don't bother me; it's rats and spiders that I want nothing to do with!"

"Vivian shoots rats all the time at the dump. If I had a rifle, you wouldn't have to worry about them."

"Yes, so your father tells me."

"Don't worry, honey, there's no rats in here. Need anything while we're in town?"

"How about some of that co-op ice cream? Whatever flavor you two decide on."

"All right. Should be back in an hour or so for the second load. Don't go overboard with cleaning; those guys are going to do a major tear-out of everything but the floors."

"I'll just sweep it out and scrub them to get an idea of their condition and coloring."

"Enjoy that." He smiles and pecks my cheek.

I watch the pickup truck vanish over the rise and return inside to begin my chores. After climbing the narrow staircase to the empty loft that once served as Edna's bedroom, I envision her queen-sized bed centered under the dormer, her Bible on one end table and *Roget's Thesaurus* on the other. Opening the window, I begin knocking down a few cobwebs with the broom before giving the floors a good sweep while thinking about the placement of my own minimalist furnishings set to arrive at the end of next month from Del-Teet on Broadway.

The entire cabin is going to be reconfigured, with the exception of these original wide-plank floors and their characteristic scratches with a gouge here and there. These are to be left as is, and once they are cleaned and oiled, their imperfections will exude a rustic touch and the nostalgia that I crave. After bringing the final few boxes of clutter onto the porch, I finish sweeping out the downstairs and pull on my rubber gloves before filling a pail with Spic and Span.

In less than five minutes of scrubbing, my mind wanders. My first thought is of how many steps my feet have taken across these floors. It has to be tens of thousands over the summers, but I still remember those first ones after Edna moved in.

Obviously coached by my father and Samantha, she inquired about the girl I spent my days playing with. She listened intently to the encounters I so vividly described, even stopping me to ask questions along the way. An ally at last, I thought. Little did I know that Edna would cleverly use those stories to ignite my interest in creative writing, and her first assignment was to commit these and future installments to the page.

It never once occurred to me that Edna doubted these stories. If so, she found a way to draw the goodness from the tapestries I wove and not crush the fragile little girl who spun the yarns.

I pause on the sweetness of that memory, not wanting it to advance further, but despite my dread, it has to . . .

Twelve summers we spent together, and in one day it all vanished with the outgoing tide as if it had never existed. The episode left a hole through my heart, and in part tribute, part promise, I wrote a novel rooted in those years; but I had regrets. I could never anticipate the hollowing of losing so much so quickly and the unrequited bargaining with God as I desperately struggled to maintain my grip on water.

~

I refill the pail as a rap on the doorframe brings me out of the kitchenette, where I find Vivian in the doorway holding a small bucket of apples.

"Hi Vivian, the boys went to the dump, but they should be back shortly if you'd like to wait."

"Hi, Ms. Meredith. I brought y'all some apples. Are you OK?" she asks, stepping inside the cabin.

"Yes, dear, thank you. It's the Spic and Span—it always makes my eyes water."

"I can scrub the floors for you if you want."

"That's sweet of you, honey, but I don't mind it."

"This is where Edna lived, right?" Vivian's eyes begin to roam the space.

"It sure is; I was just thinking about her."

"So, it wasn't the Spic and Span then."

"Vivian, please forgive my underestimating you."

"It's all right. 'Tears are cleansing, nothing to be ashamed of.' I think you wrote that about Amanda."

"Are you reading *The House of Long Shadows*?"

"I started, then put it down when it got too spooky."

"Oh my . . . I hope your folks won't be upset with me," I say, as I resume scrubbing.

"They aren't. That was last year. I'm going to try again, and between us, I want to tell Edward that I've read it before he does," she laughs.

"Your secret's safe with me, but I'll warn you, he's going to start with the first two books and then finish up his summer with *The House of Long Shadows*, besides a few comic books, I'm sure."

"I know he likes Thor; I still read Archie."

"I read my share of Archie too—many of them right here in this cabin, much to Edna's chagrin."

"Mary Ellen doesn't mind me reading Archie, but she laughs at me and says it's for commoners."

"I recall hearing that a time or two as well. Don't let it spoil your fun—we all need a break now and then."

"Edna must've been a really neat lady. Mary Ellen only talks about her if she's been into her dandelion wine, and she gets teary, too. What happened to her?"

"Edna? What does Mary Ellen say about it?" I pause and look up from the floor as she answers.

"Nothing, only that she's been gone a long time now."

"Honestly, that's part of the tears—I don't know what happened to her. We lost touch after I left Orcas, and a year or so later, I heard that she passed away somewhere back east. It's usually cancer or a car accident when something like that happens."

"My grandmother died from cancer."

"I'm sorry to hear that, Vivian," I reply, emptying the pail into the sink.

"This place is really cool—I bet it's going to be great all fixed up! Will you write books here?"

"I sure hope to! I'm working on another one now, but it's still just rattling around in my head. Maybe by the time I sit down at the typewriter, the characters will show up long enough to tell me their stories."

"Is that how writing a novel works?"

"For me it does, and that's when I know it's going to be a good one."

"That's neat. Do you think it will be a ghost story?"

"I'm not sure yet. Why do you ask?"

"I really enjoy ghost stories and adventure, and I'm even starting to like some romance too."

"That certainly gives me something to consider." I smile.

"I think it would be dreamy to be a writer!"

"It can be. Is that something you've been pondering?"

"Maybe, I don't know . . ."

"Come now, Vivian, writers can't be shy about such things."

Vivian's face lights up as she says, "Yes, ma'am, I'd like to give it try."

"Well, then, what's stopping you?"

"Starting, I guess."

"Do you mean finding the story to tell or the fear of telling it?"

Her eyes shift slightly, and her nose wrinkles in deliberation before responding with a smile. "I think it's a little of both."

"May I offer you a suggestion, then?"

"Yes, ma'am, please!"

"Go to your favorite place where you won't be disturbed. Doesn't matter if it's the actual location or if it's only in your mind—the important part is that you won't be disturbed. Then sit there in silence and clear your mind of all the chores and anything else that is knocking around in there. Take a few long, deep breaths to open your heart, and try to focus on a single sound—I like listening to the water as it washes against the rocks below, and after a few minutes I begin to hear a voice from the waves. You can even do the same with the wind on a blustery day or a stream in the woods."

"Wow! Does it sound like a real voice?"

"You're going to have to try it for yourself and tell me!" I wink.

"Yes, ma'am, I sure will."

"One more thing, Vivian: rather than grappling with the long form of a novel, start with a short story, and make it something you're familiar with, so you don't have to do a lot of research. That way, you can concentrate on managing the arc. That's the beginning, middle, and end."

"Thank you, Ms. Meredith. I'm going to do just what you say and see what happens."

"You keep me posted, OK?"

"Yes, ma'am, I will for sure. Ms. Meredith, can I tell you something else?"

"Sure, what's on your mind?"

"I'm really glad y'all are here, and I think this place is too."

"Thank you, sweetie. That's such a wonderful sentiment, and it warms my heart." I'm touched and place my hand gently on her shoulder.

~

Hearing the truck come over the hill draws Vivian and me outside as the boys pull up to the cabin.

"Hey, Vivian!" Edward shouts, jumping out of the truck with a swagger I hadn't noticed before.

"Hi, Edward. I was wondering if you want to take a hike up to Twin Lakes tomorrow morning after my chores."

Edward looks to me, curious if I have something else planned for him to do.

"You two have a great time; I've got plenty of my own projects to keep me busy around here."

"Thanks, Mom!"

"Meet me at the foot of our water tower at nine o'clock, and we'll leave from there. It'll take us about six hours round trip."

"Can we go for a swim up there?"

"People do in Big Twin, but you might get the itch."

"The itch?"

"I'll tell ya on the way. It's a really pretty hike. Wear jeans or long pants in case of nettles. It can get a little buggy in the woods, but I'll bring some stuff that Mary Ellen makes from plants—it helps keep 'em off."

"Anything else?"

"Can't think of anything. I've got a couple of day packs and canteens; Mom will make sandwiches and snacks for us. Peanut butter and homemade raspberry jam OK?"

"Fine with me!"

"OK, see you at nine sharp. It was nice talking with you, Ms. Meredith, and thank you for the advice."

"You too, Vivian, I enjoyed our chat—drop by anytime. Thanks again for the apples, and tell your folks hello for me."

10

Twin Lakes

With packs loaded, Vivian and I walk up her driveway to the shared gravel road and enter the thick woods just beyond the no-trespassing signs posted at Mary Ellen's gate.

"This is part of Mary Ellen's property, but I have permission to be on it whenever I want."

"That's cool."

"I don't think she comes out here much, says it gives her the heebie-jeebies."

"Why? What's over here?"

"Just woods 'til we reach a field. After that, her property ends, and we start climbing."

"Maybe she just doesn't like the woods."

"Who doesn't like the woods!" Vivian exclaims. "Once we cross the field, it gets a little steep and rocky, but it's not all that bad; we just keep going northwest 'til we hit the Twin Lakes."

"Are there fish in there?"

"Trout, but they're not real big. Dad and I camped out once and fished Big Twin, but we let them go because they were too small. There's some cute salamanders with brown bodies and orange bellies, though!"

"What's the itch thing you were talking about?"

"It's a parasite that bores into your skin and dies. It's like the worst mosquito bite you ever had, and they are all over you. The only way to not get it is if you shower right after you come out, but there's no place to do that there."

"I hate mosquito bites more than just about anything," I say, cringing at the thought.

"I can't stand them either, but with Mary Ellen's stuff they should leave us alone."

We eventually clear the woods and find ourselves at a rolling field of tall grass, with the foothills Vivian described in the distance. After a short deliberation over whether to follow one of several deer paths or blaze a trail of our own through the waist-high grass, we opt for the latter and wade through the field, careful not to trip over the occasional rock or fallen tree branch.

"The last arrowhead I found was in here a while back," Vivian says.

"How'd you spot it in all this grass?"

"Just dumb luck; I tripped over something and wanted to see what the hell it was. There was a small ring of rocks overgrown with grass, like when you build a campfire—the arrowhead was just lying next to that. I bet a deer-hunting party was camped here and it fell out of an Indian's pouch or whatever."

"That's really lucky!"

"Yeah, it was far out. You never know when you might find one, but you'll also give yourself a headache if you go looking for them. I like to think they find you instead."

"Then I hope one finds me soon."

"You never know; this might be your lucky day."

With the field now behind us, we begin the rocky climb without much conversation, concentrating on our footing and handholds until we reach the top of the first knoll and pause for a second.

"It's a bit easier for the next half-mile, mostly woods, so the sun won't beat down on us, but it's all uphill. You ready?"

"Yeah. I'm used to the hills—Seattle is full of them."

"How do you like being on the island so far?"

"It's cool, but it was a huge surprise."

"Surprise?" Vivian looks over in disbelief.

"The whole thing was a big secret. I thought we were just going to be camping for a week or two, like at a cabin or something; didn't even know we were coming to Orcas until we were about to dock!"

"Wow, they kept it from you? That's huge! What did you think your dad was doing all those weekends?"

"I really thought he was working extra at Boeing. A lot of people got laid off over the last couple of years; some neighbors had to move away just to find work. It was pretty terrible."

"I remember hearing something about all that from my folks."

"I learned a good lesson about appearances versus facts, and I'm really glad that I was wrong, at least in this case!"

"Then, you like it here on Orcas?"

"Oh yeah, it's like a whole other world."

"I'm glad you do. I've never lived on the mainland, so I don't know any different."

"Well, something was bugging me the other day and then I figured it out."

"What was it?"

"The quiet. Seattle is noisy—the car tires rolling up and down the streets, sirens, gobs of people, and there's buildings all over. You don't really notice it when you're there, but I bet I would now."

"I guess I take the quiet for granted, except in summer when the tourists show up. You'll have to come up in the off-season—now that's quiet!"

"I saw how crowded Templin's was the other day."

"Yep, and it takes at least twice as long to get around as it does in the off-season."

"With all this quiet, I would've finished Sherlock Holmes in half the time."

"Ya think?"

"I'm going to test that theory by reading all three of my mom's books over the summer."

"I was talking with her yesterday about doing the same thing. We could have our own book club if you want."

"Hey, that's a great idea!" I respond, excited about the prospect.

"Cool. Should we start tonight?"

"I'm game!" I reply, noting her farm girl attitude. "The first three chapters—OK with you?"

"Piece of cake!"

The woodchip-covered lake trail suddenly appears on our left, and a minute later the smaller of the two lakes comes into view.

"It's pretty marshy around the edge, so keep on the trail," Vivian cautions. "You don't wanna sink down into that—it'll fill your shoes with lake muck."

"No thanks!"

"Little Twin is actually connected to Big Twin—see, there on the right." She points to the isthmus that appears to be only a trail of trees coming out of the water between the two lakes. Big Twin is about three times the size, surrounded by woods that creep close to the shoreline, with a cliff across the lake at the northeastern edge.

"What do you think?"

"Cool, this reminds me of the lake in *Creature from the Black Lagoon*."

"I double-dare you to swim across."

"Not me, I don't want that itch thing!"

"I wouldn't do it either. Look, this is the spot where those salamanders are—come on."

Vivian reaches into the tea-colored water at the northern shoreline and gently scoops one up, resting it in her open palm, stroking its back with a finger.

"See! It doesn't seem to mind."

"Might be scared thinking you're going to eat him."

"Not nice, Edward. Thank you, Mr. or Ms. Salamander. See you next time," Vivian says, and then returns it to the water, where it rejoins the others with a few wiggles of its tail.

"That was neat. There's a lot of them, that's for sure," I say, noting her care for the little creatures.

"They've been here every time—it's something I really look forward to."

We round the northeast corner, and after walking up a small hill, we drop our packs on top of the cliff overlooking the water about twenty feet below.

"This is the best place on the lake for lunch," Vivian declares, "And with a great view of Mount Constitution."

"I bet we seem like ants to anyone from that lookout up there."

"If they can even see us, but I like that you get a view of some of the other islands from up top."

"Hey, break out those sandwiches—my stomach's about to growl," I laugh.

"Speaking of sand-wiches . . . seen anything at your house yet?"

"Sand-witches . . . good one, Vivian."

"Well?"

"You have to swear not to say anything to anyone."

"I not only swear, I promise not to say anything to any-one! Now out with it already!"

"All right . . . I woke up in the middle of the night because I heard a voice calling my name."

"Get out!"

"I swear! It was like a long, drawn-out whisper saying, 'E-d-w-a-r-d . . .'"

"Man or woman?" I detect a strain in Vivian's voice with the question.

"Definitely a woman, but since she woke me up from a dream, I'm not 100 percent sure that it was even real."

"Was she in your dream with you?"

"No, I was . . . well, I was fighting alongside Thor and the Silver Surfer." I notice the corners of Vivian's mouth turning up as her eyes move away.

"What's so funny?"

"Sorry, I'm not laughing at you. I just think it's cute—the Thor, Silver Surfer thing. But if she wasn't in your dream, then . . ."

"I don't know; it only happened that one night. The rest of the time, I sleep like a rock."

"Remember back when I was telling you all that stuff about the witch, and you asked me if I'd ever seen a ghost? I never really answered you; I just said that it was not a ghost but a witch, and I hadn't seen her. Well, that was true."

"OK."

"I haven't seen a witch, but . . . I have seen a ghost."

"Bull!" I laugh, tossing a small rock off the cliff into the lake.

"I swear it, Edward, on a stack of Bibles!"

"Great, so now we have a ghost and a witch roaming around."

"I've seen her twice—the first was last November right after those guys broke in."

"What happened? The whole story, please."

"My winter chore routine is to always check the coop first thing to make sure the heater didn't go out during the night; then I cut over to the greenhouses and take care of everything growing in them. When I was walking down toward the chickens, there was a mist shimmering in the moonlight."

"What'd it look like?"

"It was just a smudge of light floating between the coop and cliffs, about a foot off the ground. At first, I thought it was fog, but there's always that breeze coming from the west, and this just hung in the air without moving. I was curious and got to within fifty feet; then I could see that it was shaped like a woman, and she was watching me! That's when I heard my name; it was exactly like you just described it: 'V-i-v-i-a-n . . .'"

"Whoa!"

"I was frozen solid! Couldn't even feel my feet and thought I was going to barf or pee myself!"

"I don't blame you a bit!"

"She had to have known that I was terrified because then she moved off into the woods, heading south toward your property."

"What about the other time?"

"Same thing, but this was back in February. I followed her into the woods until she came out by the cabin, and she kept heading along the cliffs."

"Were you scared?"

"Hell yeah, I was, at first . . . but it's like she's waiting for something or someone. You know those old houses by the sea that have that thing on the roof that sailors' wives stand on?."

"A widow's walk?"

"Yeah, that's it. Watching her felt like that's what she was doing."

"Could you see her face?" My curiosity is almost untamable when I ask.

"No, it's not like that. It's kinda hard to describe, just a form, really . . . but I can tell it's female, maybe a young woman, definitely not an old lady."

"Did you tell your folks about it?"

"Yeah, but only the first time, and they said it was just my imagination, even though I swore that it wasn't. My mom doesn't like to tell you something more than once, so I wasn't about to bring it up again."

At this point, a murmur of disembodied voices interrupts our conversation, and our eyes get even wider. Then suddenly, a stream of kids charge out of the woods on the opposite side of the lake.

"Oh great, it's a pack of Orkila kids! That's the YMCA camp over by Beach Haven. It's been around forever, and that looks like a group of ten-year-olds."

"Geez, there's gotta be twenty of them!"

"We should probably pack out because they'll be over here in no time jumping off this cliff and playing *Lord of the Flies*."

"What about the itch?"

"It's a bitch, and they'll find out soon enough." Vivian laughs and shrugs her shoulders as we gather our stuff and head south along the eastern shoreline before retracing our route toward home.

"It's practically all downhill from here, Edward."

"How far do you think it is?"

"Only about two miles by sight, but it feels like twice that because there aren't real trails. If we didn't have a compass, it'd be hard to get back as quickly, and I wouldn't want to be wandering around out here at night."

"Sasquatch?"

"I can't believe you just said that!" Vivian starts laughing.

"It stands to reason that if there's a witch, a ghost, and a sea serpent, then a Sasquatch isn't too far-fetched."

"Sasquatch—that's mainland stuff! The largest mammals we have walking around on these islands besides people are deer. Come to think of it, Mary Ellen did say a bear swam over here by going island to island, once. Maybe a Sasquatch could, too."

"Great, sorry I asked."

The return trip takes us about half the time, and when we reach the knoll dropping down to the field bordering the northern end of Mary Ellen's property, we stop for another drink from our canteens and eat a sesame seed and honey snack that Vivian's mom made for us.

"Pretty here, isn't it?" she says, as we sit with our feet dangling over the knoll.

"Yeah, thanks for showing me around, and your mom packs the best lunches too!"

"She does. So, whaddya think about what we talked about earlier?"

"I don't really know what to think . . . but the next morning after I heard the voice, I asked my folks if the house was haunted."

"Holy crap, Edward, what'd they say?"

"My mom said that it's just like in her book—we're all haunted houses. Then she said I could read *The House of Long Shadows*, but on the condition that I read *Haunted Houses* and *The Missing* first, and I have to do a book report for each one."

"I do book reports for Mary Ellen all the time. We could work on that together, too, if you want."

"That'd be great."

"At least your parents didn't think you were nuts for asking if the house was haunted."

"No, they're cool about that stuff. I even told Mom about hearing the voice; she said it was probably just my guardian angel watching over me."

"Aw, that's sweet; maybe she is."

"Hey, different subject: do you know anything about a rich guy over on Shaw Island with a bum leg—Stuart something?"

"Chase Stuart?"

"That's him! I guess he knew my mom when they were kids. We ran into him on the boat coming over. He seemed like a weirdo."

"He's from an old San Juan's family, one of the richest out here. His mother burned alive in a house fire about four summers ago. I know someone who was passing by in their boat and heard her screaming before the propane tank blew everything up. That's how he got crippled."

"He showed us his mangled leg in a brace."

"Gross! I've only seen him a few times and I've lived here my whole life: once when he was yelling at some guy on the ferry for bumping into his car, and then one time at the Farmer's Market. He gives me the creeps."

"That's what I said after he left, and my dad agreed."

"I've heard folks around here say to keep away from him and that he even drowned a pg girl from Lopez and got away with it. But my mom says it's gossip, and I shouldn't pay attention to it."

"Pg?"

"Pregnant, Edward." Vivian shakes her head.

"He murdered a pregnant girl?!"

"Shhh—it's just a rumor—but remember, you didn't hear it from me!"

~

It's four o'clock by the time we arrive back at the water tower and say our goodbyes.

"Thanks, Edward. I had a lot of fun today. See you bright and early tomorrow."

"Me too! I'll be there at four-thirty and ready to work. Happy reading tonight!"

11

The Orcan Cowboy

Rather than cut through the woods after our hike I head for home along the shared road where I pause to examine the old iron gate at the driveway entrance. Vines of ivy wrap around the two stone pillars and climb the arch where they overlap one another in the center, then continue down the opposite sides. There's a cluster in the middle that catches my eye, and upon closer examination I make out the letters barely visible beneath the leaves. L o n g S h a d o w s.

I resume my way down the driveway until the fork in the road that leads to the barn and spot the top of a pickup truck parked next to it. Two men are talking with Dad. The scraggly bearded one leaning against the oxidized red truck could have stepped right out of a Western movie, complete with worn jeans, boots, shoulder-length blond hair, and a cowboy hat tipped slightly forward, just enough to keep the sun from reflecting off of his mirrored sunglasses. The other man looks businesslike in his dark blue jeans, red-and-white-checked shirt, and nicer boots.

"Edward, come on over; I'd like you to meet these gentlemen."

"Hi Edward, I'm Rich Steinle from Olga Livestock; it's a pleasure to make your acquaintance," says the well-dressed man, greeting me with a firm handshake.

"It's a pleasure to meet you, Mr. Steinle."

The other man bounces his wiry frame off the truck, spits tobacco juice into the dirt, and steps toward me.

"Howdy, Edward, the name's Alf McClure. I wrangle for Mr. Steinle over at Olga Livestock."

"It's a pleasure to meet you, too, Mr. McClure."

"Well, now, let's get one thing straight, hombre: folks around these parts call me Cowboy," he says as he intercepts my hand with a firm shake and a smile revealing a missing lower tooth.

Mr. Steinle turns to Dad. "Thanks again, Robert—we're very appreciative of the hay. We typically take it in mid-August. Cowboy will check on it a couple times before then, if that's all right."

"Sounds good, Rich. Cowboy, will you need our tractor?"

"If it wouldn't be too much trouble, sir. We'll cut and rake it into windrows a day or two before, depending on weather, and run the rake through it again the day we bale, just to make sure we're good and dry. We like to get an early start on pickup days, especially when we're doing two fields; that way, we can finish by suppertime."

"That'll be just fine—glad we can help out."

"Thank you, we'll let y'all get on with your evening, and thanks again for asking Meredith to sign those books. I hope it's not out of keeping."

"Trust me, Rich, it's no problem at all. She'll be thrilled to take care of it for Tracy."

"Cowboy can drop by tomorrow afternoon on his way back from Indian Point to pick them up. It'll probably be around one if you think that would be all right?"

"They'll be here waiting for you, Cowboy; just come on up to the house."

"Much obliged. Y'all have a good 'un!" he says as the two climb back into the old truck.

Cowboy gives another spit and a final wave before putting it in gear and heading up the dirt road toward the driveway.

"He's a real character, isn't he?" Dad comments. "Reminds me of somebody from *Gunsmoke* or *Bonanza*."

"He sure does. I'm surprised to meet a real-life cowboy out here."

"He moved up from New Mexico last year; just goes to show that you never know who's going to cross yer path, pardner," Dad laughs. "How was the hike?"

"It was great—have you ever been up to Twin Lakes?"

"I've only seen it from Mount Constitution—is it nice?"

"Yeah, it's in the middle of nowhere, and I told Vivian it reminded me of the *Black Lagoon*."

"I guess you didn't go for a dip, then."

"Not a chance, but that was because of the itch."

"You know, that's caused by a parasite from ducks and geese. Green Lake has it really bad; it's why we never take you swimming there. Makes me itch just talking about it."

I follow Dad into the barn to retrieve the large stack of books Mr. Steinle left to have signed, and he hands me half as we set off for the house.

"I wonder what your Ma has rustled us up for grub."

"I dunno, pardner, but all that trailblazing today, and I'm powerful hungry!" I reply, making Dad laugh.

12

A Mystery to Solve

I mention the entry gate at dinner and propose that Dad and I cut the overgrown ivy back to reveal the letters, but for whatever reason, Mom prefers its current state. I'm more surprised when she confirms Vivian's sea serpent story, and to top that, even Dad knows about the sightings that took place from here to Vancouver Island back in the early 1900s. Fueled by revelations of an actual sea monster lurking about, I gulp down the rest of my dinner and clear the table before dashing upstairs to begin reading *Haunted Houses*.

The only thing I know for sure about the book comes from the description on the inside flap, and my excitement of finally getting to read something Mom wrote is equaled by the apprehension of wanting to like it.

The foreword of the book quickly draws me into the world of diseased minds and insane asylums; almost as shocking is the discovery that the man I have always known as Uncle Alastair wrote it.

I hunker deeper into my reading chair, and soon any fears of not liking her book are discarded. They're instantly replaced by the subtle terror of unpredictability and the predator-like cunning of those individuals walking our streets without empathy. One frightening revelation in the foreword is that psychopaths and sociopaths learn how to feign compassion by studying how most of us react to traumatic circumstances. Then they add those reactions to their catalog of appropriate consolations. According to the book, empathy is a concept so foreign to this type that creating a passable facsimile of mercy and compassion is a sick game to them.

By the time I pull my face out of the book to check the time, it's nine o'clock, and I've blown past our three-chapter goal, reading one more. Vivian is expecting me at four-thirty in the morning, so I take a quick shower and am out like a light by the time my head hits the pillow. At three o'clock, I vault out of bed in a panic, searching for fresh air as I rush outside onto my porch.

The nightmare was so real that my eyes and throat still burn, with the sting of intense heat remaining on my skin until the chill of morning air penetrates my sweat-soaked pajamas.

As I stare out over the dark landscape, still shaken by what I experienced, a shiver prompts me to strip off the wet PJs and hightail it into the shower to warm up. The chill finally retreats under the warm water, and I begin to recall what happened.

In the nightmare, I'm surrounded by heavy smoke with flames clawing at me from all sides as sparks and hot ash rain down on me. There are screams of desperation from those beyond my sight, gasping for their next breath from the cinder-filled air as it squeezes the life out of us. I'm choking and unable to breathe when an icy hand finds me in the blackness; its fingers close around my arm and snatch me from the horrible scene, returning me to my bed.

That was the entire ordeal, or at least what I remember, but there's something more to it . . . I can't quite figure out what it is, but it's gnawing at me.

I debate telling Vivian about it as I walk through the woods, concerned that she might think the nightmare was brought on from reading *Haunted Houses*, a point that would be hard for me to refute without a substantial alternative explanation. Thankfully, by the time I arrive at the chicken coop, I've had an epiphany and it's no longer an issue.

"Mornin', Edward, thanks for coming over."

"No sweat. How was your reading last night?"

"Your mom sure doesn't mess around—she gets right into the gory details."

"I know! It's a lot more graphic than Sherlock Holmes, I can tell you that! Did you stop after chapter three? I accidentally read through four."

"Hey, we're supposed to read this together, remember?"

"Sorry, I got lost in it. Won't happen again, I promise."

"Better not, and don't tell me anything about that next chapter, especially if there's blood and guts," she smiles. "Now, do you remember how to set the water valves for these lower plots?"

"I just crank them to the number marked by the colored tape. You want me to get going?"

"Yep, perfect. While you're doing that, I'll feed the chickens and open the master valve up the hill. Let's meet at the upper greenhouse in about a half hour."

"Check!"

There are ten sizable fenced lower plots on the south side of the farm to be watered, and as I go around to each one, setting the valves according to the crop being grown, thoughts of my conclusion regarding the nightmare become much clearer, and I'm now excited to tell Vivian the story.

"So, wait a minute, Edward—you're telling me your mom's book gave you a nightmare?" She cuts me off before I can finish.

"No, I swear it's not like that," I insist over her laughter as my initial fears of where this might lead are playing out.

"That's quite a coincidence, then. Look, don't feel bad—I might not have been able to read it either when I was your age."

"First off, Vivian, I don't believe in coincidence," I respond a bit peevishly. "And secondly, that's not it, I can assure you."

"Promise?"

"Yes, I promise!"

"OK, I'll hear you out, but we have to keep working and get all of these butternut squash starts planted in the lower north."

"It'll have to wait until we're done, then, because it's too important, and I don't want to be distracted."

"Now you've got me intrigued. Once we get these transplanted and watered in, we're finished and can go up to the house for breakfast. I told my mom you were coming to help out, so she'll have a pile of food for us."

About an hour and a half later, we arrive at the house and Ms. Danelle sets down plates of bacon and eggs in front of us, along with a stack of pancakes and her biscuits with homemade apple butter. Vivian warned me to keep quiet until her mom left the house because Ms. Danelle has some reservations about our summer reading plan, and Vivian doesn't want to be hassled if her mother overhears our conversation.

When she finally leaves to meet Mr. Kent in the orchard, I swear Vivian to secrecy, then give her the details about the nightmare, followed by the story of the three pictures I saw in the attic that afternoon back on Capitol Hill.

"The witch! It has to be the witch in that painting, Edward!"

"Elementary, my dear Vivian . . . but it's also the other one. The one that I always thought looked like a bad finger painting—it made no sense until the nightmare; now I think those two paintings are connected."

"Whaddya mean?" She says between bites.

"I mean that picture isn't a bad finger painting at all; it's the fire burning in my nightmare."

"That's crazy."

"Really? In the dream I'm suffocating inside clouds of smoke, where I can't even see my hand in front of my face, with flames burning my skin—it was like being inside that picture."

"Sounds like being in hell with the witch to me."

"Well, if it was hell, then she's the one who pulled me out of there."

"Edward, everybody knows only Jesus can get you out of hell."

"Duh! So, it couldn't have been hell, but it had to be her—the one we've been calling the witch."

"Or maybe it was the ghost—the one that knows our names."

"Huh . . . I didn't think of that." I grin, impressed by her insight. "All I can say is that she snatched me out of that nightmare and into my bed in one go!"

"Are you scared?"

"Not really. More curious about it, I guess. She kinda rescued me, so if it's the witch, she's not a bad one, if there is such a thing. I know this all ties together somehow; I just have to figure it out."

"Well, you don't have to do it alone—I'll help."

Just then Vivian's folks come tromping up onto the back porch with a bushel of apples and join us in the kitchen.

"Nice work on the transplants, you two!"

"Thanks, Dad."

"Keep this up, and we might have to hire you full-time, Edward," Ms. Danelle adds.

"Yeah, it'd be great to have some real help around here for once," Vivian smacks.

"Count me in if it always includes your cooking, Ms. Danelle."

"Now don't go all suck-up, Edward."

"Vivian Irene! You're not too old for a bar of soap!" Ms. Danelle chides, and I catch Mr. Kent's discreet smile and headshake as he exits the room.

"I was just joking around."

"Irene?" I smile but hold my laughter.

"Thanks a lot, Mom!" She's clearly exasperated by the disclosure.

"Another biscuit, Edward?" Ms. Danelle pats my shoulder as she walks by.

"Yes, ma'am, two please!" I answer as Vivian teeters on the edge of irritation and embarrassment.

"I like it."

"You like what?" she responds in a huff as Ms. Danelle walks out of the kitchen to chase down Mr. Kent.

"Your middle name."

"You're bats—it's so old-fashioned."

"No, really! Irene Adler was the only woman who captivated Sherlock Holmes. She outsmarts him in *A Scandal in Bohemia*, and from then on he only refers to her as the Woman."

"Huh, you don't say . . ." Vivian lowers her voice and leans over the table. "So tell me, Edward, do I captivate you like this Irene Adler?"

I instantly feel my face getting warmer as she stares at me, and I quickly look over to the clock on the kitchen wall.

"Thanks again for the great breakfast—I need to get back home and do some stuff for my mom."

"Oh, Edward, you're hopeless at times," she shakes her head. "All right, thanks for helping out this morning—I owe you! And remember: up to chapter ten tonight and keep me posted."

"Yep, you do the same, and don't worry, I won't go over."

"Better not, Mr. Holmes."

"I promise that I won't, Ms. Adler."

13

The Rite

I enjoy signing books about as much as I do writing them. There's a unique satisfaction at the intersection of creation and reception that I wish everyone could experience at least once in their lifetime. That reward has never dulled, and as I sit here on the rear porch this morning with my coffee and a stack to inscribe, there's a pinch-me level of gratitude for the honor that comes with each name on Tracy Steinle's list.

When I saw the name Cowboy and asked Robert about it, he relayed the man's heartrending story of losing his wife and preteen daughter to a drunk driver while living in rural New Mexico. Afterward, he and his broken heart traveled aimlessly up the West Coast until arriving in Anacortes as winter approached. It was on a ferry ride to the islands when he sat across from a woman reading the final pages of *Haunted Houses*. When she closed the book, he casually asked her the location of those houses. "They're inside each one of us. Here, enjoy the journey through yours," she replied, handing him the book.

He finished the story during his weekend on Orcas and ventured into the island bookstore, where he bought my other two. It was in conversation with the proprietor, Kim Stone, when he discovered that Olga Livestock was desperate for help to rebuild their fire-ravaged barn before winter set in. That was a little over seven months ago, and though he still lives in Anacortes, it appears Cowboy has found his next chapter here in the San Juan Islands.

I'm fascinated by the stories people share about what's helped them ford the river of their grief. Lord knows I've waded through the depths of loss myself and can say unequivocally that those of us who survive are forever changed by the process. I, for one, prefer to be outside in the sunshine or walking alone on a rainy day to soothe my emotional wounds, but over the years, a few readers have approached the table at book signings to tell me that my novels helped them navigate hard times. I don't pretend to understand how books bordering on the macabre contribute to such, but Cowboy appears to be among that small number who have found refuge in those pages.

So, on the rare occasions that I hear stories like his, I can't help but pause to consider my own path with the pen and how I arrived at this place, ever humbled that words put to the page during the ritual of the (w)Rite, no matter how obscure or horrifying to one, were preordained for another's healing.

~

It was in lieu of an extravagant honeymoon in Hawaii that we spent a long weekend at Snoqualmie Falls Lodge and used the savings toward the purchase of our first home together on 16th Avenue East. I readily embraced the role of wife, homemaker, gardener, and author, while Robert dove headlong into husband, provider, and renovator.

Writing daily throughout the fall and winter months, I submitted everything that rolled off the typewriter to get local editors accustomed to seeing my new name. The strategy paid off, and by spring, several of my short stories had appeared in smaller regional publications, providing me with much-needed encouragement and, most importantly, some professional legitimacy. When *The Haunted Houses of Capitol Hill* ran in Northwest Lifestyles magazine, it caught the attention of a senior editor at the publisher Random House, who read it on his return flight to New York.

The story portrayed haunted characters rather than dwellings, drawing a distinction between the internal voices that many of us contend with daily and the undetected psychotics living among the masses. Random House contacted me the following week, and after a few telephone conversations, Robert and I flew to New York City, where they presented me with a two-book publishing deal.

The first novel, *Haunted Houses*, is based on the same premise used in the Northwest Lifestyles short story and includes a sobering foreword about systemic mental health failures, written by my dear friend Alastair. It sold very well, receiving critical acclaim and two prestigious awards.

The second book, titled *The Missing*, is a psychological thriller set in Portland, Oregon, in the 1940s. Sarah is just out of college and flees her small town on the outskirts of Spokane for Portland and her first real job.

Thanks to a referral from her boss at the bank, Sarah lands a great apartment that's walking distance to the office and makes many friends among the scads of other women working in the secretarial pools of downtown Portland.

Life is grand until the fall, when six girls in the friend group go missing, and city officials are tight-lipped about it. In early December, when a dismembered corpse is found under a dock on the Willamette River, residents' worst fears are realized. Tensions reach a crescendo after The Oregonian runs a chilling two-word taunt on the cover of Sunday's edition, "Eye'm Here," and word gets out that the anonymous note arrived in a small box wrapped around a jar containing two mismatched human eyeballs, packed with dirt and earthworms.

As Portland descends into panic, a massive snowstorm slams into the city on December 22, preventing Sarah from leaving for the holidays until the downtown streets can be plowed. With intermittent power and frightened to be alone, she seeks refuge in Marguerite's apartment as the sun goes down.

The superintendent has been a motherly fixture for Sarah and the other girls in the building over the months, ever vigilant in reminding them to draw their curtains at night and lock their doors for safety. Marguerite assures her that the building is secure, and short of smashing the large plate glass window in the lobby, no one can get in or out until morning. It's by the glow of candlelight that she begins to notice peculiar things about the old woman, like the tilt of her head when she speaks or the eye twitch that seems oddly familiar, but when she catches a glimpse of stubble emerging from Marguerite's heavy makeup, Sarah realizes that the old woman is actually her boss, Mr. Goyle.

The Missing made the New York Times Best Sellers list its first week, winning several reader and industry awards, and yet with all of the positive hubbub, I felt unsettled.

Edward was born shortly after I'd begun writing *Haunted Houses* and was regularly lulled to sleep by the cadence of my fingers tapping out scenes on a Smith-Corona Super 5. When I submitted the manuscript for *The Missing*, he was almost six years old, and between the book tours, appearances, and interviews, I realized just how much of my attention was being devoted to writing other people's stories rather than living out my own. Thank God for Robert's level head when I seriously contemplated retirement from novel writing.

"You have to do what you love, Meredith." He knew . . . somehow he knew.

The success of the first two books wasn't lost on other publishers, and by the time I sat down with Random House for their right-of-first-refusal negotiation, I had several attractive offers on the table for them to compete with.

What we eventually agreed to was lucrative financially, but most important to me was the provision granting my final editorial approval for the next book.

That book was already gestating, haunting my waking moments and stalking my dreams as well. But this was a different kind of pregnancy altogether, one that churned up so much personal pain and sorrow that I almost couldn't acknowledge it.

The time had come to honor the one promise from my youth that remained outstanding, so I broke open the vault of my heart and searched the depths until I found the echo of her voice, and together we wrote *The House of Long Shadows*.

14

It's Always a Woman

My little meander down memory lane has faded by the time Edward comes into view on his return from the farm.

"Hi honey, it was so sweet of you to help Vivian with her chores this morning."

"Nah, it wasn't a big deal—we just watered the lower ten and transplanted about a hundred butternut squash plants."

"Sounds like they'll have some nice squash this fall. I just finished signing these books for Tracy Steinle. Are you hungry?"

"I'm stuffed! Ms. Danelle made breakfast for us—she makes the best biscuits."

"Yes, she does! I'll have to ask her to freeze some for us."

"They wouldn't last long, especially with her jam. Do you still want me to haul those boxes down from the attic?"

"No, I've decided to wait until we're closer to the cabin being finished. Otherwise, they'd just be in the way, and you know how I hate clutter."

"Maybe I'll help Dad in the barn, then."

"He's down at the cabin with Ralph the contractor. When he gets back, we're heading into Eastsound to do some grocery shopping—want to come along?"

"I think I'll just hang out here. But I have a favor."

"Sure, what is it?"

"Would you look in the comic rack for the July issue of Thor, number 201? I think it's supposed to be there now."

"I'll bring one home for you if it is."

"Thanks, Mom. Hey, know what Vivian's middle name is?"

"I haven't the faintest."

"Irene!"

"That's adorable! Must be in honor of a grandmother."

"How'd you know?"

"Elementary, my dear Edward," I laugh. "The name Irene wasn't in vogue for baby girls in the late fifties."

"Great deduction. But she hates that name, says it sounds old-fashioned. I told her I liked it, though—reminds me of Irene Adler in Sherlock Holmes."

"Isn't that a coincidence!"

"You know I'm not big on coincidences, but maybe it fits this time."

"I think that's a safe bet, young Sherlock. Now, I do hope Irene Adler is a flattering character."

"Oh, she is! She's the only person who ever outsmarted Holmes."

"It's always a woman, isn't it? Mind helping me carry these books inside to the table in the foyer?"

"What do you mean, 'It's always a woman'?"

"Literary history. Elizabeth and Darcy from *Pride and Prejudice*. Juliet and Romeo."

"And how about Anne and Gilbert from *Anne of Green Gables*!"

"You've got it!" I smile, giving him a wink.

We've just set the books down in the foyer when Robert walks in from his meeting at the cabin.

"How'd it go?"

"Really well, but you'd better get down there if you want more photos because the entire roof is coming off Monday so they can install that steel ridge beam and the supporting structure."

"You weren't kidding when you said they move fast."

"The weather forecast is good through next week, and they can't build the new roof until that's done. Just one thing, though."

"Yes?"

"At the behest of his wife, Ralph did ask about that gathering you mentioned."

"Let's do it the week the cabin is finished, and we'll host it there." I smile.

"Strategically, it might be wise to invite Carol over for coffee one morning and tell her exactly that. I'm sure it'll make her feel special, and she'll keep the heat on."

"I follow you . . . if mama isn't happy . . ."

"Exactly!" Robert grins.

"OK, I'll make the invite."

"You know, we could just stop by the bookstore today; Ralph mentioned that she's working."

"That's a great idea—I need to drop in and sign a few copies on the shelf for them anyway."

"Excellent. Coming with us, Edward?"

"No, I'm gonna hang around here. I've got some reading to do and might check out the woods to the south."

"Be careful over there—from what I remember, some spots are fairly thick with nettles. There's calamine lotion in the medicine cabinet if you need it."

"I will—thanks, Mom."

"If you leave before we get back, make sure to put the books on the porch for Cowboy with a note; he's stopping by this afternoon to pick them up."

"Yes, pardner, I remember."

"Adios, then, hombre!"

15

Home on the Range

I'm in the final pages of chapter ten when the sound of tires on gravel draws my eyes to the bay window as the old pickup truck comes into view. I lay the open book face down on the table and quickly walk outside to greet Cowboy who's just sliding out of the driver's seat as I reach the bottom step.

"Howdy, Cowboy! I have the books for you inside."

"Much obliged there, pardner."

"You can come on in and grab 'em if you'd like."

Stepping toward me, he stoops over slightly and puts his hand on my shoulder. "Well, Edward, we have an old sayin' out on the range, and it goes something like this here: Never approach a bull from the front, a horse from the rear, or let a stranger into the house when yer folks aren't home! You follow me, kemosabe?"

"Yes, sir, but I don't really see you as a stranger."

"Son, that's a mistake that can cost you mightily out on a homestead. Now, why don't I wait right here while you mosey on inside for those books."

"Yes, sir, it'll take me a couple of trips . . ."

"That's all right. Besides, it's a beauty of a day, and I got time." He smiles, taking in his surroundings.

When I return with the second stack, Cowboy hands me a Styrofoam cooler that must weigh at least twenty pounds.

"Now, here's a little something from us at the ranch to show our appreciation. All fresh-cut steaks, so load it into the ice box until your folks get home, and they can decide what gets frozen or not."

"Will do, pardner, and much obliged!"

"Nice to see you again, Edward. Adios!"

With a nod, he fires up the old truck and is about to take off when I ask him, "Hey, Cowboy, how did you know my folks weren't here?"

"Saw 'em in town, amigo!" he says with a grin as he throws the truck in gear and heads back up the driveway.

16

Mary Ellen Carter

It's the end of June, and so much of my time on the island has been helping Mom and Dad around the property. In Seattle, I'd be goofing off with my friends and riding our bikes all over until dinner time; it's weird, but as I cut through the woods this morning I don't really miss it.

Even though Vivian and I aren't any closer to solving the case, helping her with chores a few days a week has taught me a lot about responsibility and consequences. The type of stuff you don't think about in the city, like if something isn't watered, fed, or latched, it might die as a result, and that sticks with me.

As I walk out of the trees at the fenced garden by the chicken coop, I see Vivian wrestling with a large rubber hose that might as well be a python. From my vantage point, it's getting the better of her.

"Hey, Jane, me Tarzan—need a hand with that?"

"Yeah! Dad just replaced the hoses, and they're a real bitch until they break in," she says as I enter the enclosure and untangle her.

"Thanks, Tarzan, you got here in the nick of time. This needs to go back to the potting shed; do you mind carrying it while I grab that bag of fertilizer? All of a sudden the sky looks like we're going to get some rain."

"No problem, I'll get it," I reply, noticing the rare gray clouds rolling in.

We hustle across the property to the potting shed, and after we stow the hose and fertilizer, a squeal of static comes from the back pocket of her overalls.

"Go for Vivian."

"Copy, Dad."

"20?"

"Potting shed with Edward, chores done, heading to Mary Ellen's. Over."

"Copy that. Y'all better get movin'. Deer Harbor Marina says big rain is headed our way. Over and out."

"Roger that. Over and out."

Vivian puts a check mark on the chalkboard corresponding to each chore she's completed for the morning, then plugs in the walkie-talkie to recharge.

"Turn around, please."

"What for?"

"Because I have to get out of these gross clothes and put on my jeans and a clean shirt before we go over to Mary Ellen's."

"I can just go outside . . ."

"You might get rained on." She smiles and unclips the shoulder straps holding up the overalls.

I quickly turn toward the door, only to be greeted by her reflection in the shed's window glass. The darkening sky outside and the fluorescent light of the workbench present a clear image of Vivian stepping out of her overalls, which have dropped to the floor, quickly followed by her thermal. Any inkling of looking away is vanquished as she pauses in her bra and underwear for a second to bend over and run her fingers through her hair.

"Know what I did last night?"

"Uh, uh, ummm, there's no telling," I answer, spellbound by what's unfolding before my eyes.

"I made it to chapter twenty!" she says proudly in a singsong way as she slides her jeans over her hips and begins buttoning the fly.

"That's great—congratulations."

"Is that all you have to say?" She pauses, looking over in dismay, and almost catches my eyes in the glass.

"No . . . sorry, I know you've been really busy the past week; that took a lot. I'm glad we're back on schedule to finish by the end of the month."

"Have you kept reading?" she probes, grabbing her T-shirt from a nearby wooden peg.

"Nah, remember I promised not to read ahead," I answer matter-of-factly, still distracted as her head comes through the T-shirt, followed by each arm. "Anyway, it's much more fun to talk about it when we're on the same page—get it?"

"I get it . . . you're sooooo corny sometimes!"

"Only ten chapters left to go, so we'll have to read five each night."

"What do you think about this last bit?"

"Creepy . . . it makes you wonder how many freaks like those are walking around."

"That's another nice thing about living here on Orcas—we don't have as many kooks as you do walking around a big city like Seattle."

"Maybe not in the numbers we have, but if you go by percentages, there's bound to be a few genuine maniacs roaming around these islands. Just remember that the insane asylum in Sedro-Woolley isn't too far away from Anacortes."

"Don't say it, Edward! All right, I'm dressed; you can turn around now. What are you grinning about?"

"Sheesh, a guy can grin, can't he?" I smile wider, reliving the scene I've just witnessed.

Vivian and I exit the potting shed under a dark sky splintered with sunlight while paying close attention to the blanket of charcoal bearing down on us from the west.

"We'd better get moving, Edward!"

Running into the heavy woods as the wind picks up, Vivian coaches me about our visit with Mary Ellen.

"I'm warning you, she's kind of unpredictable, especially if she gets into her dandelion juice."

"Like one of the crazies from the book?"

"No, she's not a psycho, Edward!" Vivian laughs. "She just speaks her mind is all. Might even cuss and carry on just like she's talking to another adult, so if that happens, don't act like she's scalded your virgin ears."

"It's not like I haven't heard that kind of talk before, Vivian—I grew up in the city, you know!"

"Yeah, I know, and you watched *Psycho*. I think you should watch more *Love, American Style* and *Laugh-In*! You know, sock it to me, sock it to me!"

"Copy that, Goldie Hawn."

"Goldie's groovy! Smartass."

"Boy, I'll say!" I shout over the gusts.

As the wind begins to whip, Vivian stops talking and quickens our pace through the rocky maze of trees and brush, but when a large limb crashes to the ground less than twenty feet away, I question our decision not to wait this out.

"Maybe we should go back to your house until this blows over."

"Nah, we're almost there. C'mon, keep moving!"

A few minutes later, we pop into the clearing, only to be pelted with the first drops of rain.

"Run for it!" Vivian shouts as we take off in an all-out sprint for the quaint red cottage nestled between the rocks and field grass. We barely make it to the small, covered porch when the sky opens with a vengeance.

"Wow! We usually don't get this kind of rain in the summer. It's really good for the aquifer and crops, as long as it doesn't pulverize those fresh starts we just transplanted."

"Saves me a waterin' too!" A voice materializes from directly behind us, almost sending Vivian and me out of our skin and off the porch as Mary Ellen Carter's words cut through the heavy downpour. "Jumpin' Jane Eyre! Aren't you two a mess! C'mon in and I'll fix you some strawberry flower and chamomile tea to settle your nerves," she cackles.

The smell of incense—at least I think it's incense—wafts through the air as we enter the tidy cottage.

"Have a seat in here and I'll fetch your tea. Just watch out for Leo—he doesn't take kindly to being sat on."

My questioning look doesn't escape Vivian.

"Leo's her long-haired Siamese cat; he's always looking for the most comfortable place to snooze, and it's usually a lap."

"Oh, I love cats—they're cool and mysterious," I answer, as I notice his brilliant blue eyes assessing me from nearby.

"Good, cuz Leo's a big love once he gets to know you."

Mary Ellen's cottage has a large open area that serves as her living and dining rooms, with the outside wall being windows and the inside all bookshelves, stocked with hundreds of volumes.

Vivian watches my eyes wander around the space in awe. "Pretty neat, huh?"

"I'd say! Is she a librarian?"

"Ha! No, Edward, I just like to read," Mary Ellen says, entering the room with our teas. "You're the novelist's son, correct?"

She appears to be in her early sixties, with gray hair pulled back into a simple braid, revealing the crow's feet on her otherwise smooth oval face. Behind the round wire-rimmed glasses, I see that she has gray eyes, and with a medium build, she is wearing a purple-and-orange muu-muu, tube socks, and clogs. Based on what I've experienced so far with the tea, the incense, the books, and her appearance, my deductive reasoning tells me that Mary Ellen is a harmless hippie lady, just like a neighbor back in Seattle. I might even suggest that Leo, the cat, is likely named after the astrological sign.

"Yes, ma'am, and thank you for the tea." I smile, setting mine on the coffee table.

"Let's dispense with the formalities, Edward—you may call me Mary Ellen."

"Yes, Ms. Mary Ellen."

"Drop the Ms. and you have it!" she says, taking a sip from her cup. "Now, Vivian, what have you read while Leo and I have been away?"

"Edward and I have started a summer book club."

"Fabulous! How many members do you have thus far?"

"It's just the two of us, but we have an open enrollment," Vivian replies, upbeat.

"Splendid. What's your first read?"

"Our first challenge is to read all three M. G. Hawthorne novels by the end of August."

Mary Ellen gulps hard on another mouthful of tea, almost choking. "Goodness gracious, are your parents aware of this endeavor?" Her tone becomes more serious as she adjusts herself in the chair.

"Yes, Mary Ellen."

"I see . . . well, I guess one per month is practical, with all the distractions of summer. How far along are you?"

"We only have ten chapters left of *Haunted Houses*, so we'll be finished by the end of the month, and we have to write a book report for Edward's mother."

"I extend my congratulations to you for sticking with that one. If there's two things that scare the bejesus out of me, it's psychos. Regular crazies are pretty easy to spot, but psychopaths—they can be damn near anyone. Next thing you know, the trusted neighbor lady conks you on the head with a shovel and throws you in the cellar. That's another reason I don't want you hitching rides around the island, Vivian. I don't give a fat rat's ass if everyone else does it, either!"

"Yes, Mary Ellen, I don't do that anymore . . . but you said two things scared you."

"I just told you both of them. Now, Edward, what's the last book you read before venturing into your mother's world of the macabre?"

"All of the Sherlock Holmes cases."

"The entire Conan Doyle catalog, all sixty-two?" she responds with obvious admiration.

"Yes, Mary Ellen."

"Bravo, young man! I see you have the stamina for fine Victorian-era writing. Have you read *The Old Nurse's Story*, from Elizabeth Gaskell, by chance? It's short and to the point, modestly spooky, and beautifully Victorian. I only read it on a cold winter's night in front of the fire. Still gives me the willies after all these years."

"Yes, last fall. I think it made reading Sherlock Holmes easier because I was used to the differences in language."

"That's an excellent observation, Edward, one that may escape some."

"By the looks of things, I think Leo has a new lap to sit on," Vivian says, noting Leo's residency.

"Indeed! It certainly appears that way. Do you like cats, Edward?"

"I love cats. I love dogs too, but cats are different—they seem to always be around books. My mom says they're a writer's best companion and that one day when things are more settled, she'd like to have one."

"Delightful! Mark Twain once wrote, 'When a man loves cats, I am his friend and comrade, without further introduction.' I find much wisdom and comfort in those few words. Yes indeed, good words to live by."

The Missing

17

Independence Days

Robert and Edward are still fast asleep when I step off the rear porch with a rucksack slung over my shoulder and take the north fork that leads to the cabin. The first of July carries a noticeable shift in the morning air, almost as if summer arrived overnight, and as I approach the two large boulders down trail, they look like an ancient entry gate into another world. I recall that as a little girl, I pretended to be young Mary Lennox entering the *Secret Garden* for the first time.

A few paces beyond, I'm greeted by a stand of cedars as the trail begins to level once again, this time within sight of the cliffs. My steps slow as I'm nearly overwhelmed by the beauty surrounding me. There's an almost indescribable combination of morning birdsongs, layered with the scents of earth, sea air, and island fauna, that must be lived to fully appreciate its majesty. The cabin, along with its fellow cast members of cedar, pine, and madrona, now comes into view, each silhouetted against the golden line breaking out of the eastern horizon as it bears witness to the magic of Orcas Island on a summer morning.

I've kept clear of the construction site these last few weeks because watching the process is distracting and has me on pins and needles. But today, seeing the new roofline with its longer dormer and the depleted stack of steel beams and girders in the staging area brings a confidence that by this time next month, the writing retreat of my dreams will be a reality.

The smell of fresh cedar is evident as I enter the cabin and quickly locate the heavy extension cord powering the work lights. It looks twice as large without the interior walls, and the vaulted ceiling with its cedar tongue and groove is stunning against the red steel ridge beam spanning the entire apex of the roofline.

An industrial-style skylight trimmed in black hovers above to cap the roof, creating the feel of an atrium below. I can't wait to see how its diffused light will occupy the space throughout the day and the seasons.

My mind races with inspiration beneath the Northwest Native color palette that I've always loved, and I quickly tape off three sections of floor that will soon be removed when the stoneworkers build the fireplace. I retrieve the tinted oil samples, gloves, and rags from my rucksack, then work each color into the planks as a glint of sunlight begins its creep through the eastern windows. The stain needs about thirty minutes to penetrate, so I peel off the gloves and walk outside with my thermos in one hand while dragging a chair closer to the cliffs with the other. There's a peach glow as the sun filters through the marine layer, and I pour myself a cup of coffee to the sound of water lapping against the rocks at ebb tide, a moment that brings with it an exhale.

After a month of island living, my thoughts are now free-flowing like the sea below, and when a southbound eagle crosses my view, I recall another eagle-like encounter some twenty-eight years ago. That eagle delivered me from Samantha's vile intentions and revealed a painful truth about my father. Years later, this same eagle told me that one day I would create a life on my own terms. His words became the mantra I clung to like a life raft of hope when mine was sinking beneath the blackest waters of despair.

~

I didn't know the older gentleman when I arrived for my lessons at Edna's cabin that early July morning. He was a very distinguished-looking character with his white beard, silvery hair, and the twinkle in his eyes behind those round tortoiseshell glasses.

"You must be Meredith!" he said enthusiastically, bearing a big smile.

"Yes, sir, Meredith Lila Gaines," I replied with a curtsy.

"Well, Meredith Lila Gaines, my name is Alastair, and it's an honor to meet you. I understand that you have a wonderful little playmate as well, and you two girls have all sorts of adventures and fun together."

"Yes, sir, her name is Lhaq'temish, and we do have a time."

"Isn't that wonderful? I love stories; would you please tell me more about her?"

I looked to Edna, who was moving toward the kitchenette, and she smiled with a nod, then suggested that Alastair and I have a seat on the porch while she put the tea kettle on and brought us some cookies.

The following week, during his second visit, Alastair told me that he was very excited to meet Lhaq'temish and asked if I would be willing to introduce them.

"Yes, sir! Let me see if I can find her," I said, then hopped off the porch and walked into the tree line where we often met. But when I called to her, she didn't come.

"I'm sorry, Alastair, she must be off somewhere."

"I understand; maybe on my next visit. You know what, Meredith? Let's play a picture game instead. It's a very clever one where I show you some ink spots on paper, and you tell me what you see in them."

Alastair visited me three more times that summer, and on each occasion , we walked around the property as I told him of our latest adventures. I answered his questions, some of which I thought strange, like if Lhaq'temish ever told me to hurt myself or anyone else and if I heard different voices or had other friends that only appeared to me. While perplexed by the notion that nobody else could see her, I just shrugged it off.

The last time I met with Alastair as a child, it was a gloomy Seattle fall day just before Halloween. I recall it clearly, as the wet leaves gave off a heavenly aroma that will forever remind me of accompanying my mother on errands around town, as she never palmed me off on the staff that my father insisted cater to our needs.

His office was sleek and modern but had a very sedate and calming ambiance. It was a ground-level unit with floor-to-ceiling windows that showcased a stand of large trunks belonging to the cedars that seemed to grow everywhere on Mercer Island.

As calming as the space was, my father fidgeted in his chair when Alastair invited him to join us midway through the session.

"Hello, Alastair, old man—good to see you at the club last week," Father bantered awkwardly.

Alastair dismissed the clumsy social attempt and dug right into the matter at hand.

"I enjoyed the guest speaker very much. So, Marvin, I've invited you into Meredith's session today because I think we're at a critical juncture. Her pediatrician has confirmed that she has no congenital abnormalities, and after spending time with her on the island and the past six weeks here in my office, I'm of the opinion that it was Lila's untimely death and your very quick remarriage to Samantha that triggered Meredith to conjure her friend Lhaq'temish."

"Now, hold on a minute, Alastair!" Father countered. "Are you implying that it's my fault she's seeing things, because I didn't want to be lonely after Lila died on me?"

Alastair's concerned eyes darted to mine and then instantly returned to my father's before tearing into him like an eagle would a salmon.

"I'm sorry for your distress, Marvin, but your little daughter sitting in that chair didn't 'die on you'—your words, not mine. She's not responsible for this misplaced ideation of your abandonment, and most sadly, what you appear to have missed is that Meredith has, in effect, lost both of her parents in this tragedy. The point is that she now needs her father's attention more than ever. I'm singling you out because from Samantha's tepid demeanor whenever she's joined our sessions in a sober state, it's clear that this is yours alone to do. It's my professional prognosis that if you, her father, provide such support, Meredith will outgrow her playmate and avoid other developmental pitfalls that lie in wait as a result. Further, as the chairman of the Washington State chapter of the American Psychiatric Association, I'm cautioning you that it would be child abuse and parental neglect of the highest order if she were to be entered into the types of institutions Samantha has inquired about. I will not stand idle if that course of action is pursued any further."

The gravity of Alastair's words hit hard. And while at six years of age I couldn't possibly understand all that was at stake, I knew at least that Alastair cared enough about me to stand up to my father, something only my late mother had done. Alastair's strength at that moment, however, could not assuage the despair of suddenly realizing that I was viewed as an obligation rather than a subject of adoration by my own father, and I never trusted him again.

~

It wasn't until years later, on an August morning in 1955, that my excommunication from his family became absolute.

I was just seventeen when I walked off the early ferry in Anacortes, and thanks to Edna's coaching, I hailed my first taxi like someone who had done it a hundred times before. Sleeping much of the two-and-a-half-hour drive, I awoke just before we arrived at the gate to our lavish Broadmoor neighborhood in Seattle's Madison Park.

Lyle, the security guard whom I have known since I can remember, flagged us over to the side.

"Miss Gaines, a word in private if I may," he said, motioning for me to join him inside the gatehouse. "About an hour ago, I received a long-distance call from Samantha with instructions not to permit you to pass the gate. As far as I'm concerned, I never saw you. But if I were a betting man, you might expect a similar reception when you arrive at your house."

"Thank you, Lyle. I understand."

I paid the driver well, wishing him a safe journey back to Anacortes, and he wished me good luck.

"I'll need some," I replied, staring down the walk-up to the magnificent Tudor that was my home for all seasons but summer.

With each step forward, the emptiness of an outsider crept into me, and by the time I reached the arched front door, I felt like an intruder at the threshold of my own home. When Carver, the head of house, opened the door before I had the chance to insert my key, he didn't utter a word, but his eyes betrayed a sadness that I hadn't known since the day my mother was buried. He picked up my suitcases, indicating with a nod that I quickly and quietly follow him. Upstairs in my bedroom, he put the cases down and emphatically whispered, "Meredith Lila Gaines! Dear God in heaven above! Are you pregnant? Your poor mother. . . . God rest her soul; she must be shaking the golden gates of glory right now!"

"No, for crying out loud! I'm not pregnant!" I insisted as Carver fervently motioned me to keep my voice out of range from any snooping staff.

"What then? I'm under strict instruction from the drunk to have you removed should you show up here!"

"Edna says there's big financial trouble . . . something really bad with the company, and also a large gambling debt up in Victoria. My poor excuse for a father, along with that scheming souse, are selling anything to the highest bidder in order to scuttle the scandal before it reaches Seattle."

Carver rubbed his chin as he took in what I said, and then he noticed my throat.

"Meredith, please step over here next to the window," he said, steering me in that direction. "Are those bruises?"

"I guess my makeup needs a retouch."

"The hell it does, young lady! Who the devil did this to you? Your father? Samantha?"

"Neither." I paused, then wilted into his arms. "Oh, Carver . . . what am I going to do?"

"First, you will tell me exactly what happened, and I do mean every lurid or sordid detail. Then, you are to have a nice long hot shower as Mariel prepares your favorite meal. Meanwhile, I'll consider our options."

There was a chill that seemed to originate in my bones, and no matter how hot I turned the water, it persisted. Carver had always been a faithful steady hand since the loss of my mother, whom he had been devoted to. He was my only safe harbor, my Seattle Edna who would guide me through this awful day—that much I could count on.

"All right, my dear, into the deep water you go. I'm sorry it's not easier, but count your blessings that your mother had the foresight to set up a private bank account and other means, so you don't have to worry about that type of survival too!"

I looked up from the French toast I was devouring, stunned, but acknowledged his words with a nod.

"From what I recall, you have enough credits to graduate Seattle Prep early—is this correct?"

"Technically, I'm a semester away, but—"

Carver held up his hand, stopping me in the interest of time. "Then you will attend Prep for the coming semester and graduate in December. In the meantime, we must change your enrollment at the University of Washington to commence in January, and since your mother has prepaid your education—"

"Wait, she what?"

"Yes, I was with her when she walked into the chancellor's office and wrote the check: four years for two thousand dollars, including books. Quite the deal by today's standards, and I do have the receipts."

"But Carver, I'm not supposed to start until the following September."

"That's fine—I promise they'll take you early. Now the hard part."

"The hard part?" I felt my stomach drop as if I were on a roller coaster.

"While you were in the shower, I received a call from your father. He and Samantha are on the way here now, and it was made abundantly clear that he expects your room to be emptied and locked, and any photos around the house with you in them are to be removed. We have a little over two hours before they arrive, so you need to decide what's going to travel with you. Mariel and I will hide what you can't take with you today up in the eaves, but you must grab anything precious."

"My God, I'm really banished then." I slouched in the chair.

"No, my dear, you're free, emancipated!"

"I'm angry, I'm so angry! Why don't I just stand my ground and threaten to expose this charade to their precious club and all of their so-called friends? At this point, what do I have to lose?"

"Listen to me, Meredith. That's a dirty business, and I've served in these households long enough to know what happens when titans fall. Your mother was smarter than all of them put together, and it's clear to anyone who adored her that you're her daughter!" Carver slapped his hand on the table, emphasizing his point. "In this situation, I can guarantee that Lila would float gracefully above the fray while the whole damn thing is swallowed by the greed that created it. You, my dear young lady, will not be collateral damage, because just like her, you will make your own way!" He finished his statement with a resolute finger in the air.

"But I have no place to go!"

"Oh, I did get ahead of myself, didn't I? When I hung up with your father, I rang the Montlake Mels, and after hearing the story, they insisted you come live with them. We're cutting it close on time, so let's get you packed and out of here."

"Carver—"

"Calvin and I would love to have you stay with us, but Melanie and Melinda are right around the corner, so we can see each other anytime. Trust me, it's much better that you be among the girls and have a little mothering rather than living with us two old queens."

"The Mels are wonderful, but—are you sure it's OK?"

"They have that fabulous separate suite above the garage with its own entrance in the back garden. You're going to love it there, and most importantly, you'll be safe with them. It's also walking distance to Prep and a short bike ride across the cut to the UW."

"I don't know what I would do without you, Carver."

"You'd figure it out, love. Now let's get packing."

~

Two hours later Carver finds me in my room. "Are we ready, Meredith?"

"I need five minutes alone, if possible."

"Yes, of course; we have perhaps eight."

I stared intently through the windows that stretched across the dormer of my bedroom. First was a farewell to the large cedar and fir trees that stood as silent witnesses to my private world two and a half stories above the ground. Opposite the perfectly manicured golf course was the ever-changing foliage of the arboretum, which provided a view that inspired years of childhood dreams, stories, and self-reflection. The memory of those Saturday mornings when I'd fling my windows open and inhale fall's fragrance to the distant roars from Husky stadium brought a tear. I smiled as innocence flashed before my eyes, pausing on the simplest of things. Is this what happens when we're dying? I wondered.

A light tap on the door was followed by Carver's tender voice. "Meredith, dear, it's time."

18

The Farmer's Market

Cutting through the dark woods of the morning is now something of a game for me. One in which I imagine myself as Holmes, trudging across the moors of England or Scotland in the wee hours, hot on the trail of some mysterious villain. It tends to keep my mind from wandering into thoughts about some of the characters that I've been introduced to in my mother's first book. However, just like anything else that you try not to think about, it becomes all you think about, and after finishing *Haunted Houses* the night before last, I'm thankful that it's only Gerald . . .

Considered a barstool regular at Toby's Tavern on 15th Avenue East, Gerald often referred to himself as a leg man, and aside from his love of fly fishing and ceramics, his job at Washington Anatomical Services where he provided cadavers to the UW and other medical research facilities was Gerald's passion. But during his third year, customer complaints began to mount regarding the decline in cadaver quality—specifically, that an unusually large number of the female bodies had arrived shy one leg.

~

There were thirty-two kiln-dried legs in all, each one neatly detached and suspended by its femoral head from the ceiling of his Capitol Hill apartment. According to court testimony, the mummified legs were sheathed in various colors and styles of nylon hosiery, wearing an assortment of high heels—all dangling like mobiles and impossible to slip past without sending them into a morbid ballet.

Tagged as "The Leg Man" in the newspapers, Gerald spent five years in Northern State Mental Hospital before his return to society, where he was last seen working for a notable retailer in downtown Seattle selling women's shoes—I assumed it to be Nordstrom.

~

Breaking from the tree line, I'm surprised to find the barn still dark, and I quickly hit the light switch to clear my imagination of legs twirling from the rafters above me. But when Mr. Kent's booming "Good morning, Edward!" comes from behind, it nearly sends me up into the hayloft.

"Whoa there, son! Didn't mean to startle you," he chuckles.

"Good morning," I reply, grateful that it's not Gerald.

"You beat me here—I'm impressed."

"The sooner we start, the sooner we finish."

"I see you're taking the farm motto seriously!"

"Where's Ms. Danelle and Vivian?"

"Oh, they're running a few steps behind this morning, should be along any minute."

"Mornin', Edward," the two say in unison, walking into the barn immediately following his prediction.

"Vivian, why don't you and Edward bring the eggs up from the coop and put them on the racks in the van, same with the berries and cherries; we're going to need the old truck and the van today. Dad and I will finish up the bushels and other vegetables here."

"Yes, Mom." Her reply is barely audible.

Vivian is the definition of a morning person, so today when she isn't talkative, I know something is off.

"You all right?"

"Just tired. Didn't sleep all that great."

"I'll try to do extra today so you can rest a little."

"Thanks, you're sweet. I'll be OK once the aspirin kicks in and the market opens. It's going to be a madhouse, and it goes real fast when it's busy like that."

This is pretty much the extent of our conversation as we pack the van and secure the cargo for the trip into Eastsound, making it even clearer that she doesn't feel well.

After loading up, Vivian hops into the van with Ms. Danelle for a much smoother ride than what Mr. Kent and I will have to endure in the truck aptly nicknamed Old Bone Shaker, because it bounces you around like the Wild Mouse roller coaster at the Seattle Center.

"I really need to take this over to Anacortes someday and get the suspension worked on."

"Yes, sir," I chatter as we bounce and bang along the island roads.

"What do you miss about not being in Seattle over the summer?"

"Hmmm . . . probably Joe's Popsicle truck. We listen all day for the music, and when it finally drives up the street, kids come out of everywhere. Back when I was little, the driver would let us sit on the back of the box and ride it all the way through the neighborhood. It was pretty cool."

"That sounds like a lot of fun. Anything else?"

"Volunteer Park—it's the best, and just around the corner from our house too."

"I haven't been there; what's it like?"

"There's a really cool museum with white granite camels out front and a couple of other giant statues hidden around the bushes, but the conservatory is my favorite place, especially in winter. It's a giant greenhouse, with these sensitivity plants that will close up on your finger!"

"A Venus flytrap?"

"No, these are different. They have a bunch of long thin leaves that wrap around your finger when you touch them; they're not a clamshell that closes up, like a Venus flytrap."

"I don't recall ever seeing one of those. Does it hurt?"

"Not at all, it's a little weird though! Another thing: on hot days we run through the big sprinklers when the workmen have them out—they're super-powerful and shoot about fifty-feet. There's a game where you try to get control of it, and then you can blast anyone who tries to get it from you!"

"It sounds like a great place to grow up," Mr. Kent says with a smile.

"I told Vivian that if you guys come to town for a visit, I'll give you a tour."

"That's a deal!"

As we pull onto the green in Eastsound, I see Mr. Steinle and a couple of men unloading a box truck with a familiar brand on the side.

"There's Olga Livestock—I wonder if Cowboy's here."

"He usually doesn't work the weekends, but since it's going to be busy, we might see him. One thing for sure, I'm glad we're upwind from them today because every time Rich gets to cooking those samples, man alive, my stomach starts growling!" Kent laughs, rubbing his belly.

It takes about ninety minutes to set up the large stand with fruit and produce all neatly stacked in pyramids and the flats and bushels organized for the customers.

"Very nice, you two. Vivian, how are you doing—need another aspirin?" Ms. Danelle smiles.

"No thanks, Mom, I'm all right for now."

"OK, the market starts in twenty-five minutes, so if you need to use the restroom, it's over in the Municipal building."

"I'll show him . . . c'mon, Edward.

"All right, Vivian, but I want y'all back when they ring the bell."

"Don't worry, we'll be here when the market opens."

As we walk across the green, Vivian gives me the lay of the land. "That's Hattie Gil's Crow Valley Co-op booth— we should stop on the way back if we have time and get some ice cream."

"It's never too early for ice cream!"

"When we get inside the building, just show them your orange sticker, and they'll let you use the restroom. It's a longer walk but way better than using those stinky porta-potties."

"I bet those are bad for a girl. You know, with guys whizzing all over the place."

"Ewww, yeah, it's super-gross—why do guys do that?"

"Not sure . . . some probably think it's funny."

When we arrive at the municipal building, a member of the Sheriff's Department is working the newspaper's crossword puzzle and pauses to greet us.

"Good morning, Vivian, how's your summer going?"

"It's been great so far, Captain Stone, how about yours?"

"Very nice; we just had the first visit with our granddaughter—they named her Kim after her grandmother. She's going to be a real pistol, I can tell!"

"That's neat!"

"Who's your friend here?"

"Oh, this is Edward Hawthorne—he's my neighbor and a big help on the farm too."

"Ah, yes, it's nice to meet you, Edward. Your folks stopped by the Sheriff's Office a couple of weeks ago after visiting the bookshop. I hope your mother didn't mind signing all those books."

"No, sir, she loves to do that stuff, and it's nice to meet you."

"Mr. Stone is a captain with the Sheriff's Office; he also pilots the police boat, and his wife, Ms. Kim, owns the bookstore."

"Wow! I bet you've had some interesting cases."

"Every now and then we have some drug smugglers to track down out on the water, but to tell you the truth, since I transferred in from Whidbey with Sheriff Chancey and Deputy Littauer, most of what we see during the summer months has to do with litterbugs, speeders, and noise complaints."

"Your office must be doing a fine job, then, if criminals know better than to start trouble around here."

"Edward's read all of the Sherlock Holmes stories, Captain Stone."

"A real detective in the making!" he laughs. "I hope you're enjoying Orcas. From what I've seen, it's a neat place to grow up—lots of adventure for young explorers like yourselves, especially on that end of the island."

"Yes, sir, it's really great."

"Say, Edward, since you're a Sherlock Holmes buff, maybe you can help me with my puzzle."

"I can try. What's the clue?"

"The peppered room of Conan Doyle. It's seven letters, ends with an L."

"Hmmm . . . try paradol. There's a case called *The Adventure of the Paradol Chamber*, and paradol is a component of pepper, if I'm not mistaken."

"Great Scott! I believe you've solved this one, Mr. Holmes," he laughs, penciling in the answer.

With that, Vivian takes my arm and says, "C'mon, Edward, we've got about fifteen minutes before market."

After using the restrooms, we make a brief stop at the Crow Valley Co-op stall to see Hattie Gil, whose Lummi heritage is evident by her light brown skin and long, shiny black hair pulled back tight into a ponytail. Middle-aged and wearing a tie-dyed muumuu that reminds me of Mary Ellen, she welcomes us with a nice smile and two of her famous homemade strawberry ice cream bars.

"Those are made with your strawberries, Vivian," she says. "Tell your parents to have a great market and to come see me when they have a minute, OK?"

"Yes, Ms. Hattie, thanks for the ice cream."

"Yes, ma'am, thank you for the ice cream—it's delicious!" I chime in my most promotional manner as we leave her tent and head back across the green.

"You're a natural barker, Edward." Vivian laughs, waving to a few of the other vendors on the periphery.

"I'm just practicing up for today is all."

"Oh, that's right, you rode here with Dad—he's big on that!"

"He gave me a few pointers." I smile. "Are ya feelin' any better?"

"Yeah, thanks. The ice cream helps."

"Good, because that lady is walking toward the triangle and looking at her watch."

We are back at the stall just as the iron rod clangs around the interior of the triangle, and soon swarms of people descend into the market area like someone kicked a bee's nest. The rush ends at about eleven-thirty, as all but the stragglers are heading out to get on with their Saturday.

"Dad and I are going to walk around and check on how the others did. You two all right with running the stand for this last bit?"

"Yeah, Mom, we can take it from here."

As her folks walk away, I mention to Vivian that if she wants to lie down in the shade for a while, I can run the stand and just come get her if I need to, but she about bites my head off.

"Worry about yourself, I'll be fine!"

"All right, sorry . . . I was just trying to—"

"What? Be my boyfriend? I don't need a boyfriend, Edward!"

"Geez, Vivian . . . 'help' is what I was going to say."

We stand there in an awkward silence for a minute, and I feel like I have just taken a shot to the jaw when Vivian nudges me.

"Uh-oh, here comes trouble."

A lanky, long-haired boy, at least fourteen years old, comes cruising across the grass on his bike, dodging people like pylons before dumping his Sting-Ray carelessly on the ground next to the stand.

"Hey Viv, how's dem berries today?" he says while grabbing a handful of raspberries from one of the containers and shoving them into his mouth in one go.

"The name is Vivian, and that will be one dollar, Louie. That is how the berries are today," she smacks back in proper English, extending her hand for payment.

"A dollar! What a rip-off!" Louie says as he looks over at me for a second and sneers, then back to Vivian with a half-nod and his mouth still full.

"Who's the queer bait?"

Apparently offended by our dismissive snickers, Louie makes a larger error in judgment than just being a jerk and a slob.

"OK, slut. Keep your lousy berries then," he gurgles before refunding the red mush from his mouth into Vivian's outstretched hand.

I see the tears well in her eyes as Louie laughs and shoots me one of those "What are you going to do about it?" looks that guys like him often do.

My left jab was honed to piston-like precision under the tutelage of Jimmy McGhee at Seattle's Downtown Boxing Gym and well-tempered on the bullies of Capitol Hill. When it slams into Louie's face, the blow sends him flailing backward and on top of his Sting-Ray in a heap. Thankfully, nobody saw me hit him, and it just looks like he tripped and fell over his bike.

"Why don't you cut that greasy hair so you can see, Louie!" snarks a neighboring crafts vendor as Louie groans and slowly untangles himself.

When he finally regains his footing, the combination of bright red berry juice and blood from his nose is smeared across his face, making things look far worse than they actually are.

"Oh shit," whispers Vivian, wiping her tears away as she moves behind me.

"Ah, he's all right," I assure her and throw Louie a wad of paper towels to wipe his face before somebody starts screaming for an ambulance.

"Those berries pack a punch, eh Louie? Care for another?" I say, moving out from behind the table.

Still wobbly, he wipes his face off while in retreat, and I quickly bear down on him.

"Uh, yeah, yeah, no thanks, man . . . no thanks, it's cool! Here's the money!" as he digs a crumpled dollar out of his cutoffs.

"Money and an apology."

"Sorry, Vivian," he says, handing her the money and keeping an eye on me.

"Thank you, Louie, apology accepted," she replies, washing her hand in the melted ice from the cooler.

Something I know from experience is that bullies typically travel with an entourage, so when three of his pals come riding up on their bikes, I'm ready to haul off and slug the biggest one in the side of the head before he dismounts if I think it's warranted.

"Hey, man, what happened?" asks the one who reminds me of Lumpy Rutherford from Leave It to Beaver.

"Nuthin'—just got some berries is all. It's cool."

"Hey Lou, there's an ice cream cooler in the back of the co-op tent again—we should go kipe some before we hit Cascade."

"Hell yeah! C'mon guys, let's ditch these queers and get some ice cream!" Louie barks, as he and two of the gang pedal off toward Hattie Gil's stand.

"Hi Vivian, how's it goin'?" says the one who didn't seem to fit in and stayed behind.

"Pretty well, Bob. It's always busy on the farm this time of year."

"For sure, I'm just glad we're donating the hayfield to Olga Livestock, so I won't be loading it."

"Us too." Vivian turns to me with an admiring smile. "This is Edward Hawthorne—he lives next door."

"Bob Heese," he says, extending his hand.

"It's nice to meet you, Bob."

"Right on, you too. Your mom wrote that book, right?"

"Word travels fast."

"Man, around here it does. I live over at Indian Point in Deer Harbor, and we have to keep the gate shut because when folks figured out that back in the old days it was called Maple Point like in the book, they began driving up to our house asking if they could walk around."

"Sorry about that."

"No sweat, man—it's not your fault. At least once a month I'll see a boat or two in the cove tossing flowers overboard . . . it's kinda weird."

"Huh, I wonder what that's about."

"My folks are part of the island book club, and they met at our house a couple of times. They laughed about it and said it's got to do with the girl in the book. Last year when the property owners were up from Seattle, they even renamed the old cabin next to the cove 'Amanda's Cabin,' and my dad used one of those wood-burning irons on a piece of cedar to make the sign."

"Oh hell no, not him," Vivian interrupts us, as an odd clatter approaches from behind.

"What?"

"Not what, Edward . . ."

"Hello Miss, and it's Edward, isn't it?"

"Uh, yes, sir," I reply, noting that he is completely ignoring Bob, who has his eyes locked on Chase Stuart's Bermuda shorts with an obvious look of disgust.

"Seems that you've extended your 'surprise' a bit. Well, good for you! Seen any whales?"

"No, sir, not yet."

"How can I help you today, Mr. Stuart?" Vivian intervenes.

"Well, Miss, I'll take some of your raspberries, cherries, a half-box of apples, and, umm . . . some lettuce too."

"Romaine or butter, sir?"

"Oh, ah, both will be fine, and those cucumbers look good—I'll have some of those as well. I'll need a hand getting it all to my boat; I'm tied up just there at the dock," Stuart says, throwing his thumb over his shoulder.

"Yes, sir, of course."

The thought of going anywhere with him gives me a chill and I pack the two boxes as slowly as possible while praying that Mr. Kent and Ms. Danelle will soon reappear. Vivian somehow senses this and she stalls him with questions.

"Are you planning a big Fourth of July event, sir?"

"No, I don't care much for crowds."

"Do you have a cellar, then?"

"Cellar? I didn't say anything about any goddamned cellar!" he yells back.

"No, sir . . . for the lettuce. If you aren't eating it right away, it might wilt on you with this warm weather we're having," Vivian answers, snickering under her breath at his odd outburst.

"Oh, yes, yes, sorry, I see what you mean," Stuart says, peeling off bills from a roll to pay her.

The clanging triangle signals the market's end, and with Vivian's folks nowhere in sight, I'm grateful that she asks Bob to help me carry Stuart's purchases to his boat.

"Have you been enjoying the house, Edward?" he huffs, over the squawking contraption bound to his pasty white leg.

"Yes, sir, very much. We can slow down for you, if that's better."

"No need. I'll grease this squeaky son of a bitch when I get to the boat."

"Yes, sir," I reply, not daring to look over at Bob for fear of laughing.

"I remember Long Shadows well . . . nice property. People say it's cursed, you know."

"What's cursed?"

"The whole damn thing is Indian cursed, and there's a witch on it. Don't tell me she hasn't told you!" Stuart scoffs. "Ask around, and you'll see I don't lie."

"Thanks for the warning. I'll be sure to keep an eye out for her now."

"Is this your tub, Mister?" Bob asks as he pulls the stern line tight, bringing the boat closer to the dock.

"It's not a goddamned tub, you mongoloid, it's a Boston Whaler!" Stuart yells, pointing his cane at Bob before throwing it into the boat and awkwardly climbing aboard.

"I was just being nice—it actually looks more like a garbage scow," Bob fires right back, tossing the box he's carrying onto a seat before walking off.

"Hey, you come back here! Come back here right now, goddammit!"

"Have a good Independence Day, Mr. Stuart," I say, momentarily distracting his ire from Bob while handing him the box I'm holding.

"Be careful with those goddamned fireworks—they start fires and blow fingers off!" Those are his parting words before gunning the boat through the no-wake zone on his way past Indian Island into East Sound.

"That went well!" I laugh when I catch up to Bob.

"What a bastard! Know what else? I've seen that ratchet leg and his scow before, throwing flowers in our cove!"

"What?"

"No shit, I'll swear to it."

"I believe you. That stuff he was saying about the house, do you know anything about it?"

"Rumors here and there, but the last time I was over at Louie's, his big brother Scuzz and this guy Krantz from the other side of the hill in Cormorant were smoking weed and listening to records. Then Krantz asks him something about the time he and those dudes went over to Long Shadows and saw the witch. Scuzz went berserk! He kicked the record player, stuck his finger in Krantz's face, and told him to get the fuck outta there, or he'd kill him. After that, he was fuming and looked over at Louie and me and told us to split. I don't know what happened to those guys that night, but it must have been pretty bogus."

"Sure sounds like it."

"You haven't seen anything out there, have you?" Bob asks warily.

"Not a witch—at least not yet, anyway."

"I've noticed that people say a lot of things out here . . . it's hard to know what to believe and what's straight-up bullshit."

We return to the stand just as Vivian's sorting the leftover stock to be dropped off at Templin's.

"How'd that go?" She laughs in anticipation of our account.

"He's a freak!" Bob says. "Hey, I better take off if I'm going to catch up to those guys—we're hitting the tree and the cliffs at Cascade. Check you later, Vivian—nice to meet you, Edward."

"You too, man!"

"If y'all are going to watch the fireworks on Tuesday, we could do it together—I'm going to hang out with Brooke and Megan."

"Sure, let's meet up at the ice cream trailer, six sharp."

"Good call, Vivian, see y'all Tuesday."

Vivian and I continue weighing and counting stock as we pack up the booth for a quick load-up when her folks get back.

"Why didn't you tell me the Farmer's Market is this exciting?"

"Who knew?" she shrugs with a smile.

"Bob seems like a real nice guy."

"Yeah, he moved up here from Seattle about a year and a half ago when his folks became the caretakers at Indian Point. He's a smart kid, but he's in with a not-so-good crowd. It's hard that way for those of us who live here full-time—you can't help but hang out with the kids that live closest, and Indian Point is way over on the other side of West Sound."

"That's just like most neighborhoods; it's the same thing back on Capitol Hill."

"I'm glad you're my neighbor, and Edward, I'm really sorry for what I said earlier—I didn't mean any of it. I'm just not myself right now."

"Don't worry about it."

"Thank you for standing up for me with Louie. That was really brave of you—did you hurt your hand on his hard head?"

"Nah, it's fine. He's a bully and deserved that and more."

"Still, I'm not used to having someone else take up for me like that."

"From what Bob said, Louie's older brother was one of the guys who tried to burn Long Shadows down."

"Yeah, his name is Roger, but everyone calls him Scuzz—one look at him and you'll know why!"

"Get this! When Bob saw Stuart's boat, he realized that he's one of those folks throwing flowers in the water at Indian Point."

"You're kidding!"

"That's what he said, and that he'd swear to it."

"That guy's such a psycho . . . he should be in *Haunted Houses*!"

"Speaking of, now that we're done packing up, do you feel like talking about our book report? We have to finish it so we can start reading *The Missing* this week."

"Sure, I can take some notes and clean it up when we get home, so you can hand it in for us tomorrow," she says, reaching for the spiral notebook that we've used to tally the day's sales with.

"Great! I've been struggling with all the twists. It's hard to get the real theme because of the characters and their creepy behavior."

"You're overthinking it, Edward; it's a book full of psychos. Impossible for us to write a summary for each one and their special kinks—it'd take forever. I say we pull from what the psychiatrist wrote in the foreword—that about sums it up."

"Oh, I forgot to tell you: that psychiatrist is my uncle Alastair."

"Really?"

"Well, technically he's an old family friend of my mom—you know how that is."

"That's cool, but yeah, we can totally build from that. The theme shows that there's no real solution for psychos, I mean, other than sterilizing them or locking 'em up and throwing away the key. It fits with what he wrote, and we just use a couple of the cases for examples."

"Sounds good to me. Incidentally, I'd feel a lot better if most of them were still locked up; I've been looking over my shoulder and peeking out of the shower curtain way too much."

"I thought I was the only one who did that!" She laughs.

"That one maniac murdered seven people and only got five years in the asylum before being turned loose again. That means, if he's not dead, he's out walking around somewhere."

"And the leg guy got out in five years too. I mean, he didn't murder anyone, but still. It kind of makes the whole point. The adults have to do something; they can't just keep letting them back out on the streets."

"Someday we're going to be those adults."

"Brilliant deduction! I think we about have our report. We'll spruce it up a little back home and you can hand it in."

"No, we're a team, so we turn it in together. Plus my mom really likes you, and she might not grill me too long if you're there."

"Whatever you say . . . she's the best. Hey, here comes my mom."

"Looks like you two have everything sorted!"

"Yes, ma'am, it's all been weighed, packed up, and marked for Templin's."

"You know, Vivian, it won't be long until you can handle this whole market by yourself."

"Oh, the joy . . . where's Dad?"

"Here he comes now with the van. He'll get the truck for the tables and chairs while we're loading up the stock for Templin's."

After packing the truck, Mr. Kent heads for home while we go to Templin's and put the overstock into their inventory. Back in the van, Ms. Danelle hands Vivian and me each a nice crisp twenty-dollar bill and thanks us for the hard work.

"Thanks, Mom!"

"Yeah, thanks, Ms. Danelle, but you really don't have to pay me for helping out."

"You do farm work, you get paid. That's how we do it at Madrona Cliff—got it, Edward?"

"Yes, ma'am!"

"Good! Now, when we get back to the farm, I'm going to make us a nice big lunch!"

~

Vivian and I retreat to the back porch with her notes, and we almost have the book report done by the time lunch is ready.

"I'm beat, Edward," Vivian says after the last bite of her ham and cheese sandwich.

"Yeah, me too. I think I'll head home and crash after this."

"Thanks again for everything. I'll walk you to the tree line."

"No problem, you don't have to."

"I actually do—gotta check the relief valve at the upper plot by the barn."

After I say my goodbyes to her folks, Vivian and I cut across the ankle-high grass and walk toward the barn trail.

"Since I only have a couple of chores in the morning, I was thinking maybe we can do something after handing in the book report," she says.

"Sure, if you're feeling better."

"I should be fine after a good night's sleep; today is usually the worst of it."

My bewilderment registers with her, and she just shakes her head with that "Oh, Edward" look.

"Thanks for walking with me. Need any help with that valve?"

"Nah, I just have to push a button and make sure it doesn't stick. See you tomorrow, and thanks again for everything today." She smiles and kisses me on the cheek.

Walking back through the woods with a grin of my own, I chuckle, thinking about how right I am about girls. Guys are way easier to understand—no wonder Holmes never got married!

19

The Montlake Mels

Edna's instruction and guidance laid a formidable foundation for my independence, but without the timely intervention of Carver and the Mels, I'm not sure how I would have managed to scale the crevasse that swallowed me that day.

I arrived on the Mels' doorstep with little sleep and too emotionally exhausted to comprehend the shock of it all. Melanie and Melinda cared for me so gently as I hid away in the suite above the garage and cried for those first two weeks while they consoled me with words of encouragement and great home cooking. Then school started up, and their set of house rules kicked in.

"We expect you home by six o'clock for dinner, which we will eat together; you will bring home nothing but a 4.0; no dating. And one more thing, Meredith: enough with the waterworks—let's see that beautiful smile of yours again."

Over that final semester at Prep, I endured the sideways glances and murmurs without retort. The few friends I did have became formers as the clique got wind of my father's financial woes, and soon afterward, the scandalous rumors circulated that I was out of Broadmoor and now shacked up with a couple of *lisbons* on Montlake. In their eyes, this provided irrefutable evidence that I wasn't to be trusted in the post-gym-class showers.

My isolation from the high school herd presented me with the opportunity to stare down a churning that was just below the surface of every moment, and I returned to the one resource that I felt understood most of the moving parts from my past: Alastair.

He was every bit as gracious and kind as I remembered from our meetings twelve years earlier, and I sat across from him now in the outward confidence of my young woman's body while feeling like a fractured little girl inside as I brought him current over the next several sessions.

"Meredith, it wasn't your fault! Your mother's death, your father's poor decisions, the departure of the girl, and losing Edna; with all its cruelty and pain, this is part of what life is, my dear child."

"And the loss . . . Alastair, how do I cope with this cavern inside of me?"

"Yes, and the loss. It's a lifelong grieving process, and the joy, as you will soon discover, comes with the reconciliation in acknowledging each sorrow as it nudges you. And that cavern? Well, you're going to fill it up with life, but it will be with a life on your terms."

"Do you really believe that?"

"Unequivocally, but only if you choose to do so."

As I stood up to leave, I asked him a question that had lain dormant for over a decade, one I never even broached with Edna.

"So, the girl, do you think I imagined her?"

"Your playmate? Oh, I did for a time; however, opinions devoid of facts must be pliable. I'm fairly certain the word I chose that last session with your father was conjure; I still think it's suitable when used in the proper context."

~

The University of Washington provided the anonymity I craved and set me on the path to that promised life on my own terms. The Mels were determined for me to remain with them until I graduated from college, and after working most of my sophomore year at the school paper, I began to seriously consider becoming an author. Over dinner one evening at our favorite small bistro a few blocks away on Montlake, I mentioned my leanings to the table, and what happened next changed my life.

"Look here, if you're going to write novels, it's all about characters, characters, and characters—you need characters!" Melanie declared.

"Calvin has plenty of characters all day long at the salon," Carver offered.

"Ain't it the truth, honey! You can borrow some if you want, but my stars, some of the stories they tell even make me blush, and that's saying something!"

"Meredith needs her own characters, you two! Not some wash-and-wear fancies from the hair salon," Melinda opined.

"Well, Miss Smarty Pants, where do you suppose she'll find them? Y'all have her locked up in that tower like Rapunzel. She never gets out and meets people—probably has a chastity belt on under that cute skirt of hers. Poor girl."

"Oh, stop it, Calvin! Meredith's savvy enough to be the guardian of her own gate! I simply propose that she get a part-time job to find her own characters!"

"As far as characters go, I'd say the four of you are a pretty good start!" I shouted over their clucking.

"I guess we are at that!" Carver laughed and finished the last swallow from his glass of beer.

"What do you propose, Aunt Melinda?" I leaned closer to hear her over the noisy restaurant.

"Why don't you wait tables a few nights a week? It'll get you out of the house, and you'll meet plenty of real characters, I'm sure of it."

"And where, pray tell, do you suggest I do this waiting of the tables?"

"Why not right here? There's nothing but characters that haunt this place." Melinda flung her arms wide, amplifying her point.

"I guess I could—"

"Hey, Harvey! You need a waitress a couple nights a week?" Melinda cut me off and yelled to the owner, who happened to be passing by with a tray of food.

"Who? You?" he shouted back over the commotion of the busy restaurant.

"No! Meredith!"

"Well, why didn't ya say so? Can ya start Thursday for training and then work Friday and Saturday nights?"

"Sure!" I answered as Harvey squeezed his round midsection through the patrons on his way back to our table.

"Good, I'll see ya at four on Thursday afternoon. If you catch on, you'll make good tips on Friday and Saturday. See me on the way out—I'll give ya an apron and a menu to study."

"Now, that's how you get things done!" Melinda smacked the table.

"Well shit fire, you go, girl! Friday and Saturday nights too," grinned Calvin, admiring Melinda's get-shit-done ability.

"It's all in who you know," Carver affirmed.

On Thursday before I left for work, the Mels handed me a small notebook that fit easily inside my apron pocket, sending me off with a kiss on the cheek and some advice that has stuck with me to this day.

"I read somewhere that real authors write down the names of characters they randomly meet—just a name and a quality is enough—and I bet you'll hear some humdinger tales too if you keep your ears open. Just be sure you change the names in your stories," Melanie advised.

Harvey's Bistro was a short walk up Montlake, and I enjoyed working there over the summer, plus the tips on Friday and Saturday nights added up and I didn't have to dip into the small trust Mother had set aside for me. I filled my little notebook with names, character ideas, and circumstances, but between summer classes and work, I found little time to develop those stories. So, in mid-August, I swapped my Friday and Saturday shifts for Wednesdays and Thursdays. Though a lot less money, I was out of there by nine o'clock rather than midnight and could actually put pen to paper.

On that first Wednesday night, a handsome young man was seated in my section—a regular, the others told me.

Over the next several Wednesdays, I noticed that he rode a bike, arrived promptly at six o'clock, and always ordered spaghetti and meatballs. His only dinner companion had been the same textbook full of mechanical drawings and other technical papers jammed with calculations and what appeared to be his notes.

He was friendly but so engrossed in his work that I didn't think he even noticed me. So, after a few weeks I took a chance and placed his order ten minutes before he was due to arrive. As soon as the hostess seated him, I walked out of the kitchen with his spaghetti and meatballs and sat the plate down in front of him.

He looked up at me with his blue eyes and jet-black hair.

"Am I really this predictable, Meredith?"

"Uhhh . . . ummm, well, apparently not!" I stumbled, with a smile to match his, shocked that he knew my name.

"Robert Hawthorne," he said, extending his hand.

"Meredith Gaines. It's nice to meet you, Robert Hawthorne."

"English Lit?"

"My, you are full of surprises, aren't you? Yes, how'd you know?"

"Your fingernails."

"But I haven't any!" I replied, embarrassed by the badly chipped polish but unable to escape the blue eyes that hadn't left mine.

"Exactly. It's the typing. English majors have to be the best typists around, or they'd never get all their course-work done."

Relieved that he understood my plight, I relaxed into his gaze and responded in kind: "OK, it's my turn. You're studying for your master's in engineering; you appreciate punctuality in regard to time and precision when it comes to deed."

"I feel like I just had my palm read! Are you part gypsy as well?"

"More like I've seen that textbook before. But I prefer your version of the story—it's much more mysterious."

Robert chuckled, and with a smile, he said, "Maybe you're onto something there. . . . this might be out of line, but a pal just gave me two tickets for the game against Minnesota this Saturday. They're really good seats, and I don't have anyone to go with—want to join me?"

"Hmmm, let's see . . . a handsome young man, a beautiful fall morning in Husky stadium . . . that sounds like a wonderful time."

"It could rain, you know."

"I'm the English Lit major, remember? And my story calls for a cheery fall morning."

"Fair enough, Meredith Gaines, and I do like your optimism."

"Good. Now you have to pick me up early because the Mels are going to want to know everything about you before I go traipsing off with a graduate student, especially if he's a regular at Harvey's."

"The Mels?" He grinned.

"Kickoff is at ten, right?"

"Yes."

"Come to this address at seven-thirty; breakfast will be served," I said, handing him the house number.

"But this is just down the street—it'll only take us five minutes to get to the stadium from there."

"As I said, seven-thirty . . . but if it's too much trouble, I understand."

"No, no, not at all! I'll be there."

The Mels had just finished cooking when I stepped outside to greet Robert that Saturday morning. Apart from the French toast and bacon, there was the smell of fall in the air that I had lost track of since my days in Broadmoor. Robert stood awkwardly on the walk-up as I exhaled the fragrance with a smile and invited him inside.

"Welcome to our home, Robert," said Melinda. "You're just in time for breakfast; please have a seat and help yourself."

"Yes, ma'am."

"My, you are a handsome devil, aren't you," Melanie piped in. "Coffee, orange juice, or both?"

"Both please—that is, if it isn't too much trouble."

"Oh, and manners too!" Melanie smiled.

As we all sat down for breakfast, Melinda released a barrage of questions that made me want to crawl under the table.

"So, Robert, tell us a little about yourself. Where'd you grow up, what's your GPA, are you a jailbird? I see you have a letterman jacket—is that the icon for swimming or diving? Are your folks rich? Ever been married? Are you an alcoholic? Where are you planning to work after school?"

"Let's see . . . ah, I grew up about two miles from here on 17th Avenue East, four years on the swim team, graduated with a 4.0 and honors, but right now, to be honest, school's challenging."

"Oh, a little too much brainpower for the jock?" Melinda poked.

"That could be . . . but I honestly think it's more that I'm working almost every weekend at Boeing to get the experience needed when I graduate. The money earned barely covers what I didn't get in scholarship funds. No, I haven't been in jail, and my folks aren't rich, not even close. In fact, at one time both my parents worked, and I helped with my little brother and sister so we could make ends meet. Haven't been married; I've never been one to date around a lot. I do enjoy a glass of wine, a beer or two, and a stiff drink on occasion, but that's about it."

"You poor dear, I'm sorry I was so rough on you. As Meredith is our girl, we can't allow her to go off with just anybody, you see," Melinda explained.

"Bless her, the poor thing works so hard, she never even goes out and has any fun—you'd think we had her locked up or something!"

"Thank you, Aunt Melanie!" I rolled my eyes as my face flushed.

"Oh, I can relate," said Robert.

"You kids enjoy the game—the Huskies are on a winning streak!"

"It's only the second game, Melanie," Melinda countered.

"Don't be so negative—everyone knows that all winning streaks begin with one." Melanie laughed.

"Robert, you'll have her back here by six, won't you?"

"No, he won't, Melinda! It's Saturday night, for heaven's sake! If you two are having a good time, you may keep her out until eight-thirty."

"Yes, ma'am, thank you, Ms. Melanie."

From that moment on, Robert never missed a Sunday dinner at the Mels'. He even helped with the dishes afterward, endearing him all the more to them and to me.

He had been working at Boeing full-time for six months when he took me to dinner at Harvey's Bistro and proposed over spaghetti and meatballs at the table where we'd met.

When we arrived home, it was obvious that he had asked the Mels and Cs for their approval, as the foursome were anxiously awaiting our appearance and greeted us on the walk-up.

"And . . . ?" Aunt Melanie coaxed.

When I presented my left hand with a smile, their screams brought neighbors from both sides running outside to see if there'd been a murder on the historically quiet street.

"Break out the cake, Pa, our baby girl is getting hitched!" Calvin cried out, clinging to Carver.

~

We were married on a beautiful autumn morning in the heart of the arboretum, cloistered among the silent trees and nestled in the scent of changing leaves and rich fall earth. Until that moment, I had never known such peace.

When Carver walked me down the aisle of brightly colored leaves, a familiar face came into view, and tears of joy filled my eyes. As we passed, I smiled and mouthed, "You were right, Alastair. Thank you."

20

Never Break a Promise

Edna was a retired English teacher who left the classroom after the authorities insisted that she cease teaching classical education and, according to her, "follow their new illiterate trends." My father liked her spunk, and she was hired on the condition that she move onto the property immediately and tend to my summer education as well as other needs. With the recent death of her husband, Eugene, and having no children, she hated being in their house alone, so the cabin by the sea was a fresh start in life.

When not with Edna, I spent my days playing with Lhaq'temish, as I still called her, because for those first two summers, it was the only actual word she had spoken. Our communication came through expressions or signs, although I still talked to her as if she understood everything I said. She led us all over the landscape from dawn to dusk, providing ample material for the writing assignments from Edna, who appeared to marvel at my imaginative ability and the reams it produced.

Regardless of what Alastair or anyone else thought about Lhaq'temish, Edna never discouraged me from writing about her and our adventures together. She did, however, advise me not to prattle on about them within earshot of my father or Samantha, something that proved more challenging from the third summer forward.

Until then, Lhaq'temish and I were about the same stature common for girls our age, but when I arrived on Orcas that third summer, she had grown a full head taller than me in the months apart. Then one August afternoon, as we walked hand in hand through a field at the far northern end of the property, I pointed to our shadows side by side, hers much bigger than mine.

"Look at your long shadow," I giggled.

She stopped suddenly and for several seconds stood entranced by our images stretched across the dry grass bending with the breeze. When I asked what was the matter, she turned toward me with a look of astonishment and eyes full of tears, and then smiled and said:

"My name . . . my name is Long Shadow."

We were nine years old when this happened, and from that day on we talked about all the things that little girls do. She told of the taunts from others in her tribe who made fun of her height and uncoordinated nature and of being chosen last for games. There was one dear friend, but she struggled with the memory and hadn't seen her in ages. I, in turn, shared my deepest fears and secrets, many of which I wouldn't dare tell Edna.

By sixteen, Long Shadow had grown into herself. The once-unsteady movements of a young fawn were now elegant, intentioned, and powerful, and she was now known throughout the islands for that beauty, poise, and strength. We typically spent the first days of summer together catching up on all that had transpired during those nine months apart, but when I arrived the following year at age seventeen, Long Shadow was distressed. She was in love with a boy, a wonderful and honorable boy from the tribe, but there were rumors.

Haida were coming from the north, and every Lummi was on edge. When Haida raided, they killed and took slaves. Her love would fight alongside the men, but Lummi were a peaceful people and no match for the brutality of Haida. Long Shadow feared for their future and spent every night in my room. I prayed constantly, and when I did sleep, it was with one hand resting on her swelling abdomen. Many times I awoke to find her standing outside on my porch, staring off into the darkness as she anticipated the inevitable.

Then, in the middle of August, I awoke from the worst nightmare I've ever had. Everything around me was ablaze with smoke so thick my eyes burned, and I could barely see the ground beneath my feet as I choked and gasped for air. The screams, God in heaven, the screams of suffering, and the hopelessness of impending death . . . I can't escape! There is no quarter! Then suddenly, it all went black and quiet. I bolted up in bed, panicked and drenched in sweat.

Long Shadow stood at the foot of my bed in the moonlight, soaked to the skin and shivering in the ice-cold room as she delivered an ominous warning:

"You must leave this place while you still can—promise me you will, promise me!" She struggled desperately to get the words out, as if she were once again losing her ability to speak.

"I promise! But what's happening to you? I won't leave you here!" I jumped out of bed and frantically reached out to grab hold of her, but my arms passed through her frigid form, and the desperation I felt in that moment paled before her reply, which gutted me:

"Meredith, my time has passed with the tide; I am no more."

Those were the last words she spoke as her misty figure dissolved before my eyes and was pulled through the bedroom window, leaving nothing behind but a puddle of seawater.

Within days I made good on that promise to Long Shadow and left my father's fiefdom, never to return. That fateful morning when the tires of Edna's truck found the gravel lane exiting the property, I covered my eyes as the tears began to fall. But like Lot's wife, I looked back, and what I saw in those few seconds scarred my soul.

Through my tears was the girl I loved—my best friend in the world, now ravaged by a cruelty whose depths I could not fathom. I screamed my pledge to her: "I love you! I'll come back, I promise—I'll come back for you, Long Shadow!"

My head remained in my hands as I sobbed uncontrollably the entire way to the ferry dock. Edna, God bless her, drove with one hand on the wheel and the other on my back until we pulled into Orcas Landing, where she helped me compose myself for the life ahead.

That memory was like a painful splinter of glass in my soul that took years before I could see it clearly enough to extract it. Today I still bear the burden of that promise yet to be fulfilled. How long will she linger among the waves, unable or unwilling to answer my morning calls?

21

Fireworks

After helping unload the station wagon Vivian and I walk around checking out the scene before the fireworks show.

"There's Bob!" Vivian points and waves at the same time.

"Oh, yeah, I see him at the picnic tables next to the co-op trailer; looks like he's pretty busy."

"I'm not surprised. Megan, the dark-haired girl, lives over in the Palisades on the cliffs across from Rosario. Her folks own Garrison Dredging—they put in the pilings for most of the docks in the San Juans, including the whole ferry system. The other one is Brooke Carlson—her parents own a fleet of fishing boats, and they live somewhere outside of Seattle but have a summer place on Shaw. Their families are loaded, and those two are about as boy-crazy as it gets."

"Kinda like Betty and Veronica?" I laugh, referencing Vivian's Archie comics.

"Yeah, kinda like. . . . C'mon, Eddiekins, we might as well get over there."

Vivian grabs my hand and leads me through the maze of blankets, ice chests, and families sprawled across the grass, eating and carrying on with each other.

The Fourth of July in Eastsound reminds me of the potlucks we have back on 16th Avenue East, where we block the street and the whole neighborhood turns up with their family favorites to share. The smoked salmon today is from the Lummi tribe, and Olga Livestock is handing out beef and chicken shish kabobs, while the sides and desserts are a hodgepodge of what other island businesses have contributed. Ms. Danelle supplied the spuds and herbs for Mom's potato salad, which gives her legendary status among my friends back on Capitol Hill, and Hattie Gil makes the ice cream that her co-op is famous for throughout the islands.

"Hi guys," says Bob, "I've already tested the ice cream— so far, so good!"

"How was Cascade Lake?"

"Didn't go. We were just out of Eastsound when those guys suddenly dumped their bikes and ran into the woods squirting diarrhea all over themselves." Bob laughs.

"Serves 'em right for stealing from Hattie!"

"When your mom told us that Hattie put Ex-Lax in that ice cream, I figured they'd regret it." I shake my head.

"It worked! They had—"

Bob's two companions don't care to hear more details of that afternoon and intervene in the conversation.

"Hi Vivian, haven't seen you around all summer. It appears you've been busy."

"That's the farm life, Meg, always something to do."

"Aren't you going to introduce us to your friend?" asks the tall, suntanned blonde with clear blue eyes and skin so smooth I want to reach out and touch it.

"Brooke Carlson and Megan Garrison, meet Edward Hawthorne—he's my next-door neighbor."

"Is that all Edward is, Vivian?" asks the raven-haired Megan with a devilish grin as her dark eyes shift to Vivian's hand still holding onto mine.

"Just being neighborly, Meg," Vivian answers in a tone somewhere between innocence and sarcasm before casually releasing my hand. "I was surprised y'all didn't come by the stand on Saturday—it's unlike you to miss that market."

"By the time we got back from Victoria, it was closed. Dad wanted to take us up there Friday in the new boat, and Mother decided to spend the night at the Empress—you know how persuasive she can be."

"I remember," Vivian answers with a smile.

"So, Edward, I've heard stories about that house of yours; I'd love to see the inside sometime. Maybe walk around a bit?"

"Um, yeah, sure, Brooke, I'll have everyone over for a picnic when we finish up a few things."

"Did your mom really make the potato salad?" Bob asks out of nowhere, freeing me from the noose of girls I feel tightening around my neck.

"Yep, I helped her peel about a hundred potatoes and chopped the herbs myself."

"It's the best I've ever had, and no BS either!"

"Thanks, man, I hear that a lot back home."

"Where is home, Edward?" Megan cuts in.

"Seattle. A place called Capitol Hill."

"I've been there. Great art museum and a cool old water tower, if I remember correctly," Brooke says.

"Yep, that's just a little over a block from where I live."

"School field trip," Brooke smiles, preempting my next question.

"I see . . . so, where do you live?"

"North Seattle, a neighborhood called The Highlands. But I have my hair done in downtown Seattle. I love the excitement of the city—there's so much more to do there."

"Sorry to butt in, but we'd better claim a spot to watch the fireworks from—it's getting pretty crowded," Vivian suggests.

"Why don't you and Edward join us on the boat—we have the best view from where it's anchored off Madrona Point, and there's plenty of room on this new one, with fresh seafood and snacks aboard," Brooke says.

"Well, if you don't think your folks will mind . . ."

"Are you kidding me? They won't mind at all! I'm sure they'd love to see you, and Mother will want to meet Edward as well."

"Great, our folks are back over on the green, and we should tell them what we're doing so they don't freak out. How about we meet you guys at the dock in five minutes?"

~

After we all pile into the runabout, Bob releases the lines and jumps aboard as Brooke starts the engine.

"Go for Völva," Megan calls over the radio.

"Copy," crackles a deep male voice through the speaker.

"Five incoming. ETA seven minutes."

"We'll roll out the welcome mat, over and out."

After slowly navigating the shallows around Indian Island, we pull out into the dark green waters of East Sound heading south toward Madrona Point, and minutes later we see the yacht silhouetted by the setting sun.

Völva is a beauty, over one hundred feet long; the only boat larger I've been aboard is the ferry that brought us to Orcas. After the runabout is secured to the platform on her stern, we find Mrs. Carlson in the main cabin refreshing her drink before the fireworks show kicks off.

"Hello, Vivian, it's wonderful to see you again. How are your parents?"

"It's nice to see you too, Ms. Elsa. They're fine, thank you, busy with the farm as usual."

"Please send them our best regards and tell them that Jens and I are excited to attend the farm event next month."

"Yes, ma'am, I sure will."

"Excuse me, Mother, this is Edward Hawthorne."

Elsa Carlson's smooth bronze skin and white Nordic hair are second to the piercing green eyes that seem to flash when she turns toward me. As she steps closer with a perfect smile, I feel as if she's looking into the depths of my soul, and I don't put up a struggle.

"Welcome, Edward. It's a pleasure to meet you."

When she presents her rose-petal-soft hand, the fleeting thought of kissing the back of it occurs, but thankfully I come to my senses and just hold it lightly between mine while she smiles as if knowing my thoughts.

"It's nice to meet you, Ms. Elsa," I answer, still suspended in her eyes.

"Your mother is M. G. Hawthorne."

"Yes, ma'am, but friends call her Meredith." I have no idea why I mention this; it just comes out.

"I've read each of her books, the recent one twice. I look forward to meeting her."

"Yes, Ms. Elsa, I'm sure she'll enjoy that as well."

"Pardon me, Edward, dear—Brooke, darling, while Megan takes our guests to the forward deck, will you help me put together the food for everyone?"

"Yes, Mother, of course."

"We'll speak further, Edward," she smiles, turning her attention to the task at hand.

Megan leads us out onto the main deck and introduces me to Jens Carlson, a towering, rugged seafaring man with a reddish-brown tan and white hair. His stature is that of a modern-day Viking, only he's dressed in shorts and a blue Hawaiian-print shirt. Mr. Jens introduces Elsa's parents, Sven and Freya. Besides their being knockouts, the resemblance of the women in the family is remarkable, even with their eyes: although Brooke's are blue and the others' green, they each have this same irresistible jewel-like quality.

Freya must be sixty but looks only slightly older than Elsa, who has to be about my mother's age; anyone might easily mistake the two for sisters.

Brooke and Ms. Elsa soon emerge from the cabin with a rolling cart full of chilled crabmeat and garlic bread, right as the first salvo of fireworks fly over East Sound.

"Perfectly timed, my dear," Freya notes as the reports ring out over the water, followed by streams of red, white, and blue lighting up the sky and the deck.

We're invited to help ourselves to the food and quickly find a spot in the large horseshoe-shaped seating pit with an unobstructed view of the show. The oohs and aahs steadily increase with the intensity of the fireworks, and I periodically glance around the deck at the others as the flashes from above light up their faces. When my eyes meet Brooke's, I quickly look away, only to be caught by Elsa's, and then Freya's . . . suddenly, I find myself floating peacefully in their collective gaze as they study me.

The booming grand finale to "The Star-Spangled Banner" returns my eyes skyward and my mind back to the deck as the trio release their gentle hold.

"You all right, Edward?" Vivian nudges me with her elbow.

"Just enjoying the show."

"Apparently."

We begin helping with the cleanup when Brooke whispers in my ear, "Edward, we'll take care of this. You go inside—Mother has something for you in the lower saloon. Use the stairs behind the bar."

"Oh . . ."

"Now go on. You mustn't keep her waiting."

I make my way down the five or six steps and find Ms. Elsa seated at a table in the dimly lit room, which is laden with richly colored tapestries and unusual designs that are completely foreign to me.

"Come, dear . . . sit," she beckons, her voice soft like the velvet curtains framing the portholes with their gilded stays.

Taking the seat directly across from her, I instinctively place my hands on the worn leather tabletop covered with symbols emblazoned over a spiraling pattern. In the center sits an incised disc that reminds me of a skipping stone about the size of a quarter.

After a slow feline blink, she places the disc in the palm of my hand, gently closing her fingers over mine.

"Edward, this is a very old water symbol from my homeland. It's good to keep in your pocket while you're here on the islands. Will you do this for me?"

"Thank you for the gift, Ms. Elsa—yes, I will."

"You're welcome, dear. It's my pleasure."

~

Brooke and Megan remain aboard while Mr. Jens ferries Vivian, Bob, and me back to Eastsound, where it takes the entirety of the journey for me to emerge from my stupor after meeting with Elsa Carlson.

"Thank you, Mr. Jens, we had a great time."

"You're welcome, Vivian—you kids don't be strangers. Come see us over on Shaw this summer, and maybe we'll take a two-day cruise through the islands. I need to get more hours on those engines before taking her out on the open ocean."

"Cool!" Bob says as he shoves the runabout off, and we wave farewell.

"Do you need a ride home, Bob?"

"No thanks, Vivian—I'm supposed to meet my folks on the green."

"Yeah, us too."

Walking back across the space now clear of everything but spent firecracker paper, Piccolo Petes, and the smell of burnt gunpowder, we see seven adults sitting together on an island of blankets waiting for us.

"Looks like our folks watched the show together."

"I guess they did, and Hattie's with them, too."

After we help pack up everyone's stuff and are piling into our cars there's the toot of a horn from the caravan of Olga Livestock trucks. Cowboy leans out to wish us a happy fourth and warns us to watch out for deer before he races for the ferry dock and the last boat back to Anacortes.

Vivian and I are relegated to the rear bench seat of the station wagon and sit facing the rear window.

"I hate riding back here," I say, "it makes me kinda sick."

"Don't you dare barf on me, Edward."

"I haven't yet, but there's always a first time for everything."

"What'd you think about Brooke and Megan?" Vivian asks quietly while the adults continue to laugh and chat about their evening.

"They're nice."

"Pretty, aren't they?"

"I guess so."

"Yeah, right," she huffs. "I thought your eyeballs were going to dry out and shrivel up with your ogling."

"It's not like that . . . I'll have to tell you later."

"What did Ms. Elsa say to you?"

"She gave me some type of good luck charm or something. Here, skootch over a bit so I can dig it out of my pocket."

I produce the disc and turn on the rear dome light to have a look.

"Edward, turn that light off—it makes it hard for me to see up here."

"Sorry, Dad, sure thing."

"It's all right, I can kind of make it out," Vivian says. "It looks exactly like the one I've seen Brooke wear around her neck. It's called a rune or something. It's made out of bone; I have one too, but it's a little different."

"Bone? What kind of bone?"

"Why don't you ask Brooke when she comes over? I'm sure she'd love to tell you all about it."

"Are you mad at me about something?"

"Another brilliant deduction."

"I'm not sure why . . . I thought the fireworks were cool and way more fun than being in Seattle."

"I thought Bob looked great tonight," she says. "He's sure getting a good tan, didn't you think so?"

"Uh, yeah, I guess . . . but what—"

Suddenly, a pothole drops the left side of the car and knocks our heads together, instantly changing the topic.

"Sorry, Robert, I should have warned you about that one. I meant to have it filled in by today," Mr. Kent says. "Everyone all right back there?"

"Don't know yet," I groan, rubbing the side of my head as Vivian does the same.

"Damn, that hurt," I whisper, and then start to laugh.

"No shit, Sherlock," she responds, cracking herself up.

We're still laughing when the station wagon pulls up to the farmhouse, and I swing open the tailgate to let Vivian out.

"See you tomorrow morning?"

"Four-thirty, right?"

"Yep. It won't be too bad—we gather eggs and then sow the carrots, radishes, and chard so they'll be ready for fall."

"See you then."

She smiles, blowing me a kiss.

22

Acquisitions

We signed the closing documents on the dreariest of November days, and while Robert went straight back to his office at Boeing, I headed for Montlake and a cup of tea to share the news.

"Are you sure about this, Meredith?"

"Yes, Carver, I'm positive."

"What does Robert think about it all?"

"After living through the Boeing layoffs last year, he was a little hesitant about pulling that much out of our savings. But when the latest publishing check arrived, he stopped resisting and realized that the property for the price was an absolute steal, as he so eloquently put it."

"I'm sure it was. Poor dear Robert, he's always been putty in your hands."

"Hardly!" I laughed, thinking, if only he knew.

"What about Edward?"

"We haven't said a word to Edward yet. The house needs some work in the interim, and we'd like to keep this as a surprise until it's finished, fingers crossed by the last day of school in June. So please, mum's the word!"

"I swear, he won't hear it from me or Calvin." Carver paused with that look of deliberation I know all too well.

"Do I sense one of those 'buts' of yours on the horizon?"

"Now, Meredith . . . I've never mentioned this before because I know how much you loved being up there each summer; and with all you lost, including the death of your mother and everything else that followed, I just couldn't bear adding to it."

"Carver, you're scaring me."

"Lila had horrible nightmares about that place, something she never told your father about."

"What on earth are you talking about?"

"She said they began the very first night after viewing the property, but she was fascinated by the place and insisted on buying it the following morning. From what she told me, those dreams continued."

"Did she confide in you about any of them?"

"Just the first one, and it was hellish by her description. Thick smoke and screaming, things that would make most of us run for the hills—not your mother, though."

I gulped hard and took a sip of tea to loosen the tightening in my throat. "Carver, I know that dream."

"God, Meredith . . . there's something off about that place. You'd better take along a priest from St. Joe's and a vat of holy water."

"It's not what you're thinking—it's not demonic."

"Well, if that doesn't sound like a glimpse straight into the pit of hell, I don't know what does!"

"The only thing I can promise you is that this isn't some portal into the abyss—at least not that one."

"All I know is that a few months later, when it was evident the cancer was taking your mother from us, I asked if she wanted to spend her final days on Orcas, or at the Tudor in Broadmoor; either way, she knew I would never leave her side regardless of what your father might say."

"I remember the day she died at Broadmoor. Is that what she wanted?"

"That's the thing . . . when I posed the question, she smiled like only your mother could and said, 'Carver, Broadmoor will be fine. I've already done the other.'"

"What do you think she meant by that?"

"When she passed, I was the one charged with packing her things up because your big, tough father wouldn't set one foot into that room. He demanded that everything of hers be put out of the house. It wasn't right."

"I remember how much he changed. It's all right, Carver; it gets to me as well sometimes when I think about her."

"Forgive me, Meredith, but it's just so damned unfair. Lila was such a beautiful person. She died too young, and I'm almost ashamed to admit this, but in my worst moments, I can name plenty of SOBs much more deserving of it."

"I know how you feel. At least we can thank God for the memories we have—not even the grave can rob us of those."

"I'll give a big amen to that!" Carver replied while blotting his eyes with a kerchief.

"Now, I believe you were about to tell me something about packing up her effects . . ."

"Oh yes. There were three books on the nightstand: her Bible, of course; another book titled *Indian Tribes of the Pacific Northwest and Their Legends*; and one that was about reincarnation, of all things! By their condition, each was very well read."

"I hate to ask this, but did you—"

"Of course not! But Calvin is so damned superstitious, I've got them packed up in the attic in a box that was used for that clove gum she chewed."

"I completely forgot about that! I used to dig in her purse for it."

"Well, they're yours anyway, Meredith."

"They're ours, Carver. Someday I'd like to go through them; maybe you could bring them up to Orcas when you visit us this summer."

"Just like your mother . . ."

"Then you and Calvin will come up for a nice visit with the Mels as soon as everything is finished, right?"

"I was afraid this was coming."

"Carver, aren't you the one who taught me to face my fears?"

"Yeah, me and my big mouth!"

23

Eagle Rock

Vivian and I finish the chores early and are at the kitchen table comparing the still-tender bumps on our heads when Ms. Danelle drops another waffle on my plate and asks what we're planning to do for the rest of the day.

"We're going to review the first five chapters of *The Missing*, then, I'm thinking about heading back down to Eagle Rock."

"Eagle Rock?"

"It's somewhere on the way to Lawrence Point. I don't think it has a name—that's just what Edward calls it."

"If you come with me, Vivian, I'll show you that beach and the cool place in the woods that I've been talking about."

"Sure, I'll go."

"You two be careful around those cliffs—I'm serious."

"We will."

"Let me make you a couple of sandwiches for the trip."

"Thanks, Mom. I'm going upstairs to change clothes. Edward, grab the packs out of the utility room."

"Roger that!"

By the time Vivian returns to the kitchen, I've stowed the sandwiches, along with two pears, and filled the canteens with water for the trip.

"Have a good time, and remember what I said about being extra careful around those cliffs."

After taking the upper trail back to my house, we enter the southern tree line just behind our barn, and I lead us along a deer trail as we navigate the nettles.

"These nettles clear out pretty soon, but they're real bad for a ways yet."

"Yeah, no kidding—I don't think I've seen them as thick for this far."

"It's worth it after we make it over that little hill just up ahead."

"Just up ahead? That's like a quarter mile!"

"Where's your sense of adventure?"

After a few minutes of careful walking, we make it to the small berm at the edge of the nettle patch, and we both brush a leaf.

"Shit, Edward! I hate these things. This better be good, or—"

"Or wha—"

"Shhhh." Vivian reaches out and grabs my shirttail, stopping us cold. "I feel like we're being watched," she whispers.

An unsettling stillness surrounds us as if the woods have taken a deep breath and are waiting to exhale. The silence creates an eerie tension that sends a shiver up my spine, and I give Vivian a quick look, confirming her intuition. I ask myself what Holmes would do in this situation; clearly, he'd become the observer while not revealing his suspicion. A casual scan of the area yields nothing but woods for as far as my eyes can see, but whatever this is, we aren't imagining it.

"Follow me like everything's normal," I whisper.

With each step beyond the berm, the feeling grows stronger, like we are walking into a trap when suddenly the caws from directly above snap our heads skyward, and I gasp, grabbing Vivian and ducking behind a pine tree.

"Son of a bitch!" I say as the crows fly off. "I guess we should look up now and then."

"Let's hope it's not a foreshadowing of what's ahead."

"Murder! Bravo, Vivian!" I smile at her application of the correct term for a group of crows.

Soon the trees thin, and shafts of sunlight find their way to the forest floor, revealing a haze not evident in the heavier woods. The ferns grow larger here, with the smell of dirt and moss hanging in the air, even with the soft breeze. This place has a solitude unlike anywhere I've been this summer. . . . No, it's actually more of a solemness; it reminds me of walking along the shrub-laden chain-link fence separating Volunteer Park from Lake View Cemetery.

"What do you think this place is, Edward?"

"I don't know, but if the mosquitoes wouldn't eat you alive, it would be a great reading place; it's so peaceful and quiet."

"Yeah, great job—this was totally worth it."

"Check out those big rocks. I think it's the moss that helps make it so quiet, like a kind of insulation."

"Four of them, and they must be at least eight feet tall."

"And about as wide—"

"How do you think they got here?"

"I thought about that last time; I bet they're on almost a straight line from those huge boulders by the cabin."

"So maybe they rolled down here all the way from Mount Constitution."

"If they did, it must've been before these woods were here."

"Or the trees were like bowling pins and got knocked over when they got plowed into." Vivian surveys the area with her suggestion.

"If we walk straight between those two, we end up at Eagle Rock just above that little beach," I tell her. "C'mon, it'll only take us a couple more minutes."

We continue through the last bit of woods and walk into the ten o'clock sunshine atop a rocky outcrop covered with dry grass, about the size of a large living room. The north side is a dead end with a sheer thirty-foot drop to the rocks and water, but to the south the land falls away with a switchback to the sea.

"Impressive, huh?" I smile proudly.

"It's amazing—this would make a great camping spot too!"

"Let's go down to the beach, but be careful: there's some loose rock on the way."

Walking along the small driftwood-strewn beach below, we look for anything interesting that's washed ashore.

"Why do you call this place Eagle Rock?"

"The day I was here, I kicked back on that log there, just looking at the sky and listening to water washing onto the beach, thinking about nothing in particular. Then I closed my eyes and listened—my mom does that a lot—and I must have been like that for a while when a shadow blocked the sunlight right before a loud screech scared the crap out of me, and I opened my eyes. I looked up, and right where we came out of the woods was a huge bird perched on top of that cedar. It was an eagle—don't ask me how I knew she was female, but she was.

"I didn't dare budge while she stared at me, and honestly, I was afraid she might head my way. Then suddenly her large beak, the color of a rain slicker, darted toward the sea, and with one flap of her giant wingspan, she produced a salmon from the water and circled so close to me that I could see its blood on her yellow feet from the talons piercing the fish's side. Her wings were loud, Vivian—they sounded like a bellows carrying her up to the massive nest in those trees over there, and I watched her feed the lone eaglet."

"You saw all that right here?"

"Yes, but no. It was all a crazy dream. When I woke up, the water was getting close like it is now, and I remembered what you always say about getting stuck if the tide comes in, even though I could probably climb back through that heavy brush behind us."

"That's a crazy dream . . . pretty cool, though. Hey, look! There's some fishing tackle tangled up in that mat of kelp and sticks floating out there. Looks like a Deep Six Pink Lady wrapped up in it. I'm going to roll up my pants and go get it."

"The water is like at least waist-deep now. You can't roll your pants up that high—you'll get soaked and be miserable hiking back."

"You're right. Turn around then."

"Why?"

"Because I'm taking them off, thank you."

"You're nuts! Here, I'll do it. You turn around."

"Why? For guys it's just like you're in a bathing suit."

I take off my shoes and socks, setting them on a log safe from the tide, followed by my jeans, then shirt, and wade out into the water.

"Do you have that charm Ms. Elsa gave you?" she asks.

"It's in my jeans pocket."

"A lot of good that'll do you in there—watch your step."

"It's pretty smooth; I saw the bottom when the tide was out."

"For skates—they're like sting rays, and they like the smooth bottom. Oh, and the dogfish—they come into shallows too, with the tide."

"Great! Now you tell me!"

The raft of kelp and tackle has already drifted farther out, and I have to move fast through the rising tide, which gets colder and deeper with each incoming wave.

"Almost there, Edward!" Vivian cheers me on as I make one last stretch, grabbing the branch that everything seems to be wrapped around.

"Gotcha!" The water is over my belly button when I reach the stuff, and by the time I make it back to shore with Vivian's prize, my legs are so numb they ache.

"Wait, Edward, don't come out of the water yet."

"What? I'm freezing my ass off!"

"Just one more thing—grab that hunk of Styrofoam before it floats off, will ya? That shit is awful, and it never decomposes."

Psyching myself up with a few quick breaths, I hurry out to retrieve it, but when I pull the chunk out of the water, it has a hook attached to a large hasp that's bolted through the middle.

"What the hell? It's attached to a cable going to the bottom!" I shout to Vivian.

"That's a smuggler's buoy, Edward! Bet it's for a skiff because it's pretty shallow even at high tide."

"What should I do with it?" I chatter as a cold breeze reminds me that I'm still freezing in the water, which is now up to my chest.

"Hurry up and get the hell out of there before they come back!"

"Suits me!"

"Don't come all the way out yet—you'll never get the sand off your feet. Reach down in the water and toss a couple of those big flat rocks up here on the beach, then step on them straight out from the water. I'll grab your socks and shoes."

"But what about my pants?" I ask, shivering in the breeze.

"You plan on wearing those soggy tighty whities under your jeans? Yuck."

"That's a good point."

"You'll warm up in a couple of minutes, I promise. Here, use me for balance, and dry your feet off with your shirt, then put your socks and shoes on."

"Thanks, Vivian, I've got it."

"Now grab your jeans and go behind that rock over there to ditch those wet things before you start itching from the salt water."

"Guys call that going commando."

"Commando? Gawd, you boys . . . hurry up."

After I get dressed, Vivian and I climb back up to Eagle Rock to have our lunch before starting back.

"Why would someone have that buoy over here, anyway?" I wonder.

"First off, we don't know how old it is. It could've been here for years; like I was saying, that Styrocrap lasts forever. Might get an idea by looking at the barnacles or other stuff growing on the cable when the tide's out. How's your sandwich?"

"It's killer—your mom makes great food."

"She's always trying to teach me how to cook. I think she gets a little disappointed that I'm not very interested in it. I mean, I can make some basics like sandwiches, even pancakes and waffles, but it's always better when she does it."

"Make me some biscuits next time and I'll let you know!"

"Smartass . . . maybe I will."

"So what was that about you having a charm from Ms. Elsa, too?"

"She gave it to me a couple of summers ago when Brooke told her that I had been sleepwalking, something I mentioned to her during a slumber party at their house. I think Ms. Elsa was worried that I might wander off while I was over there." Vivian laughs.

"I think most kids do it. I did a couple of years ago— at least that's what my mom told me after she found me standing outside on the front porch in my pajamas in the middle of the night. I didn't remember a thing about it."

"One time I thought I was dreaming about walking around the farm, and when I got back and went to lie down in bed, I missed it and hit the floor like a sack of potatoes!"

"How'd you know you were sleepwalking?"

"Because, dingle, my feet were dirty, and I left footprints across the kitchen floor when I came in."

"Wow, that's scary. What if you walked off the cliff or something?"

"I'd be dead! I don't think I've done it since I got the charm. If I have, I didn't go out barefoot."

"Did you happen to go to the lower deck of Brooke's boat on the Fourth?"

"No. Why, is it really cool?"

"It's strange . . . lots of stuff I've never seen before."

"You mean like symbols, that sort of thing?" Vivian looks at me more intently.

"Yeah! I've never seen anything like that, and there's an odd feeling . . ."

"I think the word you're looking for is 'attraction.'" She laughs.

"I guess, but only if used in a hypnotic way!"

"Yeah, Brooke and Freya have that same thing." Vivian pauses to toss a clamshell to the beach below. "Their place on Shaw has all sorts of Norse history books; I mean, like really old stuff. Some are in an ancient writing that looks different than the runes or whatever. Brooke said she has to read all of them before she's eighteen."

"That'd be something to ask her about."

"I did; she just said it was hard to explain, and that's all she'd say about it."

"Speaking of books, what do you think about The Missing so far?"

"I think Sarah's boss is a creepy perv."

"He was pretty helpful in her finding the right apartment, that's for sure!"

"She should get a boyfriend or find another job," Vivian declares. "All alone in a new city—that's scary."

"At least she has some friends, and they can watch out for each other."

"Judging by the title, somebody eventually falls down on the job."

"A brilliant deduction!" I smile. "It's already got that tension building up, the kind where you know something bad is about to happen."

"I predict it will be in the next chapter—you watch."

"You didn't read ahead, did you?"

"Edward Hawthorne, what kind of girl do you think I am?"

"All right then, we'll see!"

"I promise I didn't. By the way, this place is great and definitely worth a nettle sting!"

"Told ya!"

"You did, I admit it. Think we can make it home along the cliffs?"

"We can try—the last time, I cut back into the woods, so we'll be charting this way together."

"I hate to leave; we should come back here again soon."

We sling our packs and are walking close to the edge of the woods along the cliffs when suddenly there it is!

"Vivian, look!" I yell, bending down to pick up my first arrowhead.

"Wow, Edward! It's a real beauty, too! What'd I tell ya—they find you!"

24

Mary Ellen's Cottage

I leave the cabin at eight and set out along the cliff trail toward Mary Ellen's cottage. The waves washing over the rocks below and songs of seabirds above calm my nerves for the coming encounter, as I can only guess at what dredging up old memories might bring along with it. The one time we met was while I was shopping with Edna in Eastsound, and that gives me some comfort about using Danelle's suggested method of showing up unannounced since Mary Ellen rarely answers her telephone.

To my knowledge, she's the only person alive who can fill in the gaps about the woman who had been so much more than a summer tutor: Edna was my surrogate mother three months out of the year for over a decade, and also where Edward got his name. So, if I return home today with some insight about the woman whom I've held in such high esteem, the closure will be worth any pain associated with it.

During our years together, Edna taught me how to use my voice constructively, and though she was a tyrant at times regarding English literature and ladylike etiquette, it was her ethos on the importance of self-respect and dignity that provided me with the temerity to survive out in the real world. Curiously, it was the passing of her final exam that resulted in my immediate expulsion from the life I knew.

The day my father asked if I would consider going to the Jazz on the Green concert in Eastsound with Skip Stuart, I wasn't interested. But despite Samantha's influence, my relationship with Father seemed to be improving, and in a conciliatory gesture to preserve that progress, I agreed. Skip had been around the house before and seemed intelligent enough for conversation, and while he didn't possess movie-star good looks, he was far from a troll. My summers on Orcas were fairly isolated, and I preferred it that way, but because of that choice, I was unaware of Skip Stuart's darker reputation.

The first evening was fun, which led to a second, and Skip was a perfect gentleman on both occasions. Even so, I wasn't hinting that this would develop into a romantic interest by any stretch of the imagination. It was the evening after the shocking departure of Long Shadow, and my distress was obvious around the property. My father had informed Skip of my vulnerable state, and he called me to go out for a quick cruise. I agreed, thinking it might help to get away for a few hours, just to break the routine of wandering around and chasing every shadow I saw.

The plan was that Father would drive me to the dock in Doe Bay on his way into Eastsound; Skip would pick me up in his boat, take me out for a short sunset cruise, and then drop me off back at the dock, where Father would collect me on his way home.

"It'll cheer you up, Meredith," is what Father said as we pulled into the marina.

I stepped down into the boat as Skip and my father exchanged words on the pier above, and a minute later, Skip joined me and started the motor. We pulled out of the bay and soon ducked into the calmer waters of the inside channel that separates Doe Island from Orcas by only a hundred yards or so. He dropped anchor at the northern end and tossed me a bottle of beer from the ice chest. Unable to locate the bottle opener from his captain's chair, he asked me to grab the spare in a compartment next to the back seat, where I was sitting. After digging for a second, I found it beneath a can of carburetor cleaner, but before I could grab it, he was on top of me from behind.

"Get off of me, Skip!" I screamed as his hands slid around my breasts and down to my crotch, groping me as he tried to undo my shorts. I writhed around and grabbed as much of his face skin as I could, trying my level best to get him off of me.

"You little tease, you've led me on long enough!" he laughed, licking my neck.

I managed to raise my knee between us as he attempted to unzip his pants and pushed him off of me and onto the deck.

Jumping to my feet, I screamed, "You take me back right now, you son of a bitch! I'm going to tell my father!"

When he got up from the deck, he grabbed my throat and choked me before slapping my face, knocking me back down onto the seat. Then he opened his belt and dropped his trousers.

"You're not too bright, are ya? I have your father's blessing to make a woman out of you any way I see fit. Now, I'm going to teach you a thing or two about pleasing a real man, so you can make a good wifey someday! Come to the skipper, baby! Captain's orders . . ."

As he began waddling toward me with his pants around his ankles, I had the presence of mind to grab the can of carburetor cleaner and spray a stream at his face, sending him down to the deck screaming.

"My eyes!!! You fucking bitch! You've blinded me!" he howled, scrambling to the port side in a desperate attempt to flush his eyes with the saltwater.

Fearing for my life, I dove off the starboard side into the cold water and swam the short distance to Orcas on pure adrenaline. When I reached the shore, I frantically banged on doors until I found help at the cottage of an older couple. I phoned Edna, and she raced down to get me while I jumped in the shower to warm my body and stop the shivering.

When we arrived back home, I was still clad in my host's bathrobe, and Edna marched me straight into the house to confront my father in his study.

He was furious and called me a selfish, spoiled brat, while that sloppy drunk Samantha stood in the doorway drinking straight from her bottle of pink Chablis, egging him on with her slurring. When Father ordered Edna out of the house, she refused for fear of what would happen to me.

"No, Mr. Gaines, I will not leave this child's side. You should be ashamed of yourself."

"No goddamned schoolmarm is going to talk to me like that in my own house! You're fired! Now get out of my sight before I throw you out myself, and you better be off my property by first light with your belongings, or I'll toss them over the cliff!"

"As you wish, but I pity you, Mr. Gaines. You are a badly broken man."

"Father, no! Please!" I pleaded with him.

"Meredith, I have given you every opportunity to make something of yourself, and how do you repay me when the time comes? You behave like a goddamned prude!"

"Yeah, a gwaddam p-pwwude!" Samantha gargled.

"And it's all that prude's fault!" he yelled, pointing his finger at Edna.

"So, my virtue is less important to you than whatever mess you have gotten yourselves into, is it?"

"Oh, you know so much about the world, don't you, Meredith? You and your damn books! I should have listened to Samantha and put you away in the nuthouse! Now, I'm going to make a few phone calls and try to smooth this over. Hopefully, you didn't blind the poor chap, and he'll chalk it up to the old Gaines spunk, eh? Go to your room!"

Edna's look told me all I needed to know, and once upstairs, I gathered my most precious things and waited. A few hours later, when the house fell silent, I left for Edna's cabin.

We spent the rest of the night packing her books and other belongings, then loaded them into her pickup truck, finishing at daybreak with just enough time for one last cup of tea together on the porch.

"Beautiful morning for a ferry ride."

"Yes, ma'am."

"The statement you made to your father back at the house, the one about your virtue—magnificent," she said, resting her hand gently atop mine. "You're ready to take on the world, Meredith."

~

I arrive at the clearing a little queasy after recalling the tragic end to our story and pause in the shelter of the tree line to gather myself. A minute or two later, the feeling subsides, and I'm walking toward the cottage when a sombrero-style straw hat emerges from the giant sunflowers and then seems to vanish. Drawing nearer, I see that she's down on her knees, tending the garden in the company of a large, long-haired Siamese cat.

When I'm almost there, she looks up from the starts she's planting and says, "I wondered when you'd come; please follow me inside."

Bereft of words, I accompany her into the quaint space as she points to a spot on the sofa where she intends that I sit.

"Watch out for Leo—he's right behind us, and he'll end up on your lap. I'll pour the tea; still take it with a little honey and a dash of cream?"

"Y-yes, yes, Edna," I stammer in disbelief bordering on shock, wondering if my memories have conjured her, the way I had once been suspected of conjuring Lhaq'temish.

She continues talking from the kitchen, and as predicted, Leo finds his way onto my lap. "You know, I stayed at the dock until the ferry was out of sight. The term 'empty nester' fails miserably when it comes to the hole that opened up inside of me when that boat vanished from the horizon. I could never return to the house where Eugene and I spent our married life, so after leaving Orcas Landing, I made a left on Deer Harbor Road and moved in with Mary Ellen. We worked in the garden, read our books, and enjoyed each other's company, as well as a simple life with our cats and other critters that found us. I wouldn't have made it through that first year without her. I swear they would have locked me away in the state asylum."

Edna soon rejoins me in the living room with our tea, and understanding the unmoored state I must be in, pats my hand reassuringly before taking the seat opposite.

"Mary Ellen was an isolationist, and like me, she had no other family members. Back then, Deer Harbor was sparsely populated and almost convent-like on her forty acres off in the woods. I only left the grounds once a month that first year because it was just too painful. When she fell ill at the end of '56, I cared for her until she died that spring, then honored her wishes and buried her on that property."

At last I'm able to put my initial feelings into words; "But Edna . . . why? I heard you died somewhere back east, and it left me with scars that nobody but Jesus can see."

"Au contraire, I did die, Meredith . . . three times."

"Ma'am?"

"The first was when my dearest Eugene had that heart attack on the dock in Olga, the second was the moment I put you on that ferryboat to a new life, and the third time was when that fucking cancer took Mary Ellen away from me," Edna answers flatly, staring out the window as if looking away from the painful recollections.

"Of course . . . forgive me. That's devastating."

"Third time's a charm—I won't say that the thought of throwing myself overboard with a weight belt didn't occur to me."

"I know a lot about that kind of loss too."

"Within a week of you leaving Orcas, that degenerate Skip knew he was permanently blind in one eye and had some trouble with the other. He donned a black patch and began running his mouth at the marina bar about watching the great Marvin Gaines and his whore of a daughter lose everything. It didn't take long for Samantha to throw herself at the Stuarts' mercy. When the old man had his fill of that hose bag, he passed her off to Skip, and from what Hattie said, even the psycho had a go."

"Disgusting, but not too surprising."

"Based on other gossip, they blamed you, and Mary Ellen was worried that they might eventually come after yours truly for retribution. She wanted me to move to the mainland, but I had already lost enough. I wasn't about to lose my home, much less my ability to put flowers on Eugene's grave every month. When she was diagnosed with cancer, she said, 'Look here, Edna, Mary Ellen's been a pretty good name for me, and I won't be needing it where I'm going. Try it on for size—everything I have is yours anyway.' The kids had just taken over for their folks at Templin's grocery and confused us all the time, so we knew it would work. I just put on a few pounds, changed my hair, started wearing her clothes, grew a few pot plants, and fermented dandelion and strawberry wine in her honor. I'd say the hardest part of the transformation was learning to let the foul language fly out in public! Hattie helped get the gossip moving in the right direction by telling a couple of the island busybodies that she heard from someone in Anacortes that Edna died while on a trip back east. You remember how it is here—gossip spreads like a grassfire in August, and a few months later, people forgot all about old Edna, just as if she had moved to the mainland."

"Hattie Gil knows?" There's a flash of anger inside at the thought of others knowing all along.

"Yes, the only one. She was such a dear friend to both of us. The Lummi understand what it means to live and to die in nature. When the time came, she brought her backhoe over and we buried Mary Ellen together."

"I have so many questions . . ." My posture shifts to one of softness with her story.

"I'm sure you do, and I'll try my best to answer them, but I want you to know that I'm more Mary Ellen Carter these days than Edna Wilhite, and I rather enjoy the freedom of it."

My eyes begin to well, and I feel the nausea in the pit of my stomach. "I never had the chance to tell you that I loved you. Without your teaching, I wouldn't have made it through." I feel myself going to pieces but hold it together while petting Leo.

"Oh, my dear little Meredith . . . do you think I haven't been paying attention? Look at all you've accomplished— I'm so proud of my girl! A famous author, and what about that clever young man you're raising? He reminds me a lot of you at that age, he and that pip Vivian," she replies, handing me a box of tissues.

"He is a special child. I challenged him early, just like you did with me, even named him in memory of you."

"The highest of honors, dear; I'm humbled."

"I'm very proud of him."

"I was thrilled to hear about his Sir Arthur Conan Doyle conquest! Victorian-era literature is not in vogue these days among the youth," she smiles, knowing that I have passed along the torch she handed me.

"Between him and Robert, I couldn't have asked for more."

"You see Meredith, it's all as it should be."

"But what about you? Are you all right?"

"Age is a clever gardener, dear. It helps us grow strong enough to survive the dry seasons; other times, it reminds us of our duty to go to seed after we bloom for the last time. You, Meredith, are one of my prized seeds, and I've long been at peace knowing that you landed on such fertile ground."

"What a beautiful perspective. Then you approve of the books?"

"The first two, marvelous, absolutely tip-top, had me on the edge of my seat! And thank you for the lovely words in your dedications."

"I couldn't have done any of it without you, ma'am."

"Well, we were put in each other's lives 'for a reason and a season,' as Mary Ellen used to say."

"Forgive me, but do you not care for *The House of Long Shadows*?"

"That latest murder book of yours? Splendid work, darling! It even pried reclusive me out to the island book club just to hear the conversations."

"Thank you—I've always wondered what you would have thought about the parallels."

"It gave me a glimpse of what life may have been like for you after stepping off the ferry that day in Anacortes, and it's abundantly clear to anyone with history here in these islands what thread is being pulled. But the ending . . . I'll confess, I didn't see that one coming. What are you playing at there?"

"Yes, well, that's a bit of an excursion."

"You realize that it won't take Edward and Vivian long to figure out who the principals are when they read it."

"Yes, I know . . . it's a concern," I reply, allowing my eyes to wander around her bookshelves.

"Why did you come back, Meredith? Surely not just to rewrite your childhood memories through Edward's eyes of innocence."

"Isn't that what all novelists do? Idealize our origins or savagely distort them into catastrophic tales of grief and loss?"

"You do seem to have mastery of the latter, my dear," Edna says, pausing for a sip of tea.

"Thank you. But now's the time for me to dip my toes in the soothing waters of the former."

"So, you're here to write another book, and from what I understand, you've been remodeling the cabin to be your retreat."

"Yes, ma'am, the very spot where my journey with the page began, thanks to you."

"Excellent news. Now, tell me what prompted the *Long Shadows* book."

"It was the churning."

"Churning?"

"That's hard to explain. It's like a whisper over my shoulder that nags me until I sit down to write, and when I do, it's as if I'm lending my fingers to the keys. Alastair says it's an expression of my inner creative voice; the first time I noticed it was when the idea came for *Haunted Houses* and it also showed up for *The Missing*. With *Long Shadows*, it came after reading the account of pregnant Angela Wagner being fished out of the water just off Blakely—it became relentless with an urgency I hadn't experienced before."

"That was an awful shock here on the islands, and then those corrupt police ruled it a suicide, even though Chase Stuart was the last person she was seen with, and on his boat, too!"

"Exactly—and the fact that she was found within days of the fire that killed his mother made it even more suspicious."

"Ruled accidental, my dear, just like the drowning of his old man in Deception Pass while they were on a father-son fishing trip. That's been at least fifteen years ago now."

"Yes, ma'am, and of course, it all leads back to the boat fire that killed Skip less than a year after I left."

"I see the correlation." Edna flashes a familiar studious look and nods.

"I do recall that Skip was the favorite, and Casper didn't think very much of Chase. There wasn't any love lost between those two boys either."

"Ha! That's putting it mildly: nobody could stand Chase, especially after he set fire to the Deer Harbor dock."

"So if Chase was to be the heir when his father died, then Skip had to go."

"True. But rumor was that Casper changed the will after Skip's death to reflect that Chase would only receive a small stipend from the trust controlled by their attorney. Years later, when that attorney went to jail for embezzling from the estate, Priscilla became the executor of the trust—that is, until she died, and then the remainder went to Chase as the sole survivor.

"So in the end, Chase got it all anyway."

"Besides their place on Shaw, there wasn't much left after the attorney went through about seventy-five percent of their accounts."

"No wonder he was rubbing his hands together when he talked about the insurance checks he received."

"What are you saying, Meredith? You've seen him?"

"Yes, on the ferry coming over back in June."

"Meredith, it's not safe! He has to know that the book is pointing a finger at him. Lucky for you that those dirty cops are long gone from the islands, or you might have already been disposed of."

"That's good news, then, isn't it?"

"Not if he feels at risk—the last thing he'd want is someone poking around in the past, especially with this new no-nonsense Sheriff's Department on the islands. Good God . . . Have you mentioned any of this to Alastair? He'd be aghast."

"No, I haven't considered Stuart a threat."

"You might want to revisit that conclusion after some of the unpublished details, but fair warning, it's a little untoward."

"Ma'am, you've read my books." I chuckle, despite the topic.

"Sorry, dear, it's a habit. I'm used to having Vivian and Edward as my audience. Every old-timer knows that Hattie curates the juiciest island gossip, and it usually proves to be true. According to her, it wasn't long after Angela and Chase hooked up at the Rosario Resort bar that they were going at it like the rabbits on San Juan Island!"

I can't help but smile at her reference to the fact that San Juan Island has been overrun by uninhibited bunnies for as long as I can remember.

"But that's not the untoward part," Edna continues. "Folks around here may have a tolerance for gossip, even some scandalous sex, but incest . . . well, that's frowned upon."

"Incest!" I almost spit out my tea.

"Yes, dear," she smiles as I wipe my chin with a tissue.

"When Priscilla heard about what was happening over there, she washed down a few Valiums with her nightly bottle of wine and broke the news to Chase that he was the literal bastard of the family."

"I had no idea."

"Neither did he!" Edna laughs. Turns out he was fathered by the same traveling salesman who sired the only other ginger in the San Juans: Angela Wagner!"

"Now, just a minute, I clearly remember the photos of Angela Wagner as a brunette."

"You're right. Hattie said that when the kids began calling her 'rusted brain' back in grammar school, her mother started having Angela's hair colored on the mainland. She was a regular over at Curl Up and Dye in Anacortes until that monster murdered her."

"But didn't Priscilla have red hair too?"

"It was auburn, but Casper demanded she go more red after Chase was born. She stopped coloring it after his funeral."

As Edna ventures into the kitchen for more tea, I stare out the window and take in the revolting nature of what I've just heard.

"So, he knew Chase wasn't his child and was trying to avoid a scandal."

"Probably suspected it from the moment the lad popped out," Edna laughs as she rejoins me. "It also gave him a license to philander about, which, of course, was his favorite hobby all along."

"And what's the unpublished story about how Angela ended up in the water?"

"The day following the revelation from Priscilla, Chase took the poor girl for a ride in his boat and tossed her overboard somewhere in the middle of Rosario Strait. Sometime that evening, he burned the place down with his mother in it and spun up that 'flannel nightgown and hairspray' horseshit. He collected on three insurance policies for his efforts: one for the house, one for dear dead Mommy, then last year he finally settled with the insurance company and received a sizable check for his dead leg."

The details help fill in the gaps of my own research, and I look to Edna for more.

"But how could they get away with ruling Angela's case a suicide so easily?"

"Simple. The police cited the coroner's report to substantiate their claim that her motive for suicide was pregnancy out of wedlock. Of course, you know it was Chase's baby, just like the Stewart girl in your book."

"Yes, ma'am, I gathered that was the case," shaking my head in disgust.

"You're toying with a psychopath, dear," her tone grows resolute. "One who's much more dangerous than the Sullivan Shaw character in your *Long Shadows* novel." Edna's eyes lock onto mine. "Chase Stuart is nonfiction!"

"Yes, but he'd never get close enough to do anything to me. He's lamer than Tiny Tim without a crutch."

"I'm glad you recall your Dickens, dear, but Chase Stuart is a certifiable nutjob who holds a grudge. Perhaps you should reread the last chapter of your own book; isn't Sullivan Shaw fairly incapacitated?"

"You have a point. At least our Sheriff's Department is responsive. According to Kent and Danelle, Sheriff Chancey was Johnny-on-the-spot last year when those boys broke into the house."

"He stopped by here to introduce himself when he moved to Orcas. Nice enough, appears to be on the up and up. Brought his own deputies with him from Oak Harbor, and they had those hooligans in jail within a day. Also raked them over the coals about the Olga Livestock fire a few weeks earlier."

"Ah, yes, I didn't put that together."

"Of course, they denied any part of that, and there wasn't any evidence, so no charges were filed, and that whole witch story they concocted garnered more attention than it deserved, especially among the few old guard still around." Edna chuckles.

"So, you don't believe that they were run off by her?"

"Who knows what stopped them from burning it down? I'm just glad they didn't."

Edna drops her chin and looks at me over the top of her glasses, then rises from her chair and walks to the closest bookcase. I continue stroking Leo's coat as our eyes follow her up the stepladder to the top shelf, where she retrieves a thick binder that's out of place among the leather spines. What she returns with leaves me speechless.

"This belongs to you, my dear," she says, handing me the three-ringed denim-covered notebook.

"You... saved them!" I stammer.

"Twelve summers' worth of your adventures, all graded and in order, mind you."

"Thank you—I'm at a loss for words."

"You're welcome. Now, Meredith, it's plain as day that you're as headstrong as ever, but please hear me out. I know I drove you very hard, albeit with only the best intentions, but my dogmatic notions perhaps were too rigid at times. Let these pages be the fulfillment of your promise to return for her. For the sake of your beautiful family and your own sanity, dear God, it's time to let her go."

"So, you believed me—what I said, the stories I wrote?"

"I knew something was there when you called her Lhaq'temish. Clearly a native word, and when I asked Hattie about it, she told me the word is Lummi and means "people of the sea." It's a statement or testament that Lummi have lived in harmony with these waters and the surrounding lands since time immemorial. So, I had to ask myself, how in the world does a six-year-old child from Seattle know this word and to even pronounce it correctly?"

"You might have told me."

"Ha! And what would I have told you? That I believed your yarns of an invisible friend, a disembodied Lummi girl no less, and the two of you traipsed around the property together? If that got out, your father and Samantha would have seen to it that we were both hauled off to the nutter in Sedro-Woolley!"

"You're right, they sure would have . . . but Edna, she's still here. She's never left. That's the whole point—I think she's stuck."

"Jesus, Mary, and Joseph," Edna replies, while making the sign of the cross; the concern in her eyes is evident. "Meredith, for heaven's sake."

"I've never lied to you, ma'am, and I swear that I'm not mad—not completely, anyway." I search those gray eyes for a clue to her thoughts, flashing back to the days when I read my stories aloud to her.

"I'm certain of both, my dear." Edna pauses as she shifts in her chair and glances out the window. "When I heard that you were looking at the property, there was a mix of emotions, firstly, the joy of my Meredith finally coming home, which was quickly eclipsed by how you might respond to me, and what it might bring about, as there are certain things that are better left in the past. Many a night's sleep evaded me because of the anxiety surrounding it all, so rather than toss and turn, fretting about it all night, I'd get up and sit in this chair with a cup of chamomile tea,

Leo in my lap, and have a puff of grass to relax me until I drifted back off.

"Now, I'll tell you, as God is my witness, on several of those nights I've seen a misty figure roaming the property."

"It's not her."

"What do you mean, it's not her?"

"I've seen that mist as well; she comes through the house occasionally, even woke Edward up once. I've also caught sight of her several mornings before sunup on my way to the clefted rock. I'm telling you, it's not Long Shadow. I'm 100 percent sure of it."

"Well, that's just dandy, another spook roaming around that can't rest in peace."

"No, ma'am, she's different."

"I shouldn't be too terribly surprised. Hattie says Lummi are buried unmarked throughout the San Juans. But hear what I say: there are things we aren't supposed to trifle with, Meredith. Necromancy is not God's way."

"I promise you, I've never dabbled with summoning anything. You said it earlier when you mentioned that there is something else lurking beyond the last pages of the book."

"Yes?"

"I've narrowed it down to an epilogue."

"A second edition, then?"

"My own . . . possibly. I'm still trying to figure it out. Perhaps that's why I haven't seen her yet or why I'm struggling to get the idea on paper for another book."

"Interesting. Some readers of that book may think of it as poetic justice if they hear the author herself is wrestling with a feeling of unfinished business."

"I've had some letters about the ending. All I can say is that I wrote the story that was given to me, and it almost cost me my family."

"I'm sorry to hear that, dear. Regarding my foremost concern, your self-confidence may lead to carelessness, something that I won't abide."

"Ma'am?"

"No, Meredith, I refuse to play the role of your Captain Alastair on this voyage."

"I'm afraid you've lost me."

"You are a marvelous writer and a very good sleuth as well. Not quite on Agatha's level, but good enough that you almost had Stuart's misdeeds correctly applied from afar."

"Almost! Isn't it fairly clear?"

Edna glances at Leo lying on my lap and grins, then once again shifts her gaze out the window as she continues.

"You know, Eugene always used to warn boaters about dry rot in their fuel lines as something that could be deadly out on the water. It's a pretty straightforward fix, really: just loosen two clamps and replace the leaking hose between the carburetor and the fuel filter. Five minutes, tops, if you know what you're doing. I imagine a couple of slits in the line with a razorblade would start to sprinkle the top of the engine with fuel from the moment you turn the key. Now if there also happened to be an aerosol can of carburetor cleaner tucked between the engine block and header, then someone would have a very serious matter on their hands as the heat built up—say by the time they got into the channel after leaving Deer Harbor."

"Excuse me, ma'am, are you talking about the death of Skip Stuart?"

"Not saying I am, not saying I'm not."

"Edna!"

"Now, before you shove me in the gas chamber, I have a question for you."

"Ma'am?"

"What would you have done if it were Edward that he tried to rape that night on his boat, and you knew damn good and well that he would continue to do the same to other children out here because those dirty cops wouldn't dare lift a finger?"

Edna's question stops my head from spinning, and I finish the last sip of tea before answering her with a callousness that surprises even me. "I would have shot him in the spine, then hauled his paralyzed body to the dump and covered it in honey for the rats. That's exactly what I would have done! Good Lord, what kind of person does that make me?"

"Well, besides being a bit of a maniac, it makes you a mother kind of person, my dear! Now, that's enough of this wretched talk. Would you care for another cup of tea?"

"I think I'd prefer a tall glass of that dandelion wine of yours if you don't mind."

25

Home Is Where
the Heart Is

I'm surprised when I walk into the house Sunday after-noon and Dad tells me I'll be going to Seattle with him in the morning. It's a little shocking at first because I love being here and I'm settled into my routine. However, while packing my bag for the four-day trip I begin to consider the big reunion with my friends and my excitement grows. Six weeks away feels like years, and I imagine telling them all about this place and my adventures with Vivian, along with the mystery that we're working on. I can't wait to see their spellbound faces when they hear all about the witch and our resident ghost.

When Dad drops me off at the house Monday morning, the first thing I do is grab my bike and head for 15th with the hope of surprising my friends, who have no idea that I'm back.

My first impression is how different things look. Cars lining the narrow streets, the litter, the racket . . . my eyes are now opened to the city's grunge, something that I didn't notice before. With no one around the usual spots, I head toward the park thinking they might be throwing a Frisbee or running through a sprinkler, but still no luck. When I arrive on Matt's doorstep, his mother tells me that the guys are hanging out with a couple of kids from another neighborhood and have already taken off to Madison Beach.

Tuesday, when we do get together, I ask if they want to ride down Interlaken through the ravine and check out the Arboretum, but they aren't interested; and when I try to tell them about Orcas and the House of Long Shadows, they just smirk and look at each other. Wednesday, when I come across a couple of them smoking cigarettes while splitting up a six-pack of beer they've stolen from the delivery truck in the alley, I finally see it for what it is. I realize at this moment that everything is different; my memories are now just like old photographs from a life that existed ages ago.

At dinner, it's clear to Dad that I'm bummed out, and of course he understands what's going on. "I know it's hard, but this happens to all of us. Sometimes growing up means growing apart."

Thursday night, when we arrive back on Orcas, Mom gives me hug, and I even hold still as she strokes my cheek with the back of her hand. "What can I do for you, honey?"

"Just always be my mom, never stop being my mom." I run upstairs as fast as I can and dive onto my bed, covering my head with a pillow.

The next morning, when I come down for breakfast, I'm surprised to find her in the kitchen, figuring that she'd be off writing somewhere or down at the almost-finished cabin.

"Good morning, how'd you sleep?"

"Morning, Mom, I was awake for a while, then dozed off."

"Dad told me that things back home weren't quite what you were expecting."

"It was really weird."

"I'm so sorry, Edward, I know how disappointing that must be for you."

"I don't understand why they acted like that . . . it's like they all agreed I was an outsider or something."

"Thirteen or fourteen is about the time when this kind of thing happens. There's a lot of changes going on as your mind and body mature, and it occurs at differing rates for each of us. Just know that it's not your fault, and you did nothing wrong. It's like Dad said, sometimes growing up means growing apart."

"But I felt alone in my own neighborhood."

"Of course you did, and that's a terribly empty feeling, one that I still remember."

"I guess they weren't really my friends after all."

"Friendships change; it doesn't mean that they weren't real for the season."

"I think what gets to me is that all the good times we had growing up and the stuff we used to do together—that's all history now." I feel tears forming but look down and take another bite of Froot Loops to distract me.

"Oh, I understand. Look, I know this might not help much right now, but you'll always cherish your memories of growing up on Capitol Hill—nobody can change that or take it away from you—and you're going to make so many wonderful new memories. Just think of what the next thirteen years might bring."

"Thanks, Mom."

"Are you going to see Vivian today? I know she's started reading *Long Shadows*."

"Yeah, we finished *The Missing* a little early and thought we'd better get started since summer's almost over."

"It's not almost over—we have a full month left."

"Yeah, well . . . they have a lot of new business over on the mainland, and she's going to be super-busy the next few weeks."

"I bet she'd like a hand," Mom says with a smile.

"I'll head over there in a minute to see. Plus, I brought her something back."

"That was awfully sweet of you!"

"When the guys shafted me, I rode over to the U-District and bought her a Huskies sweatshirt at the UW Bookstore; it's gray with purple letters, outlined in gold. It's nice and heavy for fall."

"She'll love that for sure."

"You know she's kinda my only friend these days."

"It may feel like that, but don't forget about Bob, Brooke, and Megan—they're your friends too, aren't they?"

"I guess so."

"See, just like that, you have four friends right here on the islands, and that's not counting all the adults."

"Thanks, Mom. How's the cabin—is the deck finished?"

"It's perfect, even better than I imagined. They'll finish up laying the deck boards today, then all that's left to do is attach the cable railing. We'll have a little celebration down there when it's all done."

"That'll be great! All right, I guess I'd better get over to Vivian's."

"You do that, and have a good time. There'll be too much banging going on at the cabin, so I'll be working up here in the study today if you need me."

"Thanks, Mom, you're the best."

~

I approach Vivian in the apple orchard, where she's standing on a stepladder selectively filling the canvas apple sack slung over her shoulder.

"Hey . . ." I give her a wave.

"Hey, Edward, how was your trip back home?" she asks, pausing to greet me.

"Not the greatest, and believe it or not, I'm super glad to be back here."

"Bummer! Even though it was last minute, I know you were looking forward to it."

"Yeah, I was, and it went nothing like I thought it would. But hey, I brought you something back."

"Something for li'l ol' me? Aw, you shouldn't have." She smiles, jumping off the stepladder, and tries to get a peek at the bag I hold behind my back.

"It should fit; I asked one of the college girls to try it on for me. She was about your size, and it looked smashing on her."

"Hmmm . . . a college girl, and smashing . . ."

"She worked at the store! Here, I hope you like it."

She snatches the sweatshirt from my hand and screams, "Oh my gosh! Edward, I love it!" holding it up for a look.

"I think it's the best one they had—the girls at the store all said it's perfect for the football games because it's thick and has enough room for a turtleneck—"

Vivian throws her arms around me before I can finish, giving me a big hug, and mushes her face into my cheek with a kiss.

"It's the best ever, Edward! Thank you, I can't wait to try it on—I'll do it right after I shower. There's just one more sack to fill. It'll only take a couple of minutes, then we can go up to the house for breakfast if you want."

"Yeah, I've missed that."

"I know, Mom's cooking . . ."

"I promise, that's only part of it, Vivian."

"Edward Hawthorne, you say the sweetest things. C'mon, help me fill this sack."

26

Above It All

Witnessing Edward make this passage into another phase of life is painful, but at least Robert and I are here to guide him through the rough patch—a coming-of-age moment for us all, I reckon.

The doorbell rings as I put Edward's cereal bowl in the drying rack, and on my way down the hall I see the silhouette of a man and the distinctive wide brim and low crown belonging to a sheriff's hat, standing on the porch.

"Hi, Mrs. Hawthorne."

"Hi, Captain Stone, please come in. Cup of coffee?"

"Yes, ma'am, thank you—black, please."

"What'd you discover?"

"Well, judging solely by what I can see of the cable and its lack of corrosion, I think it hasn't been in the water even a year."

"You appear fairly confident," I respond, handing him the cup of coffee.

"Thank, you. Well, as bad as Styrofoam is about hanging around, the piece being used as a float is just a chunk from a cheap cooler, and it would have broken apart if it had been in the salt and sun any longer. Do you recall anything about a buoy being over there when you lived here before?"

"No, I don't."

"If you like, I'm happy to dig it out tomorrow morning at the next low tide. The last thing we want are dope runners using that little duck-in as a drop spot or layover along their route to and from Canada."

"Thank you, Captain. I think that's the best course of action under the circumstances."

"Consider it done. I'll call you to confirm that it's been taken care of. And alert us if you notice anything out of sorts."

"Will do, and please tell Kim, I'm looking forward to seeing her at our little gathering next week."

"Yes, ma'am. It's hard to believe August is just around the corner . . . summer sure goes by quick here in the islands."

After showing the captain out, I head into the study, and I'm soon pulling the thread of an idea while writing as fast as possible to hang on to it. Just as things begin to flow, the rattling of the Olga Livestock truck pulling up breaks the thread.

"Shit!" I mutter out of frustration, snapping the tip off my pencil when I grind it into the paper. Annoyed, but not wanting to take it out on anyone else, I take a deep breath and head to the front door with a smile, greeting Cowboy from the doorway before he gets out of the truck.

"Hi Cowboy, here to check the field?"

"Howdy, Mrs. Hawthorne, yes, ma'am, if it's not too much trouble."

"No trouble at all. You feel free to drive straight over there anytime—you don't need to come to the house."

"Much obliged, ma'am. I passed a sheriff's truck on the way in. Everything all right?"

"Just a friendly visit is all—thanks for checking."

"Yes, ma'am. I'm sorry if I disturbed you, I just like to do things proper is all."

"It's quite all right, Cowboy, I appreciate that. Now you just mosey on over there and have at it—there's only a few weeks left before harvest!"

"Yes, ma'am!" and with a farewell hand to his hat, Cowboy heads off toward the barn.

Though I might be a little frustrated by the intrusion, there's something about Cowboy that I can't help but like. His down-home nature evokes a casual comfort that's been strained these days. His easygoing simple way of life is one that's tragically being paved over by the machinery of progress on a daily basis, something that's going to eventually catch up to humanity and bite us all in the ass as we put more and more distance between ourselves and Mother Earth. Still, with all he's been through in life, his resilience is something to be admired, a preeminent virtue that deserves preservation.

Before I can return to my notepad, another truck pulls up to the house, this one hauling a trailer with a large propane tank for the cabin.

"Just head on down—Robert's already there waiting for you," I say with a wave and go back inside.

Now at my wits' end with these interruptions, I stuff my notebook in a bag, throw it over my shoulder, and head toward the water tower to be far above the distractions that appear unavoidable today.

These new steps make the climb much easier and less nerve-racking than the ladder that preceded it, and by the time I reach the top, my frustrations of below have melted away. Perched with an inspiring eagle's view of my surroundings, I look south and see the matchbox-sized Olga Livestock truck leaving the property. To the east there's Robert and the man from the gas company struggling with the propane tank as they disappear beneath the trees behind the cabin. To the north I catch a glimpse of Edward and Vivian walking out of the apple orchard toward the farmhouse; and beyond the tree line, the very top of Mary Ellen's red tin roof pokes out from among the trees. With the wind whipping the way it is, I don't dare produce my notebook for fear of it being scattered all over the landscape, so I put the folder under my butt and sit down to enjoy the rejuvenating purge of solitude while listening intently to the breeze, ever hopeful that she might join me at last.

AUGUST

The House of
Long Shadows

27

Farmer Down

Robert almost gives me a heart attack when he leaps up the front steps and through the screen door with a bang.

"What on earth!"

"I'll be glad when this cabin's phone line gets connected next week," he says. "Danelle just called. They're at the airfield with Kent—he's got a high fever and can't stand up straight. They think it's his appendix."

"Oh no!"

"Doc Beam thinks it might've ruptured, and he's waiting with them until the medical helicopter arrives from the Whidbey Naval Air Station; they're flying him directly over to Bellingham General."

"That's serious! Thank God there's one available."

"Thing is, Danelle can fly with them, but Vivian has to stay behind, and she asked if Vivian could spend tonight and maybe tomorrow with us."

"Yes, of course, whatever they need."

"We should get over to the airfield and pick her up. She can ride home with you, and I'll drive Danelle's car back.

"I'm ready anytime. Where's Edward?"

"The barn, I think."

"All right, let's stop there on the way out. I'll have him open up the windows in the spare bedrooms to freshen them up while we're gone; Vivian can choose which one she wants to sleep in when we get back."

~

We park next to Danelle's car and dodge a puddle of vomit on the way inside the Quonset hut that functions as airport operations, the pilots' lounge, and the passenger waiting area for the small airstrip. Vivian's easy to spot, sitting on a steel chair feigning interest in the magazine lying open across her lap. I say feigning, because from the glazed look on her face, it's evident that she's elsewhere.

"How ya doing, Vivian, honey?"

"I'm OK, Ms. Meredith, thank you. Is it cold in here to you?"

"A little; how about we get outside in the sunshine and fresh air?"

I throw my flannel shirt over her shoulders along with my arm, and the three of us are walking toward the exit when a man pokes his head out of the air traffic control room.

"He'll be all right now, Vivian. They just touched down on the hospital's helipad."

"Thank you, Mr. Reynolds."

"That's great news! I'm sure we'll get an update from your mom as soon as he gets out of surgery."

"I've never seen Dad sick before—not this bad, anyway. He was groaning and could hardly sit up in the car on the way over, with sweat pouring off of him, and then he started throwing up out the window."

"That must've been very frightening for you to see him like that."

"Yes, ma'am," she replies, her normally strong voice cracking slightly.

"A man I work with had the same type of thing happen one day at the office. Your dad's going to be OK, Vivian. He's tough as nails, and he'll back here in no time, you can bet on it."

"Yes, sir, Mr. Robert," she says as she hands him the keys to Danelle's car.

"I'll see you two back at the house—drive safe."

On our way through Eastsound, Vivian and I stop off at Templin's to pick up a few things, and also I want to shake up the haze shrouding her typically vibrant presence.

"Let's split up and do this as fast as we can. Take a cart and grab three boxes of cereal, two gallons of Crow Valley whole milk, and some Crow Valley ice cream. Choose a couple of different flavors, whatever you want, and then get yourself an Archie comic. We'll see who gets to the register first!"

"Yes, ma'am!"

Vivian rolls up the cereal aisle while I head toward the poultry cooler in search of two large fryers for the huge cast iron skillet that's been neglected since we arrived on the island.

I've no sooner put the chickens in my basket than I hear the sickening klop and squawk of Chase Stuart's leg brace coming up the aisle behind me.

"Fancy seeing you here, Meredith," he smiles as his eyes scan me and the empty shopping cart.

"Hello, what brings you over to Orcas this morning?"

"Oh, a little of this and a little of that . . . errands mostly. How's the old place treating you—seen any play-mates around?"

"Excuse me?"

"Sorry, that was a poor choice on my part. Samantha used to joke about your make-believe friend. She thought you were cuckoo, a real loony tunes."

"It's sad—she may have fared better if she had chosen other companions than her sorority of wine bottles."

"Well, that's the goddamned truth if I ever heard it! If there's something I won't tolerate in a broad, it's being a sloppy drunk. That, and facial hair."

"Noted. I understand that you ran into Edward once at the Farmer's Market."

"Yes, I did, and speaking of choosing friends, he should steer clear of that smart-mouthed boy he was palling around with! Reminds me of a degenerate I knew in the reformatory. That little son of bitch is no good—he's a bad egg, I tell you."

"Thank you for your concern," I say, relieved to see Vivian hurrying up the aisle toward us.

"Pardon me, Mr. Stuart, we delivered some fresh fruit to the store, and there's plenty of sweet cherries over there in the case."

"Thank you, young lady. I'll have a gander before I leave."

"I'm all done with my list, Ms. Meredith. Need me to help you finish up?"

"Thank you, Vivian, I sure do! Have a nice day, Mr. Stuart, and flat water on your way back to Shaw."

"Remember what I said about that smart-mouth punk."

"Rest assured, I will," I say, grateful for Vivian's intervention.

"Thanks, Vivian, you have perfect timing."

"Yes, ma'am, I thought you might like a hand!" she laughs.

"I'm not surprised; you're very observant. Which ice cream did you choose?

"Fresh strawberry and the cherry vanilla. Hattie uses the fruit from our farm, and it's so good!"

"I see you picked Froot Loops, Quisp, and Cocoa Puffs, too."

"I know Edward loves Froot Loops."

"Yes he does, did you grab an Archie?"

"Yep, it's under the cereal, and I grabbed Edward a House of Mystery too. It has a creepy cover!"

"I think he'll enjoy that one, Vivian." I smile.

Vivian and I finish the remainder of my list and make a beeline for the register while Stuart is back in the floral section giving a clerk an earful about something or other.

"How's fried chicken with biscuits and gravy sound for dinner?"

"I love fried chicken!"

"Great, but my biscuits don't stand a chance compared to your mother's."

"I can make them for us if you want; I've been practicing."

"You don't have to ask me twice, and I know the boys of the house will love that!"

"It's the only thing so far that I've been interested in learning to cook. I think it bugs my mom because she's always trying to teach me. Is that weird?"

"Vivian, I was an absolute mess in the kitchen until I was a few years older than you are and moved in with the Mels."

"Oh, Edward's aunts."

"Yes, and when Mr. Robert and I started dating, it really lit a fire under me to learn. Thanks to them, I wasn't feeding him TV dinners."

"Mom says those are inedible."

"She's right! I'm sure you've heard the cliché about the way to a man's heart being through his stomach!" I laugh.

On the drive home, Vivian's thoughts naturally return to her father, and the concern is present in her wavering voice. "He'll be OK, right, Ms. Meredith?"

"Everyone I know who has had their appendix out is still around today and none the worse for wear, including those in similar situations. In a couple of weeks, he'll be back to normal."

"A couple of weeks! That's forever at this time of year—with fall harvest coming, there's so much to do."

"It's going to work out . . . knowing your mom, I'm sure she already has a plan."

After a brief stop at the farmhouse so that Vivian can pack a duffle for her stay with us, we arrive home to

Edward on the front porch eating an apple while reading a comic book.

"Ms. Danelle just called and said the surgeon came out to let her know that Mr. Kent is going to be fine. They just have to make sure to get all the poison out of him, and he's going to be in there for a week minimum. Here, Vivian, she left a phone number for you—it goes straight to the room."

"That's great news! Vivian, Edward will take your bag upstairs for you while you call your mom from the phone in the study. Close the door and stay on as long as you want; there's no rush."

About twenty minutes later, Vivian joins Edward and me in the kitchen with a relieved smile and some redness around her eyes.

"I put your bag in the room I figured you'd like best; you can change it if you want."

"Thanks, Edward."

"How was the conversation with your mom, Vivian?"

"It was fine, Ms. Meredith. I was able to speak with my dad for a second, too; he sounded pretty sleepy, though."

"I bet that helps some, huh?" I say, giving her an assuring squeeze.

"Yes, ma'am, it helps a lot."

"Thanks for the comic, Vivian; I love House of Mystery!"

"I knew you would—I think that might be a creepy one. Hey, my mom asked me to walk around the farm and check things over. Do you want to come with?"

"Sure, we can go anytime."

"You two be back by five o'clock, and I'll start frying up the chicken."

"It's been forever since you've made fried chicken!"

"And guess who volunteered to make the biscuits for the gravy."

"Vivian?" Edward looks over at her, surprised.

"Yep. Don't worry, Ms. Meredith, we won't be too long, probably a couple of hours at most, back in plenty of time to make the biscuits."

"All right, you two be careful, and Vivian, if you need anything from Mr. Robert, you be sure to ask him. I know he'll be happy to help out."

I smile as they leave through the mudroom door and head off toward the tree line with Vivian chatting away and more like herself. I can't write a better summer story than we're living, and although the irony of struggling over my next project hasn't escaped me, I won't allow it to spoil the magic unfolding before my eyes.

28

Charmless

I wake up to the sound of my name being called and immediately think Vivian has come into my room, but when I open my eyes and nobody's here I wonder if it's the ghost. A minute passes and I hear nothing more but a weird sense of urgency that drives me out of bed and to the windows.

The first thing I notice is the layer of ground fog under the full moonlight, and then about halfway down the slope toward the cliffs there's a form twirling in its glow. I step out on the porch for a closer look but then think better of it when I realize that Vivian will never forgive me if I don't wake her up to see this. Quickly throwing on my robe, I tiptoe down the hall only to discover an open bedroom door, and no Vivian.

It doesn't take me ten seconds to get to the bottom of the stairs, and in twenty I'm already out the kitchen door, careening down the slope while hoping the rule of never waking a sleepwalker is nothing but an old wives' tale. Vivian briefly vanishes from sight as the hill terraces, and after my second time tumbling over the robe, I leave it behind with my one remaining house shoe as I tear over the hill, horrified that she's headed for the cliffs. By the time I'm within arm's length, Vivian is swaying with the breeze high above Rosario Strait, and there's no choice but to grab her before she falls. I hope she doesn't freak out, or we might both go over the edge, just like Holmes and Moriarty did at Reichenbach Falls.

Ready or not, I wrap my arms around her waist and pull her backward on top of me as we land hard on the ground.

"What the—!" she screams, kicking and swinging her arms wildly.

"Stop it, Vivian!" I yell, as her elbow smacks the side of my head.

"What's going on?"

"You were sleepwalking and almost got us both killed!"

"Really?" She stops flailing and begins to laugh until she realizes we're at the edge of the cliffs.

"Yeah, really! I'm glad you think it's funny—now get off and help me up," I groan.

The adrenaline is wearing off, and my feet begin to feel the sting of a thousand nicks and cuts from the rocks and straw-like prairie grass jabbing into them during my dash downhill. When I stand up, I instantly reach for the support of Vivian's shoulder.

"What's wrong?"

"My feet feel like hamburger." I wince, and sit back down.

"Yeah, the grass here will punch holes in them; that's why I don't go barefoot except in the grass around the house. Before you stand up, point the bottoms at the moon and let me look at them. . . . Does this hurt?"

"Shit, yeah! What the hell, Vivian!"

"Sorry, I couldn't tell if it was dirt or blood; there's some crud stuck in there. We have to clean them out so they don't get infected. Can you walk on the sides of your feet?"

Once I'm standing, it's clear that the only way I can make it back up the hill to the house is if I crawl on my hands and knees, but since the cabin is within a rock's throw and almost level from where we stand, I opt for it instead.

"Let's go to my mom's cabin, and I'll wash them off in the tub. She has a first aid kit there, too."

When we enter the cabin, it's under the dim light of a desk lamp that Mom purposely leaves on to accommodate her early-morning arrivals. I know that she'll have my head if we track a bunch of dirt and blood in here, so Vivian and I make our way to the bathroom at the rear of the cabin on hands and knees.

"Let's have a look at those feet in the light," she says.

"Turn the heat lamp on too."

"Wait till I see what we're dealing with first; that red light won't help."

Vivian analyzes my feet with a poker face, not saying a word until she begins washing her own in the tub.

"Here's what we're going to do: after I finish washing my feet, I'm going to find that first aid kit and some other stuff. In the meantime, you're going to wash yours and then fill the tub ankle deep with the hottest water you can stand."

"Is it that bad?"

"Well, you're not going to lose a foot if I have anything to say about it, Sherlock. Now hurry up!" she laughs, flipping on the red heat lamp as she leaves the bathroom.

"Thanks, but the first aid kit is in here, probably in this closet."

By the time Vivian returns, the near-scalding water has reached my ankles, and I crank the faucet off.

"What gives?" I ask, as it's clear that she's hiding something behind her back.

"Trust me, Edward, this is going to hurt you much more than it does me," she smiles and dumps a box of salt into the water.

"Holy—!"

But before I can fully verbalize my displeasure, she plants a kiss on my lips, and suddenly the feeling of my feet dissolving in a vat of lava doesn't matter.

"Sorry, but it's the only way to make sure we really get those cuts cleaned out. The trick is to soak them hot for at least twenty minutes, so when the water starts to cool, add more hot."

"You're good at this. I bet you'd make a great doctor." I smile, though my feet still sting.

"Farm life! When you work in the dirt and manure all day, you learn to take care of things before something has a chance to set in . . . plants, animals, and people. I think we're alike in that way."

"Makes sense; infestation or infection . . ."

"Hey, that's good!"

"I take it that you forgot your anti-sleepwalking charm from Ms. Elsa."

"Another brilliant deduction . . . didn't even think about it while packing, figured I'd outgrown this. How did you know I was outside?"

"She woke me up."

"You mean the ghost?"

"Yeah, she called my name again. I went over to the window and saw what I thought was her out there, and when I came to get you to see it, you weren't there."

"I don't remember anything after going to bed until we were rolling around on the ground."

"You were all the way to the edge, Vivian, just one more step . . ."

"Then you saved my life."

"You'd have done the same for me."

"But still, you did it. Better put some more hot water in the tub."

"Look at my feet, will ya? They're already turning into red prunes!"

"Just a couple more minutes, then you can drain it out and we'll put some hydrogen peroxide on those wounds."

"You make it sound so serious."

"Well, it's like that Fram oil filter commercial: You can pay me now or you can pay me later. If you stay off your feet for a day, the two deeper cuts will probably close up, and you'll be fine. If you don't, then you'll be going to Doc Beam, and he'll probably have to open them back up and scrub the infection out before giving you a shot!"

"An ounce of prevention, eh . . ."

"Yep. See, time's up—you can drain the water and blot your feet dry."

"Speaking of time, any idea?"

"Not a clue. Now, put your foot up with the heel over the tub so that when I pour this peroxide over it, the runoff goes down the drain."

"At least it doesn't sting as much."

"Good—other foot, please . . . this is the worst one. Hand me that spool of adhesive tape, a large Band-Aid, and the scissors. I'm going to tape this flap of skin down but use the pad from the Band-Aid over the top. That way, you won't tear it open when you pull the tape off to change it tomorrow. But no kidding, keep off this foot all day tomorrow—promise?"

"I promise. There's a clock on the stove, and will you grab my mom's slippers for me? They should be next to the door."

"Sure, I'll be right back, my hero," she says and kisses my cheek.

A few seconds later, Vivian comes running back into the bathroom and immediately turns off the lights.

"What's going on?"

"Here's the slippers—you gotta see this!"

Vivian helps me hobble up the short hallway to the main room, then over to the kitchen windows.

"Look along the cliffs toward the southern tree line. Is that a person out there?"

At first, it's a dark shape that might just be a shadow cast by the bright moonlight, but after a few seconds, it's growing larger.

"Shit, Vivian, whoever it is, they're heading our way!"

"What are we going to do?"

"We're going out the bathroom window, and I'll ditch in the woods while you run up the hill and get my folks."

"I'm not leaving you alone when you can't run."

"There's no time. He's like a hundred yards away! Where are you going?"

"To get a big knife! You lock the door and call your house!"

"The lock is still on order, and the phone down here isn't connected yet!"

"Crap . . . all right, two knives. Now what?"

"Up to the loft."

Vivian and I wait in silence for at least a minute longer than I figured from his pace.

"Maybe we imagined it," Vivian whispers.

"No, someone's definitely out there."

"I'm scared."

"Yeah, me too. But he can't get up these stairs if we don't let him."

Suddenly we hear a pop and hiss through the open dormer window, then an unmistakable odor.

"You smell that?"

"It's propane! We've got to get out of here!"

The sound of footsteps coming onto the front porch shoots an icy chill through my body, and there's immediate primal fear, which makes me gulp hard, as the door opens.

"Get ready, Vivian," I whisper, gripping the knife tightly.

"Edward . . . Vivian?"

"Mom!"

"What in the world?"

"Mom, come up here! Now!"

But heavy footsteps are already making their way onto the deck behind her. "Find them?"

"Yeah, honey, they're in here."

"This better be good," Dad says, dropping one of my house shoes by the door and tossing my robe over the back of a chair.

After hobbling downstairs under their critical eyes, we explain everything, and as kooky as it all seems, they can't dispute the fact that my feet are in pretty rough shape, and I left the kitchen door wide open.

"The propane!" Vivian suddenly shouts.

"What about it?"

"We heard something around back and then smelled it."

Dad soon confirms that the line has come free, but he believes it's due to a bad coupling because the installer had mentioned something about ordering a different version, one that he would pick up in Anacortes the coming week.

"There wasn't any danger—the line just decoupled is all. What you smelled was just the gas in the line. There's a safety valve so we don't lose all the propane if something like that happens. The replacement part will take care of it."

"What about the guy, then?"

"That guy was either your mom or me. Now, it's one o'clock in the morning—I think it's high time we all get back to bed."

I know Dad's irritated tone, and I'm not about to argue with him, so I hold my reservations and my tongue.

"Since Edward's in no shape to make it up the hill, y'all wait here and I'll bring the truck down."

"Thanks, honey. Would you mind grabbing my bag? It's on the desk in the study."

"You staying up, huh?"

"Yeah . . . I'm afraid the churn might be giving me a prompt."

"I'll bring it down for you. It's a little chilly in here; Edward, why don't you build a fire for your mother."

"Sure, Dad, I'll take care of it."

The fatwood kindling is so full of pine resin that it ignites with a single match, and by the time Dad returns, the fire is already burning bright and warming the cabin.

"All right, you two, pile in . . . we must leave M.G. to her task."

"Robert . . ."

"It's OK, honey. I'll pop down in the morning and check on you." Dad smiles.

Back at the house, he piggybacks me upstairs and dumps me in my bed, then brings a glass of water to my bedside table.

"No reading; go back to sleep. I love you, and you did a good job." He rubs my head.

"Thanks, Dad."

As he leaves my room, I hear him yell down the hall, "You all set, Vivian?"

"Yes, sir, Mr. Robert, sorry for all the trouble."

"No trouble, honey. You get some rest now, and no more sleepwalking!"

29

All Two of Me

I have a strong suspicion of what's at the root of my unease, and it doesn't take long to confirm—in fact, it's right after the sound of the truck fades over the hill.

The revelation that Edna had not died the way I imagined all these years was a huge shock. My cycle of emotions over this past week has spun like a roulette wheel, only with red and black replaced by anger and sadness, feelings that I was well acquainted with growing up. When I left Edna's the other day, it was clear that she had good reasons for killing herself off, so how could I blame her? But deep inside I do.

Sitting by the fire, betrayal is the word that first strikes my heart, but that isn't the best description; desertion soon follows. That's closer, and then I feel something pressing into me for more. My lips literally struggle to form the word, and once there, it's as if my vocal cords don't want to release it. Abandonment!

The nauseating wave created by its utterance confirms the prompt, and as I sit here with it for a moment, I realize that this runs far deeper than Edna, the one who taught me to never break a promise. She's a convenient target for my tarnished childhood, someone to be villainized just as my father has been throughout the decades. But that's not the answer this morning, as my eyes wander about the cabin under the firelight with so many dreams fulfilled. Then a hint of clove passes through the space, followed by the scent of wet fall leaves. Mom . . .

Scratching the surface is a simple exercise: My mom died of cancer when I was five. I must have repeated that sentence several thousand times over the years. Even Alastair didn't excavate beyond the cosmetic nature of this loss, and with everything else going on during that period, it's understandable. But stuffed into a dark corner of my soul, there's been a bitterness toward her from the day she left me.

Your mother didn't leave you, Meredith, she died—big difference! I recall echoing a facsimile of Alastair's words to my father, shoring myself up for the first visit to her gravesite, a visit that to this day hasn't been realized. My shameful secret that nobody besides she and Jesus knows. . . . So now, Meredith, tell me again, who abandoned whom?

The last time I saw my mother, she was propped up in bed and asked Carver to lift me so I could lie next to her. She held me close and stroked my back, saying that I was her biggest accomplishment in life, her unburied talent that she was so proud of. When she began to get sleepy and called for Carver, she told me it was time for her to rest, but she'd see me again. Later that afternoon, I remember the house went oddly silent, and from a window I watched two men in black suits roll a sheet-covered something out of the service entrance and into their black station wagon. It was Carver who, through his tears, tried to explain that she was now in a much better place. I guess those words meant for comfort somehow got twisted in my five-year-old heart, and I took them as, her better place was one without me.

I sit here with my tears until the fire is nothing but fading embers and the sun peeks into the cabin with an amber glow.

When Robert silently walks in with a large thermos, it's half past seven, and after pouring two cups of coffee, he joins me on the hearth.

"Morning."

"Morning . . . thanks for the coffee."

"M.G. or Meredith?"

"Meredith . . . God, Robert, I'm such a mess," I respond, barely holding it together.

"Well, you're my mess. Don't tell me you haven't budged since I left."

"I used the bathroom once."

"Why don't you stretch out on the sofa? I'll get this fire going again, just to knock off the morning chill."

"Any word from Danelle?"

"She called a half hour ago. Kent was restless through the night; they think it's an allergic reaction to the antibiotic they used, so they're looking at options. Once she feels he's better, she'll take a cab to Anacortes and hop the ferry home."

"If she needs to stay another night there, it's no problem."

"I told her that. Is there anything you want to talk about, or just thoughts you need to keep to yourself for the moment?"

"It's my mom."

I pause to collect myself before sharing this moment of shame.

"I–I've never even been to her grave," I confess with a stammer.

"I'm so sorry, Meredith, I didn't know. Is there a particular reason?"

"Completely misplaced emotions. Abandonment issues, anger that I wouldn't admit."

"I can see how that might happen. Think you've made some headway?"

"I believe so . . . funny how when you get to the root of something you didn't consciously know existed, you see other things more clearly, including your own folly."

"Anything you'd like to share with your nonjudgmental husband?" he smiles, taking a sip of coffee.

"It's a little obtuse, but for the first time, I see how a five-year-old girl shaped much of my life."

"Because your mother died when you were five, so a huge shift."

"My entire world."

"And then Samantha comes into the picture, and the apple cart really gets flipped over. That took a lot of strength, Meredith; it's amazing you didn't go off the rails."

"I see you paid attention in your developmental psych classes—and full disclosure, at times I'm not so sure I haven't."

"Yeah, well, I was a lowly freshman trying to impress the blonde senior TA!"

"Now doesn't that figure!" I laugh and smack his arm.

"I'm glad you're making peace with things . . . tell me how I can help."

"You already have; thanks for listening. Did everyone get back to sleep?"

"I think so. I woke up to the smell of bacon, eggs, and biscuits, courtesy of Vivian. She's practically militant about Edward staying off his feet today—even brought his breakfast up to him in bed."

"She's a real peach. Do you think we should take him to the doctor?"

"Vivian's over at the farm doing her chores; she'll be back by lunch. I say we let her pull the bandages, then we can all have a look. If there's any doubt, I'll carry him downstairs and throw him in the truck myself."

"Sounds good. Last night was a frightening ordeal."

"Besides the dramatics, I'm glad that's all it was and not the two of them sneaking out of the house."

"Don't even say it, Robert!"

"Well, it's a normal part of growing up . . . surely you're noting the changes."

"Afraid so. You know, at some point, you're going to have to give him the talk."

"Me! My talk came from the neighbor kids behind the garage with some medical book one of them found in the trash." Robert laughs, prompting the same from me.

"That's exactly my point!"

"All right, but you'll have to coach me. I'm not joking."

"And we're going to have to speak with Danelle and Kent about it too."

"Over cocktails, then."

"I'm sure they're dreading it as much as we are!"

"I suppose they are."

"I almost forgot—Vivian made sure I brought you some breakfast too. I'll heat it up for you in the oven before I take off."

"That Vivian . . . Robert, no need to rush. I've been so focused on myself lately, how's work going?"

"We've had a healthy rebound, considering the whole 2707 SST debacle. If things hold together, we should have a nice bonus this year."

"Now, that's a word I haven't heard you say in a long time."

"Keep those fingers crossed!" His smile wears the warmth that I need. "I'll let you get back to it—see you at lunch."

"I love you, Robert, I really do. Thanks for putting up with both of me."

"I love you two!" he laughs, kissing me twice before walking out the door.

30

The House of Long Shadows, Act One

Madrona Cliff Farms are having their busiest year ever, and with Mr. Kent in the hospital until tomorrow, I've been working the last week and a half alongside the men Hattie Gil loaned to Ms. Danelle to keep pace. Mr. Steinle even had Cowboy come over for a day to turn the soil in the large patch reserved for the late fall crops.

With Dad in Seattle for big meetings this week and work on the cabin finished, I spend the afternoons with Mom up in the attic going through boxes so she can determine what goes to the cabin and what gets tossed into the burning barrel.

While looking through one of the boxes yesterday, I found a folder labeled "LS Pub" just as she called me downstairs to the kitchen for dinner. I brought it along and laid it on the table, where she took note of its presence and smiled before moving it over to the counter and away from the food.

"That's my original publishing file for *Long Shadows*; it definitely goes down to the cabin."

"What's in it?"

"Generally, your publisher wants an outline of a book before you're given an advance to write it. That's in there, along with our correspondence and that of my agent."

"So, if they don't like your outline, then what?"

"If you're lucky, it's not far off, and they coach you into something they believe will sell. If not, they send you back to the drawing board, and you'd better get it right or they might release you."

"Fire you?"

"Yes, honey. It's a business—they can fire you if you aren't doing the job they've hired you to do."

"Huh, I never thought about any of that stuff before. Mind if I have a look?"

"Sure, you can read through my original pitch. Be careful with it, though. I'd like you to examine it in the study, and please, clean hands and no food or drinks."

"I promise I won't mess it up."

"My other condition is that you'll have to tell me if you think it lives up to the final product."

"Oh, for sure I will!"

Despite working on the farm for ten days straight, Vivian and I have only shouted and waved to each other from across the fields, something that feels weird after hanging out all summer together. We've talked on the phone each night but have both been so beat that the conversations are reduced to how sore and tired we are and about our progress in reading *The House of Long Shadows*, which we somehow finished yesterday.

Reading through Mom's pitch gives me a great idea about how Vivian and I can save a lot of time writing the final book report, and I make a hand copy of it to share with her this morning when she comes over.

~

Mom has just taken off for Templin's, and I'm at the sink washing up the breakfast dishes when Vivian comes into view, making her way up the slope. She's far enough down that I know she cut through along the cliffs instead of taking the deer trail from the chicken coop, which is the usual route.

As she walks toward the house carrying a notebook, it's clear that the sun-drenched days have lightened her hair, with pieces now almost indistinguishable from the golden dry grass that's everywhere on the island. She pauses and smiles as a gust from the stiff breeze pushes her hair around the tan face I've missed over the last week and a half. She continues on up the slope, wearing a faded pink-and-orange tie-dyed T-shirt, with cutoffs that reveal her long, lean legs and a shape that I've rarely seen out of her overalls.

I ask myself how Vivian could transform from the girl next door into something much more within a couple of weeks, but it's happened, and the tingle I feel as she gets closer proves it. With the last dish in the drying rack, I step out onto the rear porch, trying to greet her as I would normally.

"Hey, long time no see. How's it going?"

"Pretty good. I'm so glad to finally have a day off— we've never been this busy before!"

"Whatcha got there?"

"Oh, I picked this apple for you from the big tree on the way over," she smiles.

"Thanks! I was just thinking about Eve and the Garden of Eden." I laugh.

"Funny—well, it's a good thing there's only garter snakes on Orcas."

"For sure! Hey, you smell different."

"Mom got it for me when we went to Bellingham last week to see Dad in the hospital and make that delivery. It's musk—it's not old-lady smelling, is it?"

"Not at all, and much better than compost."

"Thanks a lot, Edward!"

"Do you want a snack or anything to drink before we get started on the report?"

"I'll take some Froot Loops, if you have some."

"Sure, but we're out of milk; Mom's picking some up at the store if you can wait."

"I'll just snack on them dry. Oh, and a glass of water too, please."

"I have our stuff all set up in the study so we can close the doors for privacy when my mom gets back. My dad's coming home tomorrow."

"Oh, he might be on the same boat with us, then."

"He said the six o'clock, so depending on traffic."

"I'm glad you'll be coming with us tomorrow on the Mount Vernon and Bellingham deliveries. I know it's a lot to ask, especially after the last ten days, but we can really use your help."

"No problem. You think we'll grab breakfast at the Farmhouse Restaurant again?"

"For sure—no way Mom's going to cook that early."

"I always look forward to that place! Are you ready to talk about the book?"

"I'll say! Out of the three, this is the one that really got to me."

"Me too. It's more disturbing than the others."

Once we're seated in the study, I share my idea about writing this particular report based in part on Mom's summary of the early chapters, since, as she put it, "it hints at the trajectory of the story."

"It'll cut through a lot of stuff that doesn't belong in the report."

"That sounds like a great shortcut to me," she smiles, tossing a Froot Loop into the air and catching it in her mouth.

"I'll start by reading the summary, and you can write down any highlights that you think fit. Then I'll begin reading directly from passages I've marked in the book."

"OK, let me see how much you've marked."

I hold up the book to show her the pieces of paper stuck between the pages. "It's not too bad. I tried to skip over anything particularly gruesome, or other jazz that doesn't belong in the report. You OK with doing all the writing again, while I read?"

"Yep, ready when you are," Vivian replies, tapping the pen on the pad in front of her.

～

The House of Long Shadows is the tale of a young woman who lives on Orcas Island in the mid-1920s. Her father is one of the top commercial real estate developers in the city of Seattle, where he is known as "Mr. Long Shadows" among his peers because of his propensity to construct skyscrapers on every plot of land he secures.

When he acquires the two-hundred-acre Maple Point compound on Orcas Island, it is to be their summer retreat, but he soon discovers that the isolation of island living doesn't suit his or his wife's preference as an ideal getaway. For his daughter, Amanda, however, Maple Point is a welcome enclave far away from the pretense of Seattle, and her fondness quickly grows for the place that will serve as her escape from the socialite expectations of so-called high society. When there, she whiles away the time reading at her favorite spot among the cliff-hanging madrona trees high above the cove, watching the abundant wildlife that flourishes around her private Garden of Eden.

Over the third summer, her father begins hosting friends and business acquaintances for long weekends of fishing and crabbing, something that the now-fifteen-year-old Amanda protests vehemently after the first few excursions of boozing and shooting their guns at anything that moves. The once-close relationship between daughter and parents becomes distant, and Amanda relocates herself from the main house into one of the cabins that dot the cove.

The 1929 stock market crash brings many to their financial knees, and Mr. Long Shadows enjoys no lasting immunity. Several major investors either go under or pull out, leaving him holding the bag on a debt so large that it becomes unserviceable in the current environment. At the eleventh hour, one of his local financiers, unscathed by the collapse, offers to help the family weather the trials. This young man is an unsavory individual whose family fortune was recently handed to him after the demise of his father, who fell overboard during a transit through the whirlpool-laden waters of Deception Pass. When reported that it was just the two of them aboard, it became a topic of gossip in every marina and watering hole in the San Juan Islands.

The heir never missed an invitation for those long weekends at Maple Point, and even though Amanda despised him, that invitation became permanent, only now it included her.

~

"Am I reading slow enough for you?"

"Yeah, thanks. I've got the overview—keep on going!"

"That's it for the summary. Now I'll read from the actual book, starting where Amanda has the blowout with her dad."

~

"He's a snake, Father. Actually, I take that back—it's dishonoring to snakes!"

"Oh, come now, my dear. He's a little rough around the edges, but you'll learn to accept him."

"I'm not sure I understand what you mean."

"Spare me, I didn't raise a nincompoop. He's asked your mother and me for permission to court you."

"Ha! I won't hear of it!"

"These are tough times, Amanda. We must all make sacrifices. He'll be arriving at the dock this Friday; try to be a lady and not make a scene."

"A scene? A scene? That's what you're worried about?"

"Actually, I'm more concerned about the ramifications of your tirade rather than the tirade itself."

"You mean because you and Mother are so utterly consumed with your station in life as opposed to decency?"

"That's enough, Amanda! I will not permit you to speak to me or your mother like that. Now get out of this house and take in some fresh air. While you're at it, consider how selfish you are before coming back up the hill for dinner."

"We must all make sacrifices, right, Father? I guess I'm your sacrifice . . . your only daughter sacrificed to a patricidal maniac on the altar of your illusion." Amanda storms out of the house, leaving the door open behind her.

~

"I love that part, Edward! Sorry to interrupt."

"She really lets him have it, for sure! All right, where was I?"

~

Friday before sunrise, Amanda takes one last look at the cove from her favorite spot among the madrona and whispers a prayer asking Jesus to forgive her for what she is about to do. She picks up a small travel bag containing her savings of nine-hundred-fifty dollars and a change of clothing, and then departs Maple Point on the back trail that leads to Deer Harbor.

As she arrives at the fishing boat in time to escape with the receding tide, the captain gives her a once-over and a chuckle. "You sure about all this?" he whispers.

"You sure about all this, what?" she replies, in a deeper voice.

"Oh sorry, you sure about all this, Mister?" They both smile as Amanda stands dressed in a grease monkey's outfit and cap that she discovered when cleaning out the cabin two summers earlier.

"If anyone asks, all you have to say is that you piloted a workman over to Victoria."

"You had such nice hair, Miss—I mean Sir."

"Hair grows back, but time waits for no one, Captain Alastair."

"Aye, lassie . . . I'll miss that quick wit of yours. Now it might get a little choppy in this bucket when we get into the strait. If you feel like you're going to let loose, try to toss it over the side."

"Thank you, Captain. I assure you that I will do my best."

A few hours later as the boat approaches Victoria Harbour, Amanda gives Captain Alastair a hug with a kiss on the cheek, pressing two hundred dollars into his weathered hand.

"Thank you, Alastair, I'll never forget you."

"Nor I you, Miss Amanda."

Following the captain's instruction, she heaves the bowline to a dock boy with a deep grunt and a cussword, and the pair disembark on the long walk to the top of the wharf.

Their handshake and parting words mean farewell to the only life Amanda has ever known, a fact that suddenly grips her.

"This is a rough port, sailor—keep an eye out, and take care of yourself."

Amanda barely looks up as she walks away from the waterfront, wrestling with doubt and fear for the first time in her seventeen years. Within two blocks, she reasons that the end of something marks the beginning of anything, and she will be the one to determine what her anything will be.

She ducks into a small café and has a meal. After paying the check, she visits the restroom to freshen up and change into a more suitable outfit. Then she secures a room at the Empress Hotel under the name Ms. Jane Montcliff, avoiding suspicion by paying for two weeks in advance and tipping the reservationist handsomely.

The Victoria Daily Times greets her in the room, and she devours it twice that day. Within her first week in Victoria, Jane has successfully ingratiated herself with hotel staff and guests, while managing to find work as a copy girl at the newspaper.

It doesn't take long for the journalism bug to sink its teeth into her, and Jane stays late honing her typing skills while crafting reports of current happenings around the city.

The paper's editor reads a few of her sample stories and is impressed enough to tell Jane that he would consider an occasional "short" from her for publication, provided that she works on them during off hours. True to his word, when Jane submits a piece about Chinese labor abuses on the docks, he calls her into his office, commends her for a job well done, and says that after a few minor edits, the story will run on the front page of the morning edition. He reaches into his desk drawer and gives her five dollars as a bonus for the piece, then breaks the unfortunate news that he is obligated to pass the story off to a more seasoned reporter for future investigations. "I'm sorry, Jane, this happens to every investigative journalist when they start out. Keep at it, though—you've got the natural killer instinct necessary to make it in this business."

Several more of her stories are published over the next season, but deep inside, Jane is haunted by the knowledge that sooner or later, Canadian immigration authorities will find her. She tells herself that all she needs is a couple more months and perhaps a few more published articles before heading back across the border, where she dreams of working for The Seattle Times or The Post-Intelligencer.

The week of Jane's one-year anniversary with the paper, she is called into the editor's office, where he closes the door behind her. "Ms. Montcliff, I have received a letter from Provincial Revenue regarding your employment status . . ."

Jane doesn't lie but omits details regarding her lineage, her port of origin, and anything else she feels immaterial to striking out on her own. The editor smiles, impressed with her determination and resourcefulness at almost nineteen.

"I'm not a tax cheat; I'll pay what I owe, and trust me, I do keep a record."

"I trust you; that's not your peril. Look, we've covered stories like this before at the paper. The Canadian courts like to make examples of people working here illegally, especially the Yanks. At this point, you don't exist, and if I were you, I'd keep it that way."

Jane bows her head. "This is my last day at the paper then."

"I'm afraid so, Jane, but here's what I am going to do for you: The chief editor at the Bellingham Herald is an acquaintance. I'm going to call and tell him you were the one who broke the Chinese dockworker scandal, and you're going to make a fine hard-nosed newspaperman if given half a chance."

"Do you think he will hire me?"

"He damn well better—he's my nephew! I taught him everything he knows."

"Thank you for all that you have done for me, sir. It has been an honor to work at the Times with you."

"Jane, you have the raw talent to make your mark—you hone that and don't let anyone push you around, either. Now, good luck and get the hell out of here, discreetly if at all possible."

"Yes, sir, but will you be in hot water?"

"As far as I'm concerned, you waltzed into my office today carrying a Bible and quit. Said you were off to join a convent in Manitoba or some eastern province."

~

"That's another really good twist. It makes me like her even more than I already do."

"I agree. Am I reading slow enough, the right parts for you?"

"Perfect . . . but I need to use the bathroom and grab some more Froot Loops."

"OK, I'll refill your bowl and get some Cocoa Puffs for myself."

31

The House of Long Shadows, Act Two

After a short break and a refill on our snacks, I take a drink of water to wet my throat and I'm ready to keep reading.

"Let's see, where did we leave off?"

"It was where the editor gets Jane an interview with his nephew at the Bellingham paper."

"OK, right, here we go."

~

The Victoria Times editor is good to his word, and when Jane arrives in Bellingham the following week, her interview is more of a formality than an examination.

"You broke that dockworker scandal; that took a lot of guts! Those ruffians running the docks are known to Shanghai anyone who mucks around in their business."

"Yes, I discovered that from my sources after the fact." Jane smiles.

"Uncle says you have a 'natural nose' for news, and you write well too. I need someone like you at this paper. Between investigations you will have to contribute to the daily line. That means much of your time will be banging out stories that are mundane, and frankly a bit boring by comparison. But that's how you'll make contacts and get the lay of the land."

"Yes, sir, I'm happy to start tomorrow."

"That's the spirit!"

When Jane is assigned to report on yet another in a long line of fishing rights disputes between the Swinomish Reservation and Skagit County, she does something no other reporter has taken the time to do: she visits the Tribal Council on two separate occasions and listens to their side of the story. Her reporting reflects tribal grievances that span back to a Point Elliott treaty violation and the resulting land grab by President Ulysses S. Grant. The young editor likes the story angle, perhaps as much as he likes Jane, and finds it a good counterbalance to the one-sided reporting of their competition at the Mount Vernon Herald. Because of her efforts, Jane finds favor among the tribal members and is invited out for a day of traditional fishing, a day that will bring her face to face with her past.

"Salmon is good. It's traditional and a much-revered part of our culture. But I like the taste of fried cod and sea bass better," the old Indian laughs as they pull the fish trap into the boat.

"Do you trap them as well, Thomas?"

"Some. But I like the challenge and the quiet of pole fishin' from the shore—much more satisfying, and it reminds me of the old days before, well, when it wasn't so crowded."

"*You mean whites?*"

"*No offense meant, Ms. Jane.*"

"*None taken.*"

"*When they tell us it's progress, it's never good news for the Indian.*"

"*How do you mean?*"

"*They said the logging camps and lumber mills were progress; they poisoned our land and water. Same with mining, same with population. I have never seen so much treachery. The amount of garbage these people leave behind is bad, and it makes for a sick land. The land . . . these waters . . . they feed us, not only in our bellies, but our souls. The progress, as these people call it, is only about what they can take, not about what they can give to coexist with all life. I believe you understand this principle—that's why you have heard the Indian side and recorded our words accurately.*"

"*I spent the best summers of my life on Orcas Island, a place called Maple Point. It was my refuge, where I sat high on a cliff among the madrona and read my books while the songs of the birds washed over me, and I was lost in the waters of an emerald cove. Then one afternoon in a single conversation, it was all taken from me. Even my family.*"

"*You still grieve.*"

"*I do, Thomas. Every night before I fall asleep, I imagine that I'm in that special place, and innocence is still mine.*"

"*Be grateful, Ms. Jane, you are still as God made you.*"

"*Please call me Amanda—that is my given name. Jane is just the name I use at the paper.*"

When they return to the dock that afternoon, Thomas extends an invitation.

"Ms. Amanda, meet me here Saturday morning at five, and I'll take you pole fishin' at my special place. I think you will like it, and it will do you good. My wife, Ruth, will come too."

"I'm honored, Thomas; I'll be here."

~

"How's it going—are you getting everything we need?" I ask taking another sip of water.

"Yeah, this part's easy, and you're reading great, by the way."

"Thanks, here goes."

~

Saturday morning, they set out with the tide in a small boat equipped with an outboard motor. A little over an hour later, they land at a small beach sheltered from the turbulent waters that will soon pour through the narrow passage.

"This is the best place I know for cod and bass fishing," Thomas says. "My father and I camped here when I was young, but you have to know the tide, even nowadays with a motor. Otherwise, we couldn't make it here without a two-day journey by land."

Amanda sees what Thomas means as the dark green water surges through Deception Pass, forming whirlpools with the incoming tide. Ruth teaches her how to tie the red-eyed jig to the heavy line and the proper method of casting into the swift current that's now sweeping through the channel at their feet. There's an instant yank as the pole tip dives and almost leaves her hands while the reel whines, releasing just enough line to allow Amanda to maintain a grip on the cork handle.

"You got one! Hang on, Ms. Amanda, I'm coming! Keep the tip up and reel it in, but you gotta keep it up—otherwise, you'll get hung up in the rocks."

It's an exhilarating two-minute struggle, and then Amanda lands her first fish.

"Beautiful codfish, Ms. Amanda, beautiful and a big one too!" Ruth says.

"It's my first ever!"

"Then, you have a choice to make."

"I don't understand."

"We have a household tradition for the first catch. You must decide whether to keep this fish or give him his freedom and return him to the sea."

"He's so pretty . . . I think he should go back to his home."

With that, Thomas delicately releases the beautiful codfish from the sheltered side of the boulder, and when Amanda asks why there, he tells her that the tired fish might drown if tossed directly into the current from which he was pulled.

After they fish the rest of the morning, Thomas builds a fire while Ruth and Amanda clean two of the fish, cutting them into chunks before rolling them in spices and meal. When the driftwood becomes a pile of coals, Ruth takes a heavy pot with lard, placing it over the coals, and when it boils, she carefully lowers the pieces of fish into the pot. Soon they enjoy the most divine lunch of fresh fish and dandelion greens that one could imagine. After eating, they take stock of their beautiful surroundings. Eagles soar high above them on the cool breeze, with the sounds of slack tide lapping against the rocks and the occasional squawk of a seagull searching for any scraps from their meal.

"Ms. Amanda, when you set something free as you did with the codfish, there is a debt that must be repaid," Thomas says.

"I'm sorry?"

"We Indians have many legends about these waters and the creatures that inhabit them. That was an old fish you caught, maybe ten years. He's seen a lot over that time, and to repay you he wanted me to pass along a story."

Ruth looks over at Amanda, nodding her head in a way that indicates the importance of what is about to be said, as Thomas closes his eyes and begins to speak.

"It was many moons ago when I heard a great splash in the water above me. At first I thought it was Orca or Seal and was frightened, but then a cry came; it was not Orca and not Seal, it was the cry of man. I swam toward the sound and saw a man thrashing in the water next to the hull of a boat with a green stripe. I rose to the surface and watched another man in the boat, circling the man in the water. He fought valiantly to stay with the sky, but the cold current always has its way with man, and his spirit joined the sea. Then the man in the boat left the pass heading west."

Amanda knows that boat; it is a 1928 Chris Craft, same as the one docked at Maple Point whenever her father's financier visits.

"Thomas, you're talking about murder! Everyone suspected that drowning wasn't an accident. I knew it all along."

"Of course, you did, because you have sensitivity."

"You know of this story, then?"

"Yes, I read the papers."

"Why didn't you come forward to tell what you knew?"

"It's not my place."

"Thomas, it's every man's place to shine the light of truth into the darkness."

"Not according to the society off the reservation, where a red man's word is worth less than a white man's."

"I wish I could argue that, but I can't—I won't even try."

"Indians murder each other, whites murder each other . . . there is nothing new under the sun, according to the Bible. We each have our own justice systems on earth, but after here there is only One."

"What if I write a column about this? There's no statute of limitations on murder."

"You mean a codfish's story?" he smiles.

"Thomas!" Ruth shoots him a look with her piercing blue eyes.

"I'm sorry, Ms. Amanda, you might . . . but in the end, they wouldn't believe an old Indian's tale any more than the codfish. No, if you must write about it, make it like those cliff-hangers they print from time to time. At least then the truth is spoken into the world, and the truth spoken is forever."

During the return voyage, Amanda shares the circumstances that separated her from Maple Point and her family. At least now she knows with 100 percent certainty that the man called Sullivan Shaw is indeed the murderer that she, and many others, have always believed he was.

The editor at The Bellingham Herald is intrigued by the first installment of "Death at Deception Pass" and agrees to test it in the Sunday edition. The response is immediate, and after the installments run over the next three weeks, readers are hooked. Most important, the rate of new subscribers reflects it. Now, a year after she joined the Herald, "The Jane Mont-cliff Mystery Column" becomes Amanda's sole responsibility, and she uses it to fictionalize the other activities that Sullivan Shaw is suspected of.

It doesn't take long for San Juan locals to understand that "Death at Deception Pass" has its origins straight from the demise of old man Shaw, and not only is talk around the marinas, bars, and other places where gossip is considered an art form revived, but now locals are making outright accusations that the police never even investigated the matter. If they did, they might have discovered that old man Shaw had grown to despise Sullivan, whom he found aptly named, as he had done nothing but sully the family reputation. The old man favored the older son, Fletcher, who died in a boat explosion while on the way to discuss a business merger with a group out of Everett. Convention suggests that with Fletcher gone, the old man had little choice but to bring Sullivan into his confidence. However, in a twist, he shuttered the lime business, sold off his land holdings, and retired. The story, according to his few friends, is that Sullivan would never inherit anything other than a small monthly allowance from the family trust.

When the old man drowned months later in 1928, he had not formalized his wishes, and several million dollars defaulted to Sullivan as the sole heir.

The unwanted attention ginned up from Jane's column now has people questioning why authorities were quick to call Fletcher's death an accident, while yet another was labeled a suicide, after minimal, if any investigation. Though Sullivan was disliked more than ever, he shrewdly positioned himself

*as the islands' benevolent benefactor by financially support-
ing the authorities during the Depression. It's easy to see why
they turned a blind eye to anything with his name attached
to it, no matter how untoward. During the most dire of days,
there were stories about Sullivan Shaw harvesting the virtues
of many a farmer's daughter in exchange for enough livestock
feed and nutrients necessary for island farms to survive. With
the financial duress finally lifting in San Juan County, these
farmers now have to look themselves in the mirror, as well as
their wives and daughters, with one exception: Laura Stewart's father. He only had to identify what was left of the sev-
enteen-year-old's battered nude body that washed ashore at
the northeastern tip of Blakely Island in the winter of 1932.
Laura was last seen aboard Sullivan Shaw's Chris Craft three
days earlier, and when questioned by authorities, he said that
the girl insisted he put her off at Olga, and of course, being
a gentleman, he did just that. With no witnesses to the contrary, authorities closed the case as a suicide. In a display of
monstrous cruelty, Shaw stated publicly that "she seemed like
a pretty loose girl anyway, with poor morals, probably a sail-
or's special." However, those who knew Laura Stewart were
well aware that she was a girl of fine reputation, and Shaw
a liar. According to her guilt-ridden father during a bender
at a speakeasy beneath Lopez Landing Bait and Tackle, the
coroner told him that Laura was pregnant and already almost
dead from head trauma and strangulation before she ended up
in Rosario Strait. The farmer couldn't live with himself, and
that spring he used a toe-trigger to blow his head off with a
shotgun. His poor wife, Missy, went mad, and within a month
she was institutionalized at Northern State Hospital in Sedro-
Woolley. She died shortly after receiving a botched lobotomy,*

but not before Jane Montcliff visited her twice and was able to piece together what happened before publishing the latest installment, titled "The Dead Daughter." The paper almost didn't run it because of its gruesome nature, but when the editor placed a warning in the paper the week prior, subscriptions doubled, as did Jane's notoriety.

~

"Thanks for leaving out the brutal details of Laura's murder—that really bothered me," Vivian says.

"No sweat. It sure makes you hate that guy even more, though! All right, I'm going to skip ahead now to the final chapter, if that's OK with you."

"Yep," Vivian agrees, catching another piece of cereal in her mouth and chasing it with a drink of water.

~

When Amanda docks at the Deer Harbor Marina in late fall of 1933, it's been three years, and what might as well be two lifetimes, since her predawn exodus to Victoria from this same pier.

The first stop is to inquire after her old seafaring friend, Captain Alastair. She discovers that the captain has taken ill and is convalescing in a room at the Deer Harbor Inn, just across from the marina.

"Ms. Amanda? I—I don't believe my eyes," the old sailor coughs out.

"It's me, Captain. Allow me to open up this room for you and get some fresh air in here; it will do you a world of good."

She opens the two windows of his meager lodging, which smells of aftershave and pipe tobacco.

"I hate for you to see me like this; I was much stronger in my youth, you know."

"Nonsense. After some fresh air and rest, you'll be back on deck in no time."

"It's you writing those stories, isn't it? You're that Montcliff lady," he coughs.

"Shhh . . . that's our secret, and this cough of yours is concerning."

"Ah, don't worry, lass, it's not the tuberculosis . . . at least that's what the doctor says."

"Good. How are my father and mother getting along?"

"I haven't seen hide nor hair of them in well over a year, Miss. I'd wager a bottle they haven't been on this rock the past two summers."

"Did they ever look for me?"

"There were inquiries, mostly by that devil Shaw, but nobody talks to that cretin anymore—nobody of any character, anyway, especially after that Stewart tragedy. Your parents, they kept to themselves, didn't really like to congregate with us regular folk. That doesn't help when times get tough, you know."

"I wish they weren't like that. Is Tony still living up there?"

"Oh, I'm sorry, Miss, I'm afraid our old caretaker friend died last fall. I've not seen anyone—no boats at the dock or anything else, and believe me, I look every time I pass that cove."

"That's terrible news—what happened to him?"

"They say his heart gave out; must've happened while he was sweeping the dock and he just fell into the cove. When he didn't show up to poker night, we went looking for him."

"Sweeping the dock? He never swept the dock. 'The wind sweeps the dock'—he told me that himself."

"Well, that's what the sheriff came up with when they found his broom washed up on the beach. Tony was a big fan of your writing just like the rest of our poker group. I never say a word, of course."

"Here I thought I was being more discreet. Who did I think I was fooling?"

"Maybe yourself, Miss . . . we can always fool ourselves. Those stories have caused quite a stir around these parts, especially that last one, 'The Dead Daughter.' It about gave me nightmares. I still get a shiver thinking about that part when the murderer turns around and is about to get his! Look, I have it right here," he says, shuffling through the stack of newspapers on his nightstand. "'She floats toward him, covered in barnacles, her pale green eyes staring vacantly, and with a crooked crimson smile, she presents their dead baby . . .' Obviously that's all about the Stewart girl—even the numbskulls around here know it!"

"I'm flattered, Captain."

"Why are you back here, Ms. Amanda?" he says, trying to stifle another cough.

"I'm going to visit Maple Point and was hoping to see my parents, maybe reach an understanding. But since they aren't here, I guess I'll just reminisce, maybe freshen the place up a bit."

"Let me get dressed, and I'll walk up there with you."

"Now, Alastair, you need rest, not traipsing around with me. I promise that I'll report back tomorrow morning."

"Miss, I don't like you going up there alone . . . the hardships, they changed folks, even out here, and with your storytelling, it's just not safe anymore."

"Thank you, dear Captain, but I've managed pretty well these past few years; this is my peace to make."

"Aye, so it appears. Some things never change. You're as hard-headed a woman as you were a girl."

"I accept your compliment," Amanda says with a smile, then kisses his forehead and takes her leave.

~

"OK, Vivian, I hate to do this before the final part, but I've really got to use the bathroom!"

"No problem, I'll get you more Cocoa Puffs."

32

The House of Long Shadows, Act Three

"Great idea to just grab the boxes," I laugh. "You ready? I'm not skipping anything else in the grand finale."

"Good! You left off where Amanda leaves the captain and heads for the house."

"All right, hang on! I say before clearing my throat."

~

It is just after three o'clock when Amanda leaves the captain and retraces her steps to Maple Point. Upon reaching the clearing, she wades through the tall dry grass, which hasn't been cut in at least a season, and makes her way to the small cabin by the cove that was her hideaway those final summers. The cabin is exactly as Amanda remembers, but without the anguish she felt the last time she closed the door behind her or the envelope that now lay on her bed. Written on her father's letterhead, it contains a simple sentence:

"Dear Amanda, I knew that one day you would return to us—all is forgiven."

There is no signature, no date, and judging by the dust, it anticipated her arrival for a year, perhaps two. She opens every window to allow the cross-breeze from the sea to expel the stale air of her absence, then hikes through the grass to the main house at the top of the hill. Although excited to be home, Amanda abides the promise she made to Captain Alastair and walks around the outside first, ensuring that the exterior shutters are still closed. When she climbs the stairs to the front porch, she finds an accumulation of dried leaves, confirming that nobody has been there to perform routine maintenance since Tony, the caretaker, died. At first the lock hesitates to accept her key, so she withdraws it, gives it a spit, and tries again, this time with success. The hinges let out a spine-shivering moan as the heavy door swings open into a dark void, where Amanda is greeted only by her shadow stretching across the floor into the house. The warm, stagnant air rushes to escape, carrying a musty undertone of dried flowers that fades into something reminiscent of a mortuary. When the light switch fails, she leaves the door open and hurries through the front rooms to open the windows and shutters, but what Amanda faces when she turns around stuns her.

Emptiness . . . the oil paintings, carpets, fine furnishings—everything is gone. She slowly walks through the bare house, opening windows and shutters to the echoes of her every footstep reverberating through the stillness. Her memory *struggles to retain what had been, while her heart fights to guard itself from what is now before her tear-filled eyes. Did I cause this? Amanda can't help but look inward as she ventures through each room, accompanied by the same doubt and fear she encountered at seventeen when parting ways with Captain Alastair on that wharf in Victoria. It's one thing to prattle on about the loss of her beloved Maple Point as she has done with almost romanticized flair, but it is absolutely soul scraping to experience it in person after three years gone. Eventually Amanda finds herself in the third-floor attic, standing at a large window in the waning daylight, lost in a trance as she soars over the landscape on wings fashioned from childhood memories. It's the loud creak of a stair tread that instantly brings her back inside.*

"You're trespassing," comes an icy voice from the stairwell behind her.

"I'm not trespassing—this is my father's house."

"No, this is my house, Amanda, or is it Jane? Regardless, you both are trespassing, and that provides me with certain rights."

Amanda's startle turns to fear when he reaches the top of the stairs, and his bottomless black eyes reflect the flame from the candle he holds.

"Obviously, there's been a misunderstanding, Mr. Shaw," she says, moving quickly to keep the double railing that surrounds the stairwell between them.

"There's no misunderstanding on my part. Did you get the note, the one on your pillow?"

Amanda doesn't answer him, as she now sees the large knife in his other hand, which he begins to slide along the top railing like a barber stropping a razor. She keeps moving to maintain their separation, as it's clear he has no intention of letting her reach the stairs.

"It's twilight . . . pretty soon it will be dark, just you and me, alone in this scary old attic." Then his voice suddenly changes from subdued and level to one smoldering with malevolence.

"Or perhaps you'd prefer a moonlight swim in the cove, like that knocked-up farm whore from your vile little yarn!"

The thought of yelling for help crosses her mind, but she recognizes the futility of such. She also knows that Sullivan Shaw is a murdering maniac, and a scream or plea will do nothing but excite him all the more. Instead, she speaks calmly and with confidence: "Why don't we go downstairs and chat about it, then."

"Chat about what?" he flashes an oily grin.

"Murder, of course . . . Jane says it gets easier and more gratifying with each one, and she's killed plenty. I'd like to know what you think."

Clearly caught off guard by her words, Shaw chuckles and steps back in deliberation. His half-second pause and weight shift to his heels allows Amanda to do something she did many times as a child playing in the attic: without hesitation, she deftly slips her thin frame under the lower rail, dropping to the bottom of the stairs.

Enraged, Shaw screams and lunges over the rail, losing his balance in the process and toppling headlong onto the steep staircase behind her. Amanda hears the cry and the sickening crunch of his body landing awkwardly on the steps but doesn't look back as she slams the attic door and races downstairs to get out of the house.

She flees under the light of a full moon rising, making her way across the slope as quickly as she can without tripping over anything buried in the chest-high grass. The moan of the front door hinges echoing into the night snaps her head around, and what she witnesses freezes her to the core. The terrifying sound of an injured Shaw shrieking as he drags himself across the porch is second only to the contorted bloody face illuminated by the moonlight, and Amanda knows that this knife-wielding psychopath will not be satisfied until he captures her last breath. She drops to her hands and knees, but it doesn't matter—the places where the high grass is pushed down during her escape are like footprints in the snow, and the full moon, a spotlight. Mere seconds behind her, those will soon evaporate in the heat of his rage, and he will find his quarry.

Amanda knows the trails of Maple Point better than anyone, especially along the craggy cliffs of the cove, and that's where she runs. Shaw is hobbled by his injuries, but the relentless stilted laughter and taunts drifting through the air are near-paralyzing to Amanda as she considers the irony in playing the role of his next victim.

"They're all dead, you know. They aren't coming to our party, dear!" he shouts into the night, laughing, then switches to a menacing tone. "I'm going to peel you like an apple from this orchard! Now come here, you dirty bitch!" followed by howling and more laughter.

She presses on until reaching the cliff band, where she picks her way around the polished trunks of the madrona trees to a narrow crevasse that is perhaps a yard wide with a drop of fifty-feet to the jagged rocks of the cove below. Amanda almost fell prey to this natural trapdoor when she first discovered this place, as the gap was partially concealed beneath a patch of broadleaf starflowers and vines creating the illusion of solid ground. Since that close call, Amanda made this leap every day in her youth. This is no different, she tells herself before crossing the chasm with a smooth jump, her left foot landing squarely on the other side. This island of its own, tethered to Orcas by a sliver of land, was her hideaway in the trees, the spot where she spent those summer hours reading and communing with nature. If this is her end, then so be it—there is no other place Amanda would choose for her grand finale.

Sullivan Shaw has gone silent. He's somewhere in these woods hunting her, and Amanda is certain that one way or another, tonight marks the final installment of "The Jane Montcliff Mystery Column." She walks to the rocky ledge and rests her hand against the trunk of a large madrona that leans out over the cove. Here, she will wait for Shaw under the watchful eye of the full moon as it dances across the water to the rhythm of the tide.

The footfalls in the woods draw closer, then his labored breathing and animal-like grunts, as he creeps nearer to the edge and a place where he can surely see her. The shivering tingle of instinct screams at her to run like hell, or at least turn around, for heaven's sake! She won't. Instead, Amanda focuses on the cove and her memories of those endless summer days when she was one with Maple Point.

~

A glow from the midnight blaze alerts the harbormaster, who rings the bell and brings out every able-bodied person from

Deer Harbor in the middle of the night. Fortunately, they are able to stop the fire from spreading beyond the house and tall grass that surrounds the property, saving the community of Deer Harbor from further disaster.

The smoldering earth and foundations give an eerie pre-dawn perspective when the four massive chimneys gradually appear as if stepping out of a heavy fog. It's by the light of daybreak that Captain Alastair discovers Amanda in the cold gray shallows, unblemished by the jagged rocks and yet to be discovered by the crabs. Her once-soft, pale skin is now firm and in the shade of death blue. He weeps and blames himself as he carries her body to the cabin a few yards away. Alastair does not leave her side until the mortician begins the embalming procedure.

The first clue appears when the sun rises high, and a metallic glint reveals Sullivan Shaw's monogrammed knife resting at the bottom of a tidepool below the crevasse. The second, and only other, is the green-striped Chris Craft found adrift in San Juan Channel with no one aboard and the keys still in the ignition. Sullivan Shaw has simply vanished. Depending on whether you believe island gossip or legend, either he fled to Canada or, as Amanda's friend Thomas insisted after testifying to what he witnessed while fishing at Deception Pass, the sea swallowed Sullivan Shaw, and the sea is where he will remain until the final judgment.

Amanda's service is held at Maple Point, presided over by Captain Alastair, with Thomas and Ruth by his side. In attendance are many locals who were faithful readers of her column, the editor from The Victoria Daily Times, and his nephew from The Bellingham Herald, both of whom ran features about Amanda and her pen-name alter ego, Jane

Montcliff. Amanda's parents, who were forced to make sig-nificant lifestyle reductions after her departure, declined to attend the service, saying that their daughter had died long ago.

~

The years pass, and Captain Alastair faithfully visits the cove each month to place a bouquet of wildflowers in the emerald waters where they had released Amanda's ashes. He utters a prayer, sheds some tears, and then looks up the slope at the four crumbling chimneys rising out of the overgrown landscape.

A decaying reminder of the innocence stolen by the House of Long Shadows.

~

"Gosh, I really hate that ending, Vivian."

"I know... It's so full of sadness, it made me cry. I hardly slept, and that was the night we were both exhausted from work!"

"I didn't sleep well either. Maybe I was holding out for a happier ending. It's OK to put that in the book report, right? I know my mom would want me to be honest about it."

"To tell you the truth, I've been so caught up in farm work and worrying about my dad that I haven't been able to think clearly about how to approach this."

"I hear ya!"

"As long as we spell it out, Edward, then it doesn't sound so bad, like instead of just saying it's a total bummer;

because it's a really good story, we just didn't care for the ending."

"I'm still mad about it." I laugh.

"Have you said anything to your mom yet?"

"No, and she won't ask, but she's curious—that's for sure."

"You know there's bound to be a reason for the way she ended it."

"We'll have to ask her when we hand in the report. I wonder what Mary Ellen would say."

"I can guarantee you that she'll have some highfalutin theory about it."

"I just don't like the unfinished business end of it!"

"See, that's the stuff we can use in the report. By the way, I think you feel that way because of all the Sherlock Holmes you've read." Vivian grins.

"I guess you've got something there, Nancy Drew."

"Excuse me, but I'm more Agatha Christie than Nancy Drew."

"Sorry, but I've seen shows with them both, and Nancy Drew is much better looking." I grin.

Vivian blushes and smiles. "Shallow end of the pool, Edward, but I'll take it."

"The end reminded me more of some Italian folklore tales where everything's great and then they kill off everyone at the end."

"I prefer happy endings too, but you have to admit that it's like real life."

"I suppose, guess that's part of reading modern adult fiction or just growing up," I say, a bit resigned.

"Aww, I think you're a romantic, Edward, that's sweet."

The ring of the phone interrupts our analysis, and when I pick up the receiver, Ms. Danelle is on the other end.

"Yes, ma'am, she's right here."

"Hi Mom . . . all right, yes, on my way . . . I will—see you in a minute." She turns to me. "Sorry, Edward—so much for a day off! She asked me to apologize to you because she knows we had this planned. Anyway, I think we have enough, except for structuring our opinions, but we can talk about it on the road tomorrow; it's not like we won't have plenty of time."

"No sweat—I'll be there at four-thirty sharp to help load up."

Vivian leans in closer, and her voice softens to a whisper. "It'll be the longest day, but I'm glad we're doing it together."

There's a tension bordering on awkwardness when she kisses my cheek, this time lingering with her nose lightly brushing against the side of my face. I'm enjoying the sensation of riding up a high-rise elevator, when suddenly the sound of tires on gravel brings me back down to the lobby.

"I—I guess my mom's home."

"Sounds like it . . . see you tomorrow."

33

August 17th

A second cup of coffee down the hatch, and I'm still mesmerized by the date jumping off the calendar only a few feet away. The seventeenth day of August, the seventeenth anniversary of my departure, and at the age of seventeen; the synchronicity gives me angst.

The day I left Orcas is something I only think about once a year, and in our family, it's exclusively referred to as the anniversary of my adoption by the Mels. A smile comes as I pour my third cup, thinking about the years of celebratory dinners out on the town with Melanie, Melinda, Carver, and Calvin, along with their reminiscences, which grow grander by the telling. Today is the first without them, and as significant as this particular one is, I know that today's path is mine alone to tread.

Within a month of acquiring the deed to the property, I noticed the mysterious alignment of timing and numbers, something that even a devout skeptic might arch an eyebrow over. I've always believed that there is another chapter to my story here; I just never imagined it would be written in real-time.

Beyond the obvious ego-stroking accolades and financial benefits, my rewards as an author have been many, but it's the relationships that I cherish above all. I never tire of the characters born out of the ether that both haunt and console me, their lives laid bare on the page with each encounter. I still marvel at the magic with each appearance, even with the feeling of the churn looking over my shoulder and whispering into my consciousness as I type. It gives me the willies every time I start, but as the stories unfold, I become more enthralled, lost in the twists and turns that land on the paper with the striking of each key.

After a sip of my now-tepid brew, I dump the remainder into the sink and return to my desk, hopeful that all this recollecting will lead these fingers to the first real paragraphs of my latest effort.

When Edna surmised that my return to Orcas was an attempt to reclaim what I'd lost by rewriting my own childhood story through Edward's eyes of innocence, she was right to a degree. It was giving birth to Edward and watching him flourish in the stable, loving home Robert and I created that afforded a much-needed glimpse through the lens of my own lost innocence. Perhaps that's why I've guarded this part of Edward's story so fervently, even selfishly at times, but no longer: his deepening voice, his change of carriage, more time in the bathroom primping, and then the tell of all tells—his attentiveness to Vivian.

Over the course of this summer, it's become abundantly clear that we've arrived at our second mother-son fork in the road. Thank God it's been easier on me than that rainy September morning when his tiny hand slid from mine at the threshold of Isaac Stevens Elementary School. That afternoon, when I arrived to collect him wearing sunglasses to shield my swollen eyes, the catty whispers of two mothers awaiting their broods hit me like a punch in the stomach: "She's that writer—you know the type." I just smiled and introduced myself, knowing that Madge and Brenda would suffer horrible deaths in *The Missing.*

When the bell sounded, a gaggle of children poured into the hallway, and Edward was soon at my legs, looking up with an enormous smile and proudly clutching a paper streaked with brightly colored fingerpaint. As we walked away, Mrs. Barr stopped us and placed her hand on my shoulder: "It gets easier, Mrs. Hawthorne. I wore sunglasses with my first two little ones."

I reach for a pencil from the cup in front of me and tap the eraser against the table as the tears well before spilling over and down my cheeks. But these are equal parts pride of raising him and the relief over what could have easily been a much different life for me after being so brusquely removed from all that I had known. I don't bother reaching for a tissue until the phone rings a minute or so later.

"Happy adoption day, Meredith!" the quartet shouts through the receiver.

"Oh my! Thank you!"

"You didn't think we'd forget, did you?"

"The thought never crossed my mind; in fact, I was just thinking about you."

"You sound a little stuffy, honey—you aren't coming down with something, are you?"

"No, no, Aunt Melanie, it's just the early morning marine layer; it usually clears up by ten o'clock or so. We're looking forward to your visit next week so we can celebrate together. The place has really taken shape—I think you'll approve."

"I'm sure it's wonderful. Even Carver's excited—aren't you, Carver?"

"I'm over the moon." I can picture his wry smile over the stoic delivery.

"How's your new book coming, dear?"

"A bit slower than I prefer."

"Well, you just keep at it—it'll be terrific as always!" Melanie shouts over the throng.

"How many people get hacked up in this one, Meredith?"

"Oh, shut up, Calvin!"

"It's all right, Carver. Several, actually. They're ground up and served in the chili at that truck stop along I-90. Too bad the sheriff ended up with a thumb—"

"Dear God above! You stop it right now, Meredith, or I swear I'm gonna gag!"

"That'll teach you!" Melinda laughs.

"I miss you all so much. Thanks for ringing—you really have made my day!"

"We love you, Meredith, now get back to writing, and we'll see you in a week!"

Returning the receiver to its cradle, I chuckle, proud of my quick wit for Calvin, who has the weakest stomach of anyone I know. Those four guardian angels have been my parents over the last seventeen years, and how remarkable is it to have just received a call from my future, in the very place where my former life ended, all while I'm living out a new beginning here. I wonder if this counts as reincarnation.

I give my eyes a final blot and lean back in my chair to look around the writer's retreat of my dreams. It's all I envisioned it would be, but when I finally sit down to work, nothing happens.

After three novels, several short stories, and too many articles to recall, I know my process well. I sit down in front of the typewriter, and somehow my fingertips find the tempo of the story while the keys and ribbon put the characters to the page—always.

Authors can be oblique, even superstitious, about the utterance of the B-word while working. In fact, nothing sends us in the opposite direction quicker than a perfectly innocent question from aspiring writers, journalists, or anyone, for that matter, about the topic. Never one to have experienced the dreaded condition, I have no internal reference for it other than overhearing someone at Random House once referring to it as C.A.S., or Constipated Author Syndrome, something that I laughed about in the moment. I'm not laughing now. Concerned but unwilling to concede, I lean over my Smith-Corona for the third time this morning, more determined than ever to get those first letters onto the page.

I bang out a few soulless lines until seven-thirty, hopeful that the familiar whisper will appear at my shoulder—but not even a peep. This is ridiculous, and after I mull over my predicament, it becomes obvious that my exasperation won't yield results. I decide to get out into the fresh morning air and take a stroll around the entire property as it was in my former years. Maybe this will break down the wall separating me from whatever story is brewing within.

The cliff trail gives my mind a break from the spin cycle and I eventually find myself on Edna's stoop.

"Meredith, dear, I'm sorry but I've got to make the nine-twenty over to Friday Harbor."

"It's all right. I was just out for a walk . . . working on the new one."

"Please forgive my distraction while I scurry around. Is there anything you need to talk about in the next five minutes?"

"The truth is that it's a struggle to get my arms around it. The prospectus is due to my publisher in September, and all I have are scraps with nothing knitting them together. I know it's inside of me somewhere; I'm just deaf and blind to it at the moment."

"I recall an interview with an author who said that when something similar happens to him, it's usually because there's an unchecked box. You know, like when you leave the house and wonder if you turned off the stove, or what have you. A subconscious distraction is what he called it."

"That sounds about right. I've been a little double-minded as of late."

"I've got to run, but feel free to stay here and keep Leo company. The rhubarb and strawberry wine just finished— it's under the sink in the jug. Just pull the balloon off and pour yourself some. It's a good batch, if I do say so."

"Thanks, but I think the walk may be more helpful."

"Well, here's a key in case you have a change of mind; I've wanted you to have one anyway," Edna says with a smile, handing it to me.

"Thank you—just call the house or cabin if you need anything while you're away. Edward left for Anacortes on the six-thirty express with Vivian and Danelle to help out with deliveries before they collect Kent from the hospital."

"Fabulous news! How I loathe hospitals. Vivian and Danelle must be thrilled he's coming home."

"I'm sure they are. They're coming back tonight on the six o'clock boat with Robert, so now with you gone 'til the afternoon, I have this end of the island all to myself."

"If it were me, I'd take advantage of the privacy and walk around au naturel! You never know; it might give you some clarity. Mary Ellen always said that clothes were a hindrance."

"Well, I've tried just about everything else!" I laugh.

"I'm sure you realize it's the seventeenth." She pauses long enough to give me a smile.

"You remember!" My astonishment shows.

"Remember? Ha! Yours wasn't the only life to unravel that day, dear."

"Sorry, that didn't come out quite the way I intended."

"I understand, no offense taken. Look, we'll get together for a proper celebratory reminisce over the next couple of days, all right?"

"I'd like that very much, ma'am."

"Now, I really do need to get on the road. Would you mind grabbing that canvas satchel for me? After I deliver this box of books to the library, I visit the animal shelter and read to their new batch of kittens and strays. Believe it or not, the staff swears up and down that it helps to socialize them. We'll have to do it together sometime, but it's addictive, and you may end up with a few kitties."

"That's a given!" I smile.

"You know how it is with authors and their cats!" she says with a wink.

"Yes, ma'am, I haven't forgotten Twain's words."

~

Edna leaves for the ferry, and I find a seat in the weathered Adirondack chair next to her fenced garden. The birdsongs are plentiful this morning in the natural clearing around her cottage. Long Shadow and I came to this spot often, as it was far enough removed from the main house and very peaceful, something that hasn't changed in the slightest. With more ground to cover, I continue my sojourn and a few minutes later break through the northern tree line at the field where Long Shadow found her voice. Its timbre still resonates within me, but it grows more distant by the day. Once again, there's that all-too-familiar discomfort around my eyes as I hold back the tears.

"Where are you? I know you're here; I came just like I promised," I speak into the silence, but my pleas continue to go unanswered.

By the time I reach the base of the water tower, it's eleven-thirty, and after climbing the ten-foot ladder to the platform, I scale the new spiraling stairs for only the second time this summer. The outer ring remains intimidating but yields the most beautiful views, and I push myself onward. It takes a few minutes for the stomach flutters to settle, but my back eventually comes away from the tank wall and I take in the sights as if from a stationary hot-air balloon.

Insecurity creeps in as I come to grips with the fact that summer's almost gone, and I have so little to show for it. I recognize that I'm clinging to a history that I'm not even certain of anymore.

The sting of my fear falls away with the stiff breeze and the sound from the large Olga Livestock flatbed, pulling a baler behind it.

"Oh, shit! Really?" I have to laugh, thankful that after taking Edna's advice, I had at least put my clothes back on before making the climb up the tower. I was sure Cowboy told Robert that they were going to let the hay dry another day or two before baling, but oh well, it'll be done, and we can enjoy our last few weeks here without these disturbances.

The men look like ants from this distance as Cowboy fires up the tractor and begins driving through the field, towing the hay rake behind. His two helpers disconnect the baler attachment from the flatbed and pull it over to the entrance of the field for a quick exchange when Cowboy finishes turning the windrows, which shouldn't take all that long.

I make the return to terra firma and head over to say hello and to check if they need anything.

"No, ma'am, we're fine. Thanks though," replies the man named Ronnie, as Cowboy spots me and gives a wave from the far corner of the field. "We got started a little later than we wanted to today, so we're trying to make up time. Still got to head over to San Juan, too!"

"Well, I won't bother you. Just let me know if y'all need anything, OK?"

"Will do, ma'am."

34

The Longest Day

I feel like I've just dozed off when Mom wakes me at a quarter til four with a kiss on the forehead. Throughout the summer, sleep has come easy in this room, but last night was a wrestling match with myself. I'm sure some of it has to do with the fact that summer is winding down, and that means back to Capitol Hill, a place that no longer feels like my home. It's also this last book. I had such high hopes that it would provide the necessary leads to solve the mysteries of the supposed witch, or at least the resident ghost that Vivian and I have both encountered. Instead, the only clues are those I brought here with me, and all that amounts to now are the fading memories of three paintings pinned to the attic rafters back on 16th Avenue.

Driving off the ferry in Anacortes, we see a familiar character in the boarding lanes for the first run out to the islands.

"Hey, look, there's Cowboy in the Olga Livestock truck, and he's waving at us."

"Yee-haw," Vivian laughs as we return his wave.

"I'm thinking about getting myself a pair of those mirror glasses."

"He's always got them on, I wonder if he's cross-eyed." Vivian laughs.

"Be nice to that poor man. He stopped by to check on the field yesterday and was glad to hear that we're picking Dad up today after our deliveries. He even said you were a good farmhand to have around, Edward!"

"I like Cowboy—why did you say, 'that poor man'?" I ask.

"Because the reason he's here is that his wife and daughter were killed in a car wreck back in New Mexico, God bless him."

"Gosh, we didn't know, Mom," Vivian replies with a somber tone.

"It was a happy coincidence for Olga Livestock when he arrived on the islands right after their barn burned down last year. Tracy Steinle told me herself that there was no way they could have built the new one before winter without him."

"See, Edward, that's a real-life coincidence." Vivian chimes.

"Yeah, I guess. I wonder why he just doesn't move to Orcas instead of taking the ferry back and forth every day? Seems th—"

"Maybe he likes it; not everything is a big mystery, Sherlock!"

"Knock it off, Vivian, I won't stand for that rudeness," Ms. Danelle reprimands.

"It's all right, Ms. Danelle. Mocking others is just a sign of one's insecurity," I tease.

"I'll give you insecurity!" Vivian says, crawling on me.

"Hey, stop pinching me!"

"Keep it up, and you two can forget about breakfast at the Farmhouse Restaurant—we'll be stopping at the 7-Eleven instead!"

"All right! We'll quit!" I say as Vivian and I are both laughing, trying to get the best of each other.

"Good. We don't have time for this type of nonsense today—there's a lot of deliveries before we pick up Dad from the hospital and barely enough time to catch the six o'clock boat back to Orcas."

"Don't worry, Mom, we'll get it all done, I promise!"

~

Ms. Danelle didn't overstate the tight schedule, but we managed to get everything delivered to area restaurants and obtain several new delivery agreements for the coming fall season, something that made Mr. Kent smile through his grimace of pain as he jostles to get comfortable in the delivery truck.

"Still pretty sore, honey?"

"Yeah, but I think something to eat will help."

"We're already cutting it close. But if we make good time, I'll stop at that drive-in, and you can stuff yourself silly."

"I really just want to get the taste of hospital food out of my mouth."

A wreck on Interstate 5 slows traffic to a crawl, and by the time we pull into Anacortes, even Mr. Kent doesn't want to chance missing the boat home. We bypass the drive-in and get down to the ferry terminal about fifteen vehicles back from the dock and with only twenty minutes to spare.

"The boat's late. It should be out there between here and Blakely by now." Ms. Danelle's comment carries obvious concern.

"That's a bummer—I could have had a burger and fries."

"And a chocolate malt too, Dad!"

"Yeah, thanks for nothing, Vivian." Mr. Kent replies, as we see my dad walking toward us from several cars closer to the front.

"Hey, pal, they finally broke you out of the hospital!" He says through the passenger-side window.

"I was going stir-crazy in that place. Thanks for the visit last week and all the help while I've been out."

"We're just glad you're better!"

"Me too. I'm itching to get home; figures that the ferry's running late."

"Unfortunately, one of the workers just told me there's been a fire on the Hyak after leaving Orcas. It barely made it back to the dock before losing power. Coasties, fireboats, the works. They offloaded everyone at Orcas Landing, and there's two tugs en route now to clear the dock and tow the ferry back to Eagle Harbor for repairs."

"Oh, that's just dandy . . . it's going to be a big mess."

"According to him, the best-case scenario is a two-hour delay; worst is at least double that if they have to bring the Vashon up from the Mukilteo-to-Whidbey run."

"Two hours!" We all groan.

"That's a drag," Mr. Kent says. "It's a good thing we're close to the front of the line because if the Vashon comes, about two-thirds of the cars behind us won't be happy."

"Yeah, that's a small boat. I'm heading over to the terminal to call Meredith and let her know, probably grab some coffee and a bite before word gets out and the place gets swamped. Do y'all want anything?"

"Man, I've been craving a burger, but I'd settle for a cup of coffee and a couple of hot dogs."

"No problem. Anything for you, Danelle?"

"One hot dog, a coffee, and anything chocolate, please! Need any quarters or dimes?"

"No thanks, I have a pocketful to get rid of."

"I'll come with, Dad."

"Me too!" Vivian shouts, following me out of the truck.

Making our way across the lanes of bumper-to-bumper vehicles, it's a fair guess that the other passengers haven't gotten word of the cause of our delay as they sit attentively watching the water for the Hyak to appear on the horizon.

"This is one of the things that can make island living a challenge."

"Yeah, Dad, it sure would be handy to have our own boat about now!"

"In this chop it'd take us a couple hours to even get over to Doe Bay."

"Vivian's right, and I'd be yacking overboard before we got into the open water."

"Gross, Mr. Robert!" she laughs.

"If you've never been seasick, it's awful."

"Were you green?"

"According to your cousin Jerry, I was as green as that water."

"C'mon, this way's quicker!" Vivian waves her hand, directing us around to the rear of the building.

We zigzag through the fenced parking lot reserved by commuters who prefer leaving their cars on the mainland side, because as Vivian explains, it makes passage cheaper and guaranteed as a walk-on during the crowded tourist season.

"Hey, this looks like Chase Stuart's car," notes Dad, walking by the Galaxie 500 parked a few spots from the ramp leading up to the terminal's back door.

"Oh, great. I hope he's not inside." I pause, placing my hand on the hood.

"Edward . . ."

"Sorry, Dad, but he's not in there anyway."

"How do you know that?"

"The hood isn't hot, not even warm, so it's been parked here a while."

"That's good detective work!" Dad says, and pats my shoulder.

The terminal is still relatively empty, and as I deduced, no Chase Stuart in sight. With a short line at the snack bar, we stock up on hot dogs and chips for everyone plus a few other snacks just in case we're stuck here longer.

Vivian and I want cans of Fanta from the machine rather than the tanks at the snack bar, and Dad follows us over, plugging them with dimes for the sodas and the three coffees he's taking back to the truck. As he's organizing the beverages into a cardboard carrier, we receive the bad news over the terminal intercom that they're bringing the ferry Vashon up; now we won't get home until eleven tonight at the earliest. Disgruntled moans momentarily drown out the terminal's cheesy elevator music, and Dad shrugs his shoulders. "Oh well, at least we have some food."

"If it's all right with you, Vivian and I are going to eat here and bum around a bit. We've been stuck in that delivery truck all day."

"I don't blame you. I'll be back at the truck after I call your mom. Let us know if there's any updates, OK?"

"Will do."

Vivian and I find seats across from the vending machines as folks come rushing into the small terminal, indicating that word of our plight is now common knowledge.

"Vivian, you'd better use the bathroom before it gets gross."

"Great idea, I'll be right back!" she smiles, hurrying over to the restrooms.

I've finished my dog and I'm halfway through a bag of Fritos by the time she returns with a satisfied smile.

"I'm glad I took your advice; it wasn't bad yet."

"Good, wish I could say the same about that hot dog."

"They look like a wizard's finger!" she laughs. "What's the first thing you're going to do when you get back home?"

"Probably take a shower, then straight to bed, why?"

"No, back in Seattle, summer's almost over, you know."

My heart sinks with her reply, as I've managed to escape that reality in the hectic pace of the day.

"I don't know . . . it's going to be weird."

"If it counts for anything, I'm going to miss you, Edward Hawthorne."

"Same here, Vivian," I say, averting my eyes from hers to the beige tile floor.

"You know we still have to finish the report for your mom . . ."

"I guess we do. Just need to work on our opinion, right?" I answer, still feeling the sting of her reminder.

"I was thinking about it yesterday after leaving your house."

"What'd you come up with?"

"Just that something's bugging me, and I can't quite put my finger on it."

"Duh, it's the ending!" I shake my head, not masking the dejection.

"No Sherlock, it's more than just wishing Sullivan Shaw gets swallowed up by an orca in that cove . . ."

"Yeah, it would have been way better if Sullivan Shaw was eaten by a whale!" I laugh.

"Or, Elsie—"

"Wait a second, Vivian; Sullivan Shaw and a whale . . . Sullivan Shaw, and a cove . . ."

"What are you rambling about?"

"Hold on . . . whales in Sullivan's Cove on Shaw—that's it!"

"Huh? I don't get it."

"When we ran into Chase Stuart on the ferry coming over, he said something about whales in Sullivan's Cove on Shaw Island. When he split, my mom made a big deal about that."

"So what? You know we see pods of killer whales all the time up here."

"No, she said there isn't a Sullivan's Cove on Shaw Island."

"She's right, but so what? He's a goof."

"Subtract the word 'Cove' from what he said, and you have Sullivan Shaw!"

"You're right, but why would he say that?"

"It's not a coincidence, I can tell you that! It's a taunt, Vivian. Moriarty did the same thing to Holmes all the time. Just like that psycho did in *The Missing* when he sent those eyeballs to the newspaper!"

"I don't know, Edward . . ."

"Look, remember what Bob said about seeing Chase Stuart in the cove at Indian Point throwing flowers into the water? Captain Alastair did the same thing for Amanda!"

"Oh yeah, that's right! Plus, when your mom and I ran into him at Templin's a couple of weeks ago, he was in the flower department yelling at a guy about not having any bunches yet."

"And the fact that Indian Point was once called Maple Point, just like it is in *The House of Long Shadows*!"

"All right, so let's get this straight: we're saying that your mother based the Sullivan Shaw character in the book on Chase Stuart."

"I guess we are, but why?"

"That's it, Edward! This is what I couldn't put my finger on!"

"All right, let's have it, then."

"The story is about a girl whose wealthy father gets into money trouble, and to save himself, he tries to marry her off to a wealthy sleazebag who is suspected of killing his own father to get the money—follow?"

"Yeah, so far."

"Instead, she foils his plan by running away and becomes an author who writes fictionalized accounts of a real murderer, in this case, all pointing to the guy her father tried to hitch her to. Eventually she returns home to her favorite place in the world, a house on Orcas. There's even a cabin by the sea, and she named the old captain in honor of your uncle Alastair. It's obvious, Edward; *The House of Long Shadows* is your mother's own story!"

The racket in the terminal suddenly no longer registers as my eyes remain fixed on Vivian's. The ramifications of her words land on top of me like a collapsing building.

"Vivian, it can't be."

"Why not? It's all right there, Edward!"

"Because . . . she dies at the end."

35

Take Me Away

After receiving Robert's call at the cabin about the boat delay, I decide to head for the house and whip up a spaghetti dinner for them to have when they get in. I might even take advantage of the quiet to enjoy a soak in the tub with a glass or two of wine and reflect on the significant circle closing at the end of today.

During the hill climb, I spot a few hay bales scattered along the slope, guessing that Robert must have had Cowboy leave them for another project of his. About three-quarters of the way up, my nose catches a trace of the hayfield, and I linger as the scent transports me to those childhood summers at this time of year. With closed eyes and a few deep breaths, I absorb the sensation of time travel, certain that when I open them, my sight will be through the eyes of that little girl hurrying up this same hillside for dinner.

With the sun now balancing like an orange ball atop the western tree line, I turn around to witness the grassy slope bathed in copper below me. Today my shadow runs long, and with it comes a pang of sadness as I consider my father's interpretation of the house on the hill above.

Alastair always said that I would build a life on my own terms, but were those terms predicated on subconsciously writing my way back here? I've lived half my life haunted by dreams of restoration, and now I'm questioning whether I'm trapped like my own shadow, fading with the sunset, never to realize its quest. Wouldn't that make one hell of a plot twist: "Author writes herself home, only to discover that she never writes again." Chalk up another reason for the silent keys of my typewriter this summer.

Back at the house, I continue my deliberation while making the spaghetti, concluding that the circular conversation is unproductive and creating even more frustration, not at all how I imagined this day would end.

I uncork a bottle of white wine from the refrigerator and head upstairs to fill the tub for a nice long soak and to reminisce about my summers here, hoping to make peace with the fact that I have indeed fulfilled my promise to return for her.

With candles spread about the bathroom, I turn off the lights and slip into the large clawfoot tub spiked with Calgon bath beads in the scent of English Ivy. In the soft glow, I take a sip of wine straight from the bottle and relax into those summer memories now presenting themselves in chronological order.

After I twice add hot water to the tub, my trip down memory lane arrives at the moment my father drove me to the Doe Bay dock for that alleged quick sunset cruise.

It's the first time that I allow tears to fall about his betrayal: what in the hell was he thinking to offer me up to that sicko! Deep in my soul, I still hold out hope that somewhere in his heart he was proud that I defended my honor, no matter what it cost him in the end. I exhale with a heavy sigh, acknowledging the common theme among little girls of always wanting to please their father, regardless of the circumstances.

At least Alastair was right—I have built that life on my own terms, which he talked about, whatever it brings . . . I smile.

<h1 style="text-align:center">36</h1>

<h1 style="text-align:center">Great Scott!</h1>

We sit in the terminal, mulling over Vivian's words and my observations. Chase Stuart's taunting gestures make it obvious that he knew the book was accusing him of murder, just as Jane had done to Sullivan Shaw, and we know how that played out. But there's no way a guy so badly crippled can possibly do anything to my mom; plus, she's got a .357 Magnum, and holy cow, can she shoot it. But we're missing something—I can feel it in my gut.

Once again, the loudspeaker crackles with its annoying buzz, dragging me out of the void I'm descending into.

"Paging Sybil Sinclair . . . Sybil Sinclair, please see the attendant."

"Any relation?" I ask, partly expecting a yes.

"Not to Sybil St. Clair, why?"

"St. Clair? Huh . . . I thought she said Sinclair."

"It's hard to understand anything over that staticky thing. If she'd pull her puss back from the microphone, it might help."

I laugh, but my mind immediately starts turning again. "Didn't you tell me that the Olga barn burned down the same week my dad came to look at the house?"

"Yeah, it was two days after."

"Wait here, I'll be back in a second."

"Don't fall in." She laughs.

Instead of the restroom, I ditch out the adjacent door to escape the insufferable music and squawking that reminds me of the teacher in a Charlie Brown cartoon. Leaning against the railing, I wonder why the name Sybil St. Clair sounds so familiar. I can't let it go . . . and after a solid minute of repeating her name aloud, I have it.

"Vivian!" I shout into the terminal, and she comes tearing outside to join me.

"What's wrong?"

"Coincidence! That's what's wrong!" I lean back over the rail, thinking I might upchuck that hot dog and everything else.

"What are you talking about?"

"St. Clair," I reply, after gathering myself.

"She lives over on Lopez. What about her?"

"Vivian, I have a really bad feeling. C'mon!"

"Tell me what's going on!" Her words match my urgency as I fly down the back ramp into the parking lot.

"You're sure this is Stuart's car, right?" I ask as I reach for the driver's-side door handle.

"Yeah, there's a dent in the bumper where that guy on the ferry dinged him. What are you doing?"

"Just keep watch."

"You can't just start going through his car—what if he catches us?"

"I hope he does! Now keep your voice down, will ya?"

After finding both doors locked, I cup my hands on the glass and push my face into them, looking for any evidence that will confirm my fears. The small jar of Vaseline in the front ashtray draws my attention, as does the bottle of Brut on the passenger seat. As my eyes scan the backseat, they catch a glint of metal peeking out from under his waxed jacket on the floorboard. As I focus in, I see the leather strapping and canvas slings of that familiar leg brace, and it puts a knot in my stomach.

"Of course! How stupid of me," I mutter, smacking the windows in frustration as I try to order my next steps.

"What? What is it?"

"We need to get my dad. Right now!"

"Edward, you gotta tell me what's going on!" Vivian shouts as we dash between the cars.

"My mom is in *The House of Long Shadows* with Sullivan Shaw, and she doesn't know it!"

~

"Neither the cabin nor the house line connects," Dad says from inside the phone booth.

"Call Mary Ellen, Mr. Robert. She has guns, too!"

He digs into his pocket for another dime and jams it into the slot.

"It's dead—our lines are all tied together, so the whole relay must be out."

"Isn't Mary Ellen over on San Juan Island doing her cat thing today?" I ask.

"Oh, that's right! I bet she's stuck over there waiting to get home just like we are."

"Dad, there's no time; you have to call Sheriff Chancey." My mouth is so dry the words are hardly audible as I plead with him.

"Edward, are you absolutely positive about this?"

"It's him, Dad! If you don't, I'm going to!"

Dad tells the dispatcher there's an intruder on the property, that the phone lines are down, and Mom is alone out there, unaware that she's in danger.

Slamming the receiver back on the hook, he exits the booth with a level of concern I've never seen before.

"The sheriff and his deputies are on the way, but they're coming from another call in Cormorant, and that's fifty minutes driving like a bat out of hell in the day. It'll take them over an hour in this light."

"She'll be OK, Dad." I try to mask the doubt flooding over me.

"She'd better be."

37

The Churn

The grandfather clock strikes nine and I look like a prune, so I give the stopper a yank and climb out of the old tub to the gurgling sound of water going down the drain. After drying off and recorking the wine bottle, I dress in my favorite pajamas and flip the light switch, only to remain under candlelight. I try the bedroom switch but nothing happens, and I chuckle that today of all days is the one we lose power. I grab the largest candle from the bathroom and check the electric clock on the bedside table, seeing that it stopped just after eight. It strikes me as unusual because from what I remember, outages usually happened during the day.

Donning my robe and house shoes, I step out onto the bedroom porch for a look around and immediately notice that it even seems quieter outdoors without the power on. Gazing up at the moonless sky, I watch the stars floating against the ink-black curtain, marveling at their numbers and wondering what God named each one of them, unable to comprehend how vast His language must be. The sound of tires in the distance draws me back to earth, and I smile that Robert and Edward have made it home earlier than anticipated.

Shielding the candle flame, I make my way downstairs, where I'm greeted by my ghostlike reflection in the wavy glass panel of the front door. The distorted image within the bubble of yellow light makes for an eerie vision, and I hurry to the telephone desk to jot a note and a crude sketch of the scene while it's still fresh in my mind.

The continued silence is odd. Robert and Edward should be walking in by now, but I haven't heard anything beyond what I believed to be tires on gravel, much less the familiar clunk of the station wagon's heavy doors.

Thinking it likely that they stopped at Danelle's first to help Kent get situated, I pick up the phone only to discover that the line is dead. "Well, that's just great," I grumble, leaving the candle on the desk as I walk down the hallway, watching my dark silhouette in the glass grow with each step. When I arrive at the front door, the hairs on the back of my neck stand at attention, and I chastise myself for making Robert compromise regarding his gun proposition. The pistol I eventually agreed to is in my desk drawer down at the cabin. A lot of good that does me now, but I try to laugh it off. Meredith, you've got to stop writing those kinds of books! Though the flame is tiny, the candle still bleeds enough light into the foyer to make it impossible to see anything beyond the glass, and I enter the study to escape its flicker.

As I step closer to the bay window, my eyes adjust to the darkness enough to detect the jagged horizon created by the tree line under starlight. At first, I think there's movement out there, but in the pitch black it's hard to judge how near or far away it is, and after a few seconds of nothing else, I dismiss it as the product of an overactive imagination. My stomach growls, and just as I'm about to head into the kitchen to reheat the spaghetti and meatballs, I see it again. A figure darker than the foreground, it's a peculiar triangular shape, wider at the bottom and moving in a loping awkward way—definitely not a herd of deer or my imagination. Whatever this is, it's clearly heading toward the house, and my fear takes over.

I rush out of the study, round the corner, and make it to the telephone desk in time to blow out the candle as the first footfall lands on the porch steps. I reach for the sconce, but my hands slip off when I twist it. I frantically rub my palms against my robe, desperate to remove the bath oil residue from them, and try again; this time the mechanism pops and I duck inside the small room, restoring the panel just as the knock on the front door echoes through the foyer.

My heart is pounding so hard that it almost drowns out the second knock, this one even louder and more insistent.

"Meredith, dear, it's Mary Ellen—are you all right?"

"Thank God!" I exhale for the first time in what feels like an eternity.

The banging is now frantic as I emerge from my hideaway and rush down the hallway. What I find when I open the door is incomprehensible. My eyes are instantly drawn to the flashlight lying on the porch, its beam fixed on Edna's expressionless stare and the pool of blood rapidly forming around her head.

"Edna!" I scream. She doesn't move or make a sound, and before I can tend to her, a voice emerges from the darkness as a boot lands on the bottom step.

"Edna? Well, boy-howdy, and goddamn! I thought that dyke was already dead!"

My adrenaline wants me to fly off the porch and attack, but something pulls me back inside the house. I slam and lock the door, then retreat to the hidden room just as the glass shatters.

His curses and rants fill the hallway as he bangs and fiddles with the lock until it clunks, and I feel the draft of the open door, along with the smell of gasoline.

"Deadna! Woo-hoo, now that's as surprisin' as a two-petered pony!" My mind reels with his laughter, and in complete confusion, I wonder why, Cowboy, why!

"Come out, come out, wherever you are, little filly . . ." His calls are followed by sloshes, first on the staircase and wall, then in the hallway next to the telephone desk. Seconds later, the gasoline begins to find its way through the small gaps and is leaking all over me. God, he's going to burn us down!

The dripping stops, but I don't dare move or make a sound as I try to keep the gas out of my eyes. It's quiet for almost a full minute, but a slight creak tells me he's lurking on the stairs, listening for any clue as to whether I'm up or down. Something catches his attention, and he takes off to the second floor and down the hall toward the attic. I pop the latch to make my escape and dash into the dark hallway, then trip headlong over something next to the telephone desk and fall flat on my face with a thud. It's the damn gas can! Scrambling to my feet as his boots reverse course on the attic stairs, I shed the soaked robe and flee through the kitchen and out the French doors. I clear the porch steps in two, and hide behind the rocks near the top of the slope, so full of adrenaline it's impossible to keep my thoughts straight.

"You can't hide from your book, or me, Meredith!" he screams into the night, coming out of the house carrying the gas can.

He descends the stairs and after a few paces in my direction, pauses to study the surroundings like a predator stalking its prey. The smell of fuel covering me is nauseating, almost overwhelming, even in the state of shock that I'm in. Just as I think he's going to change direction; he reaches into his back pocket for something . . . a road flare. Seconds later, under its glow, he lifts the cowboy hat and his long hair with it. I finally understand. My God, Chase Stuart!

"I know you're out there, Meredith! I can hear you breathing!"

With those chilling words, he throws the flare at one of the hay bales scattered along the slope, and by the way it bursts into flames, it's clearly been primed. The blaze lights up enough terrain that I'm easily spotted in these white pajamas, and I zag from boulder to boulder as another flare hits a bale between us, this time catching the slope grass on fire with it. Once again, I think about getting to that pistol, but the flames are advancing too rapidly, and it's obvious he's created a horseshoe of fire, flushing me toward the cliffs.

I make it behind the last boulder as a thick cloud of smoke barrels over the top, causing me to gasp for air and claw at my burning eyes. The flames are right behind it, and I know that a well-placed cinder will set me off at any moment. Out of real estate and ideas, it dawns on me that I'm inside the nightmare I had years earlier, and I frantically weigh my options: do I go over the cliff and take my chances, or remain here and burn with everything else?

Then comes the unmistakable whisper of the Churn over my shoulder: "It's not about writing the epilogue, Meredith, it's about living it."

38

No Greater Love—
The Epilogue

It's during her seventeenth summer that the war canoes of Haida arrive from the north to take slaves. They burn, kill, and capture their way from the northwest shore of the island through the interior without mercy. It seems as if Long Shadow's village will be spared this year, but then a raiding party makes landfall at a small beach to the south of the village.

Liwa was one of those keeping watch at the outpost, and known for her quick feet, she jumps from hiding and runs to warn the village. But before she reaches the cover of the forest, a lone Haida arrow finds her back and cuts through her ribs, sinking deep into her heart. A favorite memory flashes across her eyes with her final gasp: it's of her and Long Shadow sitting at this very spot, watching an eagle fish and feed her young.

Minutes later, another band of Haida assault the village from the west, and the Lummi meet them with all the ferocity they can muster, holding their ground for nearly an hour. But when the raiders pour in from the south, it's an annihilation.

With nowhere left to go, Long Shadow turns to face the carnage of her village in flames. Surrounded by the slaughter of her people, she stands defiant at the edge of the cliff as two Haida warriors approach with cords meant to bind her. Everything she knows and loves is dead, all ripped away in an August afternoon, her life stolen by those who have no right to it. She will never endure the raping and enslavement by these savages, and with resolve more than resignation, Long Shadow releases her foothold from the precipice on which she stands and enters a place beneath the waves.

It is here in the timeless solitude of the sea that she grieves until one day when the faint sounds of innocence descend from the cliffs above.

The tender voice of the little girl returns daily as she reads to her dolls while talking through heart wrenching tears to the mother who recently made the journey beyond. Long Shadow listens as the musings wash through her like a warm healing current, and though she still weeps, she now weeps for the little girl, and with gratitude for her own years above the sea.

~

Tonight as the Churn reveals this missing chapter of their story, I finally understand that it was my own innocence and heartbreak that summoned Long Shadow from the waves. Call it conjuring if you will, but the Custodian of these cold emerald waters honored the purity of our shared sorrow with a chance of redemption.

Now as I find myself drenched in gasoline and precariously perched some fifty feet above the sea, I have to wonder: am I to be her substitution?

"You just couldn't leave me alone. You should never have come back here." Stuart coughs through the cloud of smoke rolling over us and out to sea.

"I had no choice."

"There's always a choice, Meredith," he replies emotionlessly, sloshing more gasoline on the rocky ground in front of me.

After all the research and hours of conversations with Alastair, I know that Chase Stuart's personality type can't resist being lauded for his sinister accomplishments.

"Not for some of us, Chase. But I'll give credit where it's due; you fooled me and were clever enough to use my own words to do it."

"Oh, please, tell me more."

"You're clearly a psychopath, fresh from the pages of my books."

"Well, that's not very flattering now, is it?" he replies with a chuckle.

"Oh, but your creation of Cowboy and his timely arrival bearing such a tragic story—brilliant! Probably the only way to disarm these normally suspicious island folks. Now let me guess, you burned the Olga Livestock barn to lay the groundwork for all of this unquestioned loyalty to Cowboy when he comes riding in to save the day."

"I'm glad you can appreciate the necessary foresight. I admit I've always been fond of you, Meredith, even if you're a pest."

"I think that's the nicest thing you've ever said to me, Chase. Now, if I may: another thing I find admirable is that even though you didn't go with a transvestite twist like in *The Missing*, you more than made up for it by casting yourself as a harmless cripple, leg brace and all. It's really just as good as the screenplay I reviewed a few weeks back; might even be better. It's a pity you've missed your calling."

"Don't pity me, you arrogant bitch!" He screams so hard his voice cracks.

"Oh, I see, in this particular delusion, you're Sullivan Shaw, and I'm Amanda."

"Finally! Now tell me, I'm dying to know: is it irony or prophecy that your last chapter is actually your last chapter?"

"Well, we're living out the epilogue right now, so . . ."

"Suits me—you're already dead on paper anyway."

"I do have one question, if I may."

"Why the hell not?" He shrugs, indifferent to me, enjoying my suffering.

"I can understand murdering your family for money; that's completely logical—"

"Killed, goddammit! Not murdered! When Skip died, Casper would have drowned me first if given the chance; you should have seen the look on his face bobbing in that water when he realized he'd been bested by the retard, as he used to call me. Mother was a drunken, lying whore, not much better than that slut-wagon Samantha; and the way I see things, they each got what they deserved."

"Point taken, but what about the girl, your half-sister Angela, and the baby in her womb—your own baby! Did she get what she deserved?"

He sneers at my comment, muttering something unintelligible at the sky as I continue, but with a sudden boldness that overrides my fear.

"What about her poor mother, who was so heartbroken over the death of her only child that she took her own life? All this innocent blood is on your head, and now you want more? You're not the sophisticated death dealer you fancy yourself to be, Chase Stuart—nothing but a mere imitation of those I've studied, nothing more than a coward."

He's remarkably calm after the verbal scourging, as if actually weighing my words. Then, in an instant, he flips.

"If you're quite done with your tantrum, I'm going to enjoy the smell of your charring flesh. You better jump like Amanda while you still have the chance—go on, goddammya!"

"I can't do that, Chase."

"Like I said, everyone has a choice."

"No, this life isn't mine to take, and neither is it yours." If I'm going to die here, I want my last words to be the truth.

"I've given you more of a chance than the others, but know this, Meredith: when you're gone, this all burns, and it's your fault," he deadpans, striking another flare as the cloud of smoke from the grassfire rolls over us in a choking fog.

I resist the urge to close my eyes and instead watch as the red blur tumbles through the smoke until halfway to me, before slamming them shut. Suddenly a rush of sound envelops me in a blast of cold silence; then an odd peace overtakes me. I now know that burning alive feels heavy and frigid at first; I instinctively gasp for air, but as the fire enters my lungs, I choke and crumple to the ground.

My dying thoughts are of Edward and Robert; I witness their devastation and I'm crushed by the weight of our grief. My darling Mels, Carver and Calvin . . . and on our anniversary too. Then those I will soon be with—Jesus, my mother, Long Shadow, and now Edna—they all race through my mind at incredible speed. Then there's another roar, and I'm suddenly shivering in a puddle of seawater, looking up at a ghastly form hovering between us.

Her decaying flesh shimmers with the biolume of August, and thick ribbons of kelp fall from her barnacle-covered skull, forming a grisly mane. This is what I saw that morning when Edna drove us off the property; this is what has become of Long Shadow.

An icy cold fogs my breath with each shallow exhale as Stuart's face shows an initial look of curiosity, but that quickly contorts into one of horror as the penetrating hollow tone of her voice swirls about us when she speaks.

"I hear their cries, Chase Stuart . . . You! Taker of what is not yours—you will not harvest here!" Her bony, accusatory finger points at him as water pours from her outstretched arm. "No! This night the sea will try you! Your jury will be those you have slain, and your judge will be the One whose very breath gave them life."

"That's what you think!" he rages, frantically shaking the gas can at us until empty, then striking another flare. "Burn in hell, water witch!"

By the time Chase Stuart realizes that his own clothing is covered in fuel from the frenzied sloshing, the flame has already jumped, and he is instantly consumed in a pillar of fire. His scream of terror is choked by the inferno, and he hurls himself at Long Shadow, only to pass through her and plummet to the rocks below.

"Look!" She points over the cliff.

Crawling to the edge, I witness the twisted, twitching body of Chase Stuart splayed over a large rock with his face pointing to the heavens. A second later, the sea rises up to claim him, leaving nothing behind but the fading green trail of bioluminescence as he vanishes deeper and deeper beneath the waves. When I look up, the girl from my youth reaches down and pulls me to my feet.

As she stands under the starlight, at six feet tall and wearing a simple deerskin dress, her beauty defies description, and with a smile, Long Shadow joins our hands to her belly.

"You set us free, sister, thank you."

"And you set me free, sister, thank you."

"I knew you would come, because you promised."

"I did."

"She tells me you have a son called Edward and an honorable man for a husband. This is good."

"Yes . . . I would love for them to meet you; please stay, even if just for a little while."

"It is not permitted in that way, but I will never leave your heart, Meredith, nor you mine."

"Where will you go?"

"With her . . . to be where all light comes from." Long Shadow points toward the cabin.

Awaiting among the cedars is the same misty figure that I've witnessed roaming the cliffs, the one who visits the house and calls our names in the night.

"Who is she?"

"She is Liwa, the friend I told you of long ago."

I pause for a second, feeling a familiar pull.

"The Churn." I smile, understanding that it's this sentinel who's been guiding my fingers when I write.

"It is as you believe, Meredith, though Edward will call her Se'-Le'.'"

"Are you crying?" I ask, astonished by the silver drops as bright as liquid mercury rolling down her cheeks.

"I am. The time has come for me to return. Will you do something for us with the next full moon?"

"Anything, what is it?"

"You will know."

"Can I hug you? I promise that I won't survive another goodbye like the last one."

"Yes, but this is not goodbye, sister; think of it as when we were little girls, and summer was gone."

With our embrace, she whispers: "There is no greater love than to lay down your life for another." With her words, every moment we spent together permeates my being, and with them, a sense of completion; no sadness in the passage of our time, only an abiding peace of understanding that all is as it should be.

39

Some Pots Are Better Left Unstirred

I make my way up the hill with the thought of Edna heavy on my heart. Her words of refusal to be my Captain Alastair, along with the horrible twist that I'm about to play that very role for her is just too much for me, and I break down; God, how am I going to do this?

The vehicles speeding onto the property with their sirens blaring and lights flashing against the trees immediately pull my eyes from the ground, and soon a roving spotlight finds me midway up the charred hillside, followed by the bark of the sheriff's PA.

"Meredith! Lift your hand if you're OK!"

I respond affirmatively, shielding my eyes with the other as the Blazer slowly makes its way along the tree line to meet me.

"Robert called us about an intruder . . . holy smokes, you're soaking wet! You must be freezing! Let me grab a blanket."

I can't find words as he opens his tailgate and pulls out a blanket to wrap around me.

"Is he still on the property?"

I manage to shake my head no through the shivers as the truck's radio screeches.

"Go for Sheriff."

"Whaddya got, Littauer?"

"One injured to transport. She's got a pretty bad gash on her head, lost quite a bit of blood, likely concussion."

"ID?"

"It's Mary Ellen Carter, but she must've really taken a whack because she insists that her name is Edna Wilhite. Doc's expecting her at the clinic. Over."

"10-4. According to Mrs. Hawthorne, the suspect's gone . . . she's fine other than being a bit shaken up."

"Roger that. Stone's cleared the house; nothing here other than the power's out and there's at least a couple of gallons of gas dumped around the foyer."

"All right, get Mary Ellen into Eastsound. Stone, you stick around just in case; we're on the way back up the hill."

"Copy, Sheriff."

"We're heading up. Over and out."

I gather my words by the time we reach the house and relay that Chase Stuart and his alter ego, Cowboy, have met their demise over the cliff, promising a more detailed account after a hot shower and change of clothes.

By the time I return downstairs, the linemen from both OPALCO and Island Bell are already on the property tracing the faults; and in doing so, they report finding the old Olga Livestock truck just off the road in the woods.

I guide Sheriff Chancey and Captain Stone down to the spot where Chase Stuart went over the edge, and they scan the area with their flashlights, looking for any trace of him.

"If he went off here and hit those rocks, it's impossible to survive that fall. Even if he landed in the water, he's down in the current by now."

"No doubt, Sheriff. He'll show up south of here in a day or two unless a hungry orca decides otherwise."

"I'll let the Coasties know to keep an eye out for a floater. Why don't you make a pass first thing tomorrow and look around."

"Sure thing, Sheriff. One question, though."

"Sure, whaddya got?"

"That Cowboy fella, the guy who lost his wife and kid, he's actually that creep Chase Stuart?"

"It appears that way, Jeff."

"Well, that's just great . . . Kim's never going to let me live this one down."

"How's that?"

"She never did buy all that 'Much obliged, kemosabe' and 'Howdy, pardner' jazz."

"Don't feel bad about it, Captain," I reassure him, "he had me hook, line, and almost sinker: and I write books about his sort!"

"Meredith, this looks pretty cut-and-dried to me. I hate to ask, but will you drop by the office tomorrow for an official report?"

"Absolutely; I don't mind typing up my account for you, Sheriff."

"I'd need it before noon, if possible."

"I'll do my best."

"I guess the department should pay more attention to island gossip."

"Sheriff?"

"Your last book—people around here said that Sullivan Shaw was based on Stuart. You took a big risk."

"The murder of Angela Wagner and her unborn child—that was the hinge, Sheriff. Something similar happened to a dear friend of mine long ago."

"I'll see to it that the Wagner case file is reopened and updated. It looks like the guys from OPALCO just earned their paycheck—you've got lights."

"Thank you, Sheriff. Now, if I can catch a lift with you back up to the house, I have some cleaning to do before my boys get home."

Before leaving, Sheriff Chancey provides a tip for lifting the gasoline smell from the wood: wiping everything down with a healthy dose of rubbing alcohol and letting it air out. He also assures me that he'll attempt to reach Robert aboard the inbound Vashon to put his mind at ease. I smile as they drive off while holding the two bottles of rubbing alcohol they pulled from their first aid kits, and consider how fortunate we are to have this Sheriff's Department here on the islands.

Three bottles of alcohol later and the hallway smells like a doctor's office, but the runner on the stairs still reeks of gas and has to go. My attempt at removing the brass rods with a screwdriver ends after the first one, realizing that I'll never type again if I keep at it.

Shortly following my concession, the station wagon barrels down the driveway, skidding to a stop in front of the house with the farm truck right behind. As exhausted as we all are, I know this isn't going to keep until the morning, and I give everyone the same abbreviated version of the evening that I had provided the sheriff. The official story is that Chase Stuart was blinded by the smoke and fell over the cliff while pursuing me. With the tale's Cowboy twist, the gossip is going to be some of the best these islands have ever spread.

~

After Robert and Edward remove the runner, we leave the house open for the night and head down to the cabin for a very late spaghetti dinner and some much-needed sleep.

With Edward on the sofa below in front of the fire and me safely dozing in Robert's arms upstairs, he whispers, "I can't wait to hear the real story."

"You don't believe in all that mumbo jumbo, remember?"

"Yeah, I remember . . ."

40

Lost and Found

By the time we sit down in the Sheriff's Office, Captain Stone has returned from towing Chase Stuart's Boston Whaler found dragging its anchor between Eagle Rock and Lawrence Point. The boat contained a change of clothes, another leg brace, an army duffle bag half-full of rocks, and a bouquet of flowers.

When Deputy Littauer processed the Olga Livestock truck for evidence, he discovered a set of Washington State Ferry workers' coveralls, along with a map of the ferry's engine room. According to the sheriff, initial impressions of state investigators working alongside WSDOT engineers led them to believe that the fire aboard the Hyak was the result of a flammable substance being introduced into the hydraulic lines and that they were very lucky to avoid a catastrophic explosion below decks.

"Rich Steinle said that Cowboy—er, Chase Stuart— returned to Orcas from San Juan on that same boat after checking on another hayfield. It appears that this was to be Cowboy's last ride, so to speak. Looks like he planned to take care of you, Meredith, and change clothes in the Whaler, then sink his Cowboy getup in that weighted duffle on his way back to Shaw. I must admit, it was a good plan."

"Yes, it was, Sheriff, and I can't thank you enough."

"We're glad it turned out OK. You know, I was thinking it might be wise for you to have a few guns out there. We do offer firearm training at the department, and I'm sure you and Edward here would benefit from it."

I see Robert drop his head and shoot Edward a look in anticipation of my defensive retort, but I surprise them.

"I have to agree, Sheriff. We'll take you up on that."

"Good! Now, Edward, how on earth did that page in the terminal tip you off that Cowboy was actually Chase Stuart?"

"Well, Sheriff, given what Vivian and I had already gathered from my mom's book, I still couldn't work out how a guy with a mangled leg like Chase Stuart could be dangerous—not without an accomplice, anyway. It wasn't until that name came over the intercom when it became . . . elementary."

"Elementary?" the sheriff laughs.

"Yes, sir. You see, when they paged Sybil St. Clair in the terminal, her name sounded familiar; I just couldn't figure out why. Then it came to me: the Sherlock Holmes case; *The Man with the Twisted Lip*!"

"I'm not sure I know that one."

"It's where a scarred-up beggar named Hugh Boone is suspected of murdering a highly respectable London businessman called Neville St. Clair. But, as it turns out, Hugh Boone and Neville St. Clair were one and the same. When Vivian reminded me that the Olga Livestock barn was burned down right after Dad came to look at the house, and suddenly Cowboy appeared out of the blue all the way from New Mexico, well, some would call that a coincidence, but I call it suspicious."

When Edward pauses and looks over at me, I have to smile and nod, thankful for his unwavering view on coincidence.

"With Cowboy living in Anacortes and Stuart having a parking spot at the terminal, it made sense that he was Stuart's alter ego. It was just plain luck that when we spotted him in the boarding line, Ms. Danelle mentioned that Cowboy had stopped at the farm on Wednesday to check the field, and when he did, she told him the three of us were making mainland deliveries and picking up Mr. Kent the next day. So he knew my mom would be alone on Thursday, and if he was going to act, he had to do it then."

"That's mighty impressive, Edward."

"Thank you, Sheriff, and after making the St. Clair connection, it was all but confirmed when I saw that jar of Vaseline in his car. I knew it was there to remove any remaining adhesive that held on his fake beard before he went hobbling around and complaining on the ferry. It must have been pretty itchy because he had a rash on his throat both times I saw him."

"First-rate detective work if ever I've seen it, young man!"

"Thank you, but like I said, I couldn't have figured it out that quickly without Vivian recognizing that *The House of Long Shadows* was based on my mom's life."

"It's clear as day that you two make a great pair of detectives. Now because this is technically an active investigation, this information is for present company only, with the exception of Vivian Sinclair." Sheriff Chancey pauses as he picks up a paper from his desk. "When they processed Stuart's car, they found a shaving kit under that leg brace. It contained spirit gum, gelatin powder, and glycerin; also sticks of purple, yellow, and red greasepaint, and a few black tooth caps."

"So, that's how he did it." Edward smiles. "He made his burned leg look much worse out in public by mixing the gelatin with glycerin to add extra scarring and stuck it on with spirit gum. Then he colored it with greasepaint and wrapped it up in that brace for a very convincing sight. The way folks gossip around the islands, all it took was a few people seeing that image and it was as good as true—I know it worked on me."

~

That afternoon when I stop by Edna's cottage to check in on her, she's piled up in bed with my binder and a massive bandage covering her head.

"That son of a bitch! I've got twenty staples in my head! And did he call me a dyke, or did I dream that?"

"Yes, ma'am, he did, and Deadna too," I add with a laugh through the tears of gratitude that she's still around.

"Deadna?! Yeah, well, hardy the hell har . . . look who's laughing now! Oh, don't you start crying, Meredith."

"No, ma'am, happy tears."

"Got a hell of a headache, though, and some double vision, too. Thank God Hattie's dropping my medicine off any minute."

"Isn't that it on your nightstand?"

"Not on your life—I don't take that poison! Hattie's got my homegrown natural medicine. I left a baggie over there yesterday afternoon when I dropped off a couple of adorable barn cats for her."

"I didn't realize you came back early; I thought you might've been stuck on San Juan because of the Hyak."

"I was on that damn barge before the fire broke out! Matter of fact I was parked a few cars forward of that psycho in the Olga Livestock truck."

"Thank God. Are there any chores or anything I can do for you? Laundry, bring you dinner, maybe clean up?"

"Yes, as a matter of fact, there is. You can quit calling me 'ma'am' and take this binder of yours to the cabin as a reminder of your promise kept."

"Yes, Edna," I say, moving toward the door, then pause for second. "Not sure if you remember this, but when Deputy Littauer found you, you insisted that your name was Edna Wilhite. Have you considered-"

"Absolutely not! Everyone here besides you and Hattie know me as Mary Ellen, I see no reason to upset this apple cart. Do I have your word?"

"Of course you do."

"Meredith, dear, I want you to remember this as well: you are that woman I know you were meant to be. I love you."

"I love you too, Mary-"

"Edna, dear," she gently interrupts. "When not in mixed company, you may call me Edna."

～

I walk through the woods, considering Edna's words with each step of the journey, carrying a contentment that I haven't felt since the days when Long Shadow and I walked these very trails hand in hand.

The perfect term comes to mind as I emerge near the greenhouse and spot Edward and Vivian sitting beneath the large apple tree in the center of the orchard. She hands him a beautiful British plaid box; it's a pattern that I know all too well, and when he opens it, his face lights up with genuine joy and amazement.

One day in early July, Vivian had consulted me in confidence as to where she might procure a deerstalker suitable for the illustrious Sherlock Holmes; she must have sent off to England for it shortly thereafter. Undetected, I watch them just long enough to see Vivian put the cap on his head, and he immediately tackles her in the grass; I hear their giggles trail as I move away. The term is innocence.

41

A Promise Fulfilled

I can't believe that it's already September and our last weekend here on Orcas. It's the time of year when the full moon produces the lowest tides of summer, and the coolness of fall is evident with each breath and the shifting sunlight.

Two weeks have passed since my fingers once again found the keystrokes for the outline that I've struggled with these three months, and as I review this ghostly tale one final time before sending it off to my agent, Edward and Vivian come rushing into the cabin.

"Mom! Vivie and I found bones in the cave!"

"What bones . . . what cave?" I ask, snapping out of my scrutinous haze.

"The cave at the bottom of the cliff! And look what else . . ." Edward hands me the doll that he had rescued from a nook high above the water's reach.

~

Two skeletons—a tiny one nested within the larger—were reverently removed by the tribe and held for the next few weeks as the clearing in the forest between the southern tree line and Eagle Rock was examined. Their findings revealed the site to be an ancient cemetery where survivors of the massacre buried their dead.

The following month under a full moon, the bones of Long Shadow and her unborn child were laid to rest alongside the others who perished in the massacre. After the memorial service, I share the unabridged version of my encounter with Hattie, including Long Shadow's words about Edward and how he would call the Churn, Se'-Le'. Hattie takes my arm and says, "Meredith, this is our word for Grandmother."

My mind flashes back to late August when Carver handed me a box containing the three books from my mother's bedside table. Her heavily highlighted Bible, a paperback on local tribes with its spine noticeably creased at the chapters on Haida and Lummi, and the book on reincarnation that was equally as worn.

It now makes sense. The name Liwa and how closely it resembles Lila. The doll my mother gave me, as well as her obsession with this property and the nightmare we shared. Her response to Carver when asked about passing away at the Tudor in Broadmoor or here on Orcas; she chose the Tudor. Her reason: because she had already done the other.

And so it's been my own mother who has guided these fingers over countless keystrokes, prompting me with her whispers and leading me back to Long Shadow. She never abandoned me, or her—quite the contrary.

~

Our house on 16th Avenue East had been a wonderful home in which to begin our journey together, but by November of 1972, Robert and I knew it was time for her to share that special warmth with another young couple. Arthur Burke was a charming engineer who had recently graduated from the UW and started his career at Boeing. He and his new bride, Mary, who already had garnered quite the reputation around the office for her baking skills, were the perfect couple for the house to wrap its rooms around, and just in time for their first Christmas together.

Edward was beyond excited about the news of our relocation to Orcas, and though we did have concerns about his living full-time within the bubble of island life, we simply made travel a priority. Whenever possible, he would be my companion on book-related trips, and we always managed at least a day or two of sightseeing, including one very special visit to London, England, and 221B Baker Street. He also accompanied Robert on several international trips and has the passport full of stamps and great life experiences to show for it. Our other apprehension was the course that nature often takes . . . It became a topic that we parents discussed periodically through the years, sometimes laughing over a bourbon, other times crying over a glass of wine. With them now both away at the University of Washington, this end of the island is quiet, and though we miss the nonstop teenage hijinks, we're happy that the two of them are off to a good start of building a life on their own terms—just as it should be.

The Mels were ecstatic to have Vivian move into the suite above the garage, and Mary Ellen sent her off with an extremely rare 1811 first edition of Jane Austen's *Sense and Sensibility*. The following year, when Edward moved in with Carver and Calvin, she surprised him with a 1902 edition of *The Hound of the Baskervilles*, his favorite tale of them all. Although Edna makes an occasional appearance for me and Hattie Gil, it's all Mary Ellen Carter when she's at Kim Stone's book club, complete with her colorful language and commentary. We still joke about that cold winter night when she brought the wrong tray of brownies, and we all giggled our way through *The Old Nurse's Story*.

Robert left Boeing to launch what has become a highly successful aerospace consultancy firm. His office is here on the property, and he often flies clients in to enjoy a few relaxing days of island life.

My fourth book, *The Churn*, is the best seller so far. But it's a few years old now, and I hear that familiar whisper once again. So here I am in this cabin by the sea, Sherlock and Irene basking hearthside in a warm pool of light as I release my fingers to tell yet another story. This one is alive with Native lore, coming of age, and a mysterious adventure, all birthed under the watchful eyes of the doll and glass float that sit reunited within reach of my Smith-Corona. And on clear mornings when the sun rises from these emerald waters of the Salish Sea, their shadows stretch across the keys of my typewriter until eventually becoming one. A treasured reminder of that summer day when two little girls became sisters of the soul in what will forever be known as the House of Long Shadows.

~Fin~

Acknowledgements

Jennifer Pirecki, thank you for once again sharing our small house with this cast of characters that followed me home one day. Your belief and daily sacrifices are the truest reflection of your love for the two of me. I love and adore you more than you can ever know.

In memory of Aunt Ellen and Uncle Maurice, I overflow with gratitude for those years of innocence that I enjoyed on Whidbey, and Orcas. They were my safe harbor in the rough seas of a turbulent childhood, but you probably knew that all along.

To Cousin Jerry, I'll never forget our times fishing together, especially for cod and sea bass from the rocks of Deception Pass.

To Cousin Fran, much love; from the unescorted little guy who tugged at your trench coat on that Frederick & Nelson escalator one rainy fall day in 1960 something.

To Jeff and Kim Stone, thank you cousins for the nudge to write this tale. I do hope that I've done it justice.

To Bob Vine, a small tribute to our early days of wilderness dreams in Oak Harbor, and those seasons at Indian Point.

In memory of Tony Heese, an exceptional kid, always up for an adventure and willing to help anyone in need. The world misses you, Tony.

In memory of Dr. Robert F. L. Polley, my real life Alastair. Thank you for being my eagle and one for many fatherless boys. Your legacy lives on.

To Tom Beam, I hope this brings to mind those fall days of innocence and our Nerf football games along the parking strip on 57th. Thank God, for those memories.

A special bow to the Rs

Carol Lynn Rivera, aka the magnificent. This work would not be what it is without your love, and skilled pencil standing at the ready. You have truly blessed me and I'm beyond honored by your participation in my life; not only for stepping in at the eleventh hour as copyeditor and editorial advisor, but for being my wonderfully gifted dear friend as well.

Ralph Rivera, whose instincts and insight for setting and staging a scene thin the veil between worlds. Your generosity and critique made this book better, and me too! Thank you for sharing your rare talents with me, and The House of Long Shadows.

To the wonderful Bay Area poet, novelist, and my dear friend, S. Matthew Norton. Thank you, cousin, for taking this hike with me. Your knowledge, wisdom, and encouragement to unwind another emerging tale is definitely one of your superpowers.

To Andrea Reider, thank you for going above and beyond with this interior. I'm so grateful for you and your efforts.

To Dan Harding, who brought this cover into existence and made it look easy. Thank you, dear friend!

To Kent and Danelle Corrick, thank you for your friendship and inspiration. Are there Madrona in Graham?

To Rich and Tracy Steinle, thank you for all your love and support, along with your willingness to bilocate from Austin to Orcas!

To Melanie Stallings and Melinda Stickley, you are forever my Mels.

To Cash and Cho McCloy, thank you for the massive amount of encouragement, support, and friendship. It's always above and beyond when Cash is in the house!

To Scott and Judy Chancey, I'm so thankful for our long friendship and your ever encouraging words. I hope you enjoy the read.

To Ric and Ruth Littauer, Jennifer and I so enjoyed your visit to Franklin, let's do that again! And thank you for badging up!

To Doug Mann, my longtime friend and creative genius. I'm so grateful for your guidance and friendship.

To Jeff and Mia Fleetwood, thank you for your steadfast encouragement and support, it makes a huge impact along the way.

To Janet Greene, You saw my need to focus on this book. Thank you for your patient listening to the early chapter drafts. Interesting how we unravel with the (w)Rite.

To Rachel and Jim Corum, such wonderful parents to three great boys; Will, Watts, and Ben. I hope you enjoy this, Favorite!

To Duncan and Breeon Phillips, our friendship and our 219 . . . life wouldn't be the same without either.

To Phil Pirecki, I always look forward to our chinwags and catch ups. Let's keep those on the calendar.

To Judith Pfeiffer, dear big sis, I hope this book makes you smile.

To Cory and Kim Fournier, thank you for all of the prodding and encouragement to get this done.

To Monty Powell and Anna Wilson, thank you for your love, friendship, and support throughout. Now, let's ski!

To Chris Adams, that Traditional is a beast! Thank you for your friendship and encouragement.

To Troy Collins, your avid encouragement and support throughout this journey has been life giving. Thank you!

To Mark and Robin Somgynari, our daily check-ins are legendary! Thank you for the ever present support and friendship.

To Katie Mirian, thank you dearest Katie and my friends at Salon Atash.

To Les and Jo Coughran, your unabashed embrace of life is an inspiration to all you encounter. You are "unlimited opportunities." Wink.

To Kerry Miller, we all need champions in our corner, thank you Kerry for always cheering me on. I count myself as blessed to be in your camp.

To Ken Leggett and the men at Wilco AM, It's an honor to share Tuesday mornings with all 70+ of you. Special shout out to our ever-encouraging table - Rob Bomar, Mike Fisher, Gary Greene, Alan Henderson, Mike Hughes, Danny Pugh, Steve Seger, and Bobby Waechter.

To Big Mike, I miss seeing that huge smile each Wednesday. Thank you for your constant encouragement brother, we got it done!

To my friends and neighbors at Bobby's Automotive, Bobby Hollars, Billy Holt, and Jason Kelley. Thanks for being my daily sanity check. What's for lunch?

To Karen Lovelace, a non-fiction Vivian and prime example of what a farm girl knows. Thank you for the inspiration.

To Landmark Booksellers and it's talented staff, thank you for being an amazing resource for customers and authors. Your encouragement and support have been invaluable. We're blessed that you're our hometown haunt here in Franklin, TN.

Opal Lee Stansberry, I selfishly wish that you were here to catch a glimpse of yourself within these pages. I miss you Mom.